DOUBLETHINK

A Tale of Unintended Consequences

A novel by J.E. Schwartz

First printing March 2006
ISBN: 0-9778911-0-0
Library of Congress Control Number: 2006922706

Printed in the United States of America by Malloy Incorporated.
Published by Raise the Bar Press.   www.raisethebar.com
For bulk orders, please call Raise the Bar Press at 650-327-2902

"Doublethink means the power of holding
two contradictory beliefs in one's mind simultaneously
and accepting both of them."

-GEORGE ORWELL, *1984*

AUTHOR'S NOTE

While many of the social and economic impacts described in this novel have already happened, this story is entirely a fabrication of the author's mind. The author possesses no inside knowledge of potential mergers or financial events and has taken the liberty of imagining what could happen, based on present realities and trends, not only to this country but also to various public figures, organizations, and corporations whose futures are merely speculated about. Fiction extrapolates from present-day realities—and there can be many possible outcomes, some happy, some less cheerful. This work is offered as a reflection of what many in this country fear is possible if we don't take action to change our current direction. As proof this is fantasy, one need only point to the speed and efficiency with which the government programs described herein have been implemented.

J.E. Schwartz

Joe Winston woke up to the humming of his alarm. He slowly opened his eyes, smiling at the sight of his beautiful lush garden designed by his ex-wife Susan. The waterfall splashed softly into the black-bottomed swimming pool. The sturdy palm trees stood out against a backdrop of native live oak and redwoods. Not a day passed without his feeling that he was truly fortunate to have such a wonderful home and life. The Lindenwood area of Atherton was a fantastic neighborhood: serene, secure, and the property values rose every year. He was lucky to live in the best country in the world.

He got up, stretched, and turned on the flat-panel digital TV in his room to scan the perimeter security system. Everything looked peaceful and quiet, but you couldn't be too careful. Only last week, his neighbor Rich had quite a scare. An out-of-work programmer had managed to circumvent the security fence and found his way to the back door, begging for food. Fortunately, Rich's 15-year old daughter had the good sense to ask the man to wait outside while she called for Security to escort the man away.

Opening his front door, Joe walked out and picked up the folded newspaper lying neatly on the bench of his front porch. He appreciated the old-fashioned, homey touches the Lindenwood Homeowners' Association provided—they understood what contributed to a great quality of life. Personal dog walkers, dry cleaning pickup and delivery, and private armed security guards were among the other amenities they offered. Drinking his morning coffee, he scanned the headlines of the Fox Free Press *(All the Fair and Balanced News that Fits)*. Although he subscribed to the electronic version of the publication (with real-time updates), he liked the feeling of holding the newsprint with its faint smell of ink. The election stories dominated the front page. He was confident the President would win re-election but he was amazed by the polls showing Republican victories in a stunning majority of Congressional races. All legislation was under Party control, because only Republicans were allowed to participate in the Congressional conference committees that hammer out the differences between House and Senate versions of bills. The final provisions often had significant variations from the ones that were discussed and voted on originally. As a result, many Americans felt that the only way for their districts to have any chance of being served in Washington was to vote for GOP candidates. No doubt, the Republicans would get an undeniable mandate for another four years. It felt good to be on the winning team.

Joe made a mental note to log on that morning and cast his vote on the Diebold election site for the Bush-Breaux ticket. Jeb was a good man. It was his brilliant idea to choose the conservative and deeply pious former Democrat John Breaux to be his running mate, to demonstrate that he wanted to reach out and unite the country. "JB^2 Unity Ticket" made a terrific bumper sticker. Tapped for the post of Secretary of State, Dick Cheney had become as much of a fixture in the capital as the Washington Monument. It was incredible how old Dick was still hanging in there at 71 and two heart operations later. He was probably going to outlast all of them Joe chuckled to himself.

Of course it wasn't much of a contest, he reasoned, since the Democrats had managed to shoot themselves in the feet, arms and other assorted body parts. It was almost as if they'd gone hunting with Cheney. With all the cultural elitists on their side, you'd think they could create a better story to sell to voters, but then again, why go with Republican lite if you could have the real thing? They had never fully recovered from the Hillary debacle in 2008—there was just too much good material to use: Monica Lewinsky kneepads and blue dresses at the Republican convention, and Sappho Sisters For Truth who claimed to have had personal sexual experiences with the candidate. And while this time around he thought that Illinois Senator Barak Obama was a formidable prospect (and probably the better choice), the liberals were fools to think that the race card couldn't be exploited where it counted in the key Electoral College states. The other parties had fielded credible candidates too, but Karl Rove and Grover Norquist's omnipresent political machine, now run from a private think-tank, was so effective that the challengers hadn't received enough media attention to make a dent in the public consciousness.

He surfed over to www.drudgereport.com. Homeland Security forces, using the NSA's Defend America system that monitored virtually every phone call, internet message, and search in the country, had uncovered a terrorist cell in Great Neck, New York at the home of a wealthy Jewish financier. Twenty-five men, women, and youngsters had been engaged in a discussion challenging the right of the government to attack countries the President felt were imminent threats. The piece focused on the scandal of encouraging young people to disrespect the government. The parents were arrested for child endangerment and were now locked up in the Keep America Safe facility in Riverhead, N.Y., a prison run by the Safe Custody Corporation.

In another story, insurgents in Iran had just been dealt a heavy blow by the American occupation force. As usual, there were few if any details about American casualties, since such news only gave comfort to the terrorists.

He was interrupted by a knock at the back door. He looked up and saw his gardener, Javier. A graduate of the local community college, Javier had been a customer service manager for a high tech firm before he lost his job in a wave of outsourcing in 2004. When he couldn't get another office job, he rejoined the family "blow and go" business, which was subsequently bought by a national lawn services chain. Joe had found that former customer service people made the best help.

Javier wanted to know if Joe had decided whether he wanted the sod in the front lawn replaced and a new sprinkler system installed. The lawn had yellowed in spots because of the drought that season. The drip irrigation system that Susan preferred wasn't up to the challenge of the warmer weather they'd been getting the last few years. Joe told Javier to go ahead and place the order. But it brought back painful memories of one of the last fights he'd had with Susan before they were divorced. He still felt some vague feelings of love for her and thought she was a great gal, but they had sadly grown apart over the years. It wasn't anyone's fault.

Susan had wanted to fight the Homeowners' Association's restrictions and replace their front lawn with native plants that wouldn't require so much water. She had an annoying habit of openly challenging people when she thought their opinions or rules were unreasonable, and frankly, Joe found it embarrassing.

It wasn't so bad when they were first married and the kids were small. She was a teacher at a local elementary school in East Palo Alto and he found her earnestness and enthusiasm adorable. As the classes got bigger, the schools more run down, and the testing requirements more extensive, Susan became more frustrated and less fun to be around. It became a problem when they were socializing with their friends, since she was always on a soapbox about one thing or another. Her passion became too strident, in Joe's opinion.

It still bothered Joe that Susan wasn't as concerned with the reduction in teachers' salaries, pensions, and other benefits as she was in budgetary reductions that severely reduced school funding for programs like art, music, gym and special education. Thankfully, they had been in the position to overlook her loss of health insurance, because his employers covered the family. Not only did Susan buy supplies for her classes, but sometimes she'd buy a few students lunch—that troubled him too. After all, that was *their* parents' responsibility. No teacher had bought *him* lunch when he was a kid.

Susan believed in fuzzy qualitative education and hated teaching to standardized tests that she felt undermined the ability of children to think for themselves. Her favorite students were the weird ones who didn't fit the desirable profile of well-behaved, neat children who followed the rules, memorized the answers, and excelled at sports, like their own daughter Amanda. It annoyed him that Susan hadn't pushed their son Daniel enough to fit in.

She was always immersed in some cause, like The Africa Famine March. She even involved the kids. Why was it so impossible for her to enjoy their great life without worrying about every conceivable problem in the world? He wasn't unsympathetic to the difficulties other people faced, but you could make yourself crazy trying to keep up with all the various disputes or diseases. To add insult to injury, the March took place on the day of an important golf tournament at the country club. Susan missed watching Joe and his partner, Brent Newsome win their flight. Then she showed up late (wearing casual clothes, no less) to the trophy dinner. He could still remember overhearing the catty remarks of the other wives about Susan's lack of style. He loved her, but he didn't like being disrespected in front of his friends. It was the gradual accumulation of such irritants that had ultimately eroded their relationship.

Occasionally he missed her, but he had to admit that life was a lot less stressful without her around—especially with the kids gone. If he didn't have a business dinner, he would come home, fix himself a drink and nuke a frozen dinner while he watched TV or a movie. Fox had entertaining news and he loved the nationally syndicated call-in shows. Thanks to web cams, you could actually see the looks on people's faces as the host tore into them or applauded their opinions.

Susan used to like to watch dramas and documentaries on PBS, which thankfully was off the air—what a waste of taxpayer money! Besides, most of the shows were boring. Who wanted to watch all those animals mating, or tiresome documentaries about ancient Egypt, or the origins of the universe?

A warble from his mobile communicator jolted Joe from his musings. It was his electronic assistant reminding him that the executive staff meeting was starting in an hour. He put the paper down and quickly checked his email. There were a number of responses to the question he had posed to his email discussion group yesterday. He didn't bother to open them; he'd do that during the dull parts of the meeting. He rose and left the dishes on the table. His housekeeper was coming in later today. She'd take care of them.

He finished dressing and climbed into his car, the newest Humvee H12. Humvee had won the AutoCraze Car of the Year Award five years running. The bulletproof glass, extra heavy body armor, and Kevlar tires came in really handy when traveling between safety zones. He knew of someone whose Jaguar sedan had been swarmed by an angry mob of malcontents that pulled out and beat the driver; the story had made a lasting impression. You had to be careful. He checked the gas gauge. It was down to 1/4 of a tank, which wasn't ideal for a vehicle that got 8 MPG around town. He'd stop to fill up on the way home. It wasn't good to get stuck these days with so many dangerous types roving the streets. Gas was only $4.75 a gallon and his peace of mind was worth it.

The drive to work was uneventful. Joe passed the usual crowds hoping for day work on the corner of El Camino Real and San Antonio Road. Joe recalled the days when it was only undocumented Mexicans seeking employment, now it looked like a Silicon Valley job fair from the nineties. Immigration had slowed to a trickle but there still were a lot of folks who had been left behind after the Respect for Multicultural Values repatriation programs of 2008. They were in legal limbo—couldn't get work—couldn't go back home—couldn't get driver's licenses, insurance, or access to schools and hospitals. It was a tough situation. To do his part, he'd hired a few former post-docs from China to reconfigure his network at the house. Shame, really, they were bright fellows, though a bit difficult to understand.

He pulled into his spot on the ground floor of the parking garage for Organic Chemical, a Sodexho ADM Alliance Subsidiary. Jay Frost, the CEO, had talked about getting a team of valet parking attendants. Personally Joe thought it sounded extravagant. Not that he'd tell Jay that. Jay didn't like having his ideas questioned and it was safer to pick one's battles.

He passed the florist setting out the new arrangements in the lobby and took the elevator to the executive suite. Their facilities consultant had done a wonderful job. The pale gray carpets were thick and soft underfoot. The Brazilian rainforest wood furniture provided a warm glow that complemented the tasteful beige linen wall coverings and alpaca upholstery. The offices reflected the confidence and success of the occupants. You had to hand it to Jay. He had great taste, and when it came to clothes, cars, or his surroundings, only the best would do.

The guy wore $500 Lobb shoes, $600 Turnbull shirts, and $6,000 custom suits. He always paid attention to what you were wearing too, so Joe had been persuaded to upgrade his wardrobe. Joe didn't actually care about clothes, but last year Jay had introduced him to a personal shopper who took Joe firmly in hand to stores he had never heard about before. It made him uncomfortable to be analyzed and appraised so closely by strangers, but Joe did have to admit that the new clothes were as comfortable as they were impressive.

Joe stopped to straighten his raw silk tie in the reflection of the framed photo of the extended First Family that hung inside his office—a thank you gift for his work on many campaigns over the years. He dropped his briefcase on the desk, took a quick glance at the panoramic view of the bay, and grabbed his digital tablet. He stopped to say hello to his team of legal contractors and picked up his presentation for the meeting. They were a great bunch of folks and did superb work. Two of them had worked all night to prepare his materials for today. As he settled into the leather armchair in the conference room, a young woman brought him a cappuccino. It was just another example of the company's meticulous attention to detail, keeping track of management and visitor preferences so your favorite beverage simply appeared when you sat down, without your needing to ask.

He plugged the keychain drive into his tablet and flipped through the slides. They all looked good. The team had built a strong argument for why the U.S. Food Services division should be shut down and the preparation and processing work shifted to Mexico. Joe had been asked to evaluate the company's legal exposure. The executive in charge of that division, Mike Talbot, was out of town on a sales call and Jay thought it would be better to have the conversation while Mike was gone. People tended to be overly sensitive when it was their group that was being considered for restructuring. Sometimes one had to look at the big picture and sacrifice 500 jobs to save 5,000, but not everyone saw it that way.

As other executives drifted in and he was waiting his turn to present, Joe checked emails on his communicator. That liberal jerk, Paul Germain, was arguing that the current instabilities in Social Security were a direct result of the Social Security Preservation Act of 2007. The administration had stumbled on the initiative the first time around but they got their way in the end. Didn't they always? However, the stock market hadn't performed as expected and millions of young people were complaining that they hadn't seen their assets accumulating as rapidly as promised. Germain pointed out that having so many unsophisticated investors had caused problems, because far too many of them picked their stock funds based on buzz and celebrity endorsements, rather than rational financial metrics. And the really clever ones had access to solid insider information, which didn't seem to be as interesting to law enforcement these days.

Joe fired back: *I'm beginning to wonder if you're as simple a thinker as you sometimes appear to be on this thread. Are you actually unable, or merely unwilling, to see any alternatives to your hastily formed and erroneous conclusions? Can you think beyond your stereotype that everyone who's not a Democrat is stupid?*

A few moments later Paul responded: *I never said that. I honestly don't understand how you can ignore the obvious connections between policies and results. How could you think people would be better off by gutting Social Security? Who under the age of 40 will even have a pension any more?*

Joe countered: *There you go again. We didn't 'gut' social security. We had to change the rules to keep the program solvent. Market forces are the best equalizers. With an ownership society, everyone has a chance to benefit.*

Paul replied: *It's great if you own something but what if you're working two or three jobs and still can't feed your family and keep a roof over their heads?*

Joe went in with the kill shot: *"Then you clearly need to work harder and find a better job. If we don't reward people for being creative and showing initiative, we end up with lazy parasites living on the socialist dole like in Canada or Sweden. If the American people don't believe in how we're running the country, why do they keep voting for us? Just look at the polls today. We're going to kick your butts!"*

Joe liked how easy it was to express his opinion via email. There weren't many places to debate any more, which did make things a little dull. Secretly, he was disappointed that the Democratic establishment had been undermined so completely—not that he'd admit that out loud or to someone like Paul.

Even though Joe knew how easily the government could read any email exchange after the U.S.A. Patriot Act III had passed, he took comfort in the fact that *he* didn't have to worry. Congress had approved new legislation that expanded earlier law enforcement review of library records and book sales to also cover phone and email exchanges. The Supreme Court had upheld the rights of the executive branch to conduct warrantless wiretaps of U.S. citizens suspected of contact with terrorists, but it was good to get all branches of the government in sync so there wasn't any question. He was surprised that Paul was still willing to spew that brainwashed drivel. You would think he would have learned to show more restraint. One of the members of the email group had been arrested last year after she admitted she helped her sister get an abortion when they were teenagers. It was common sense—you had to know when to hold your tongue. Security was simply more important than privacy these days.

Throughout the morning Joe divided his attention between his email group and the meeting. It took a bit of concentration to keep his two personas separate. His colleagues probably wouldn't have recognized the more impatient aggressor protected by the detachment of digital exchange.

Three hours later, after the lunch break, Joe finally was invited to stand up and present his case. His main arguments were simple. The labor costs in Mexico were cheap enough to offset the additional legal challenges they anticipated. Besides, it would make the meals more palatable to a worldwide audience because more food additives were allowed over the border. Jay and the others were very supportive of his findings. The CFO was chosen to break the news to Mike when he returned the following week.

★   ★   ★   ★   ★

The armored Mercedes limousine sped down the secure highway. It passed the airport runway, gliding toward the towers of downtown San Jose, self-proclaimed capital of Silicon Valley. Joe admired the glass pyramids capping the HP Sports Pavilion rising to his right above the wooden row houses that recalled the city's past life. To his left, a compact stand of office buildings gleamed in the dusk as the pink sky darkened and the yellow sodium lights glowed.

His boss had generously arranged for cars to pick up the Organic Chemical executives at their homes and take them to a victory celebration at the Fairmont Hotel where they would watch the election returns together. Their collective mood was triumphant. How could it be otherwise?

Coming off the toll road, Joe saw a mob of agitators herded into the designated protest zone, their signs flailing wildly. As the limo raced by, dodging the potholes on the city streets, he couldn't see any TV news trucks nearby. Protest was like a tree falling in the forest. If no one heard it, did it make a sound?

The car pulled into the underground garage. Passing through the VIP entrance, the men received their electronically coded credentials and followed the signs pointing to the various receptions. The masses of sustaining members—the grassroots backbone of the Party—were in the Imperial Ballroom, while the Regents, Team 100, Majority Fund, and Chairman's Advisory Board members all had separate hospitality areas and private suites. As Pioneers who had raised at least $100,000 on behalf of the President, or Rangers who had raised at least $200,000, Joe and his colleagues were entitled to visit most of the functions.

They decided to duck into the main ballroom first. There was an all-star line up of musicians scheduled to play throughout the evening: Amy Grant, Seventh Day Slumber, Stryper, and

Whitecross. The room was packed with a jubilant throng crowding around the cash bars and dancing to the lively music with arms upraised. Joe wasn't sure if that indicated they were true believers or if it simply meant that evangelical fashion had reached Silicon Valley. He'd noticed a number of signs that the formerly blue area was turning a shade of purple lately, which made him somewhat uneasy. Flush with Congressional victories in the east and southwest, RINO (Republicans In Name Only) had set up shop in California, to ensure that conservative candidates were well-funded and supported. Personally, he preferred the more business-centric, socially progressive positions of Northern California Republicanism, but he was realistic about what it took to win national elections. Courting the faith and gun vote was as essential as promoting tax cuts.

Other groups were watching the Fox News election returns on immense plasma displays. Since exit polls had been so dramatically wrong the last few years, the networks had stopped commissioning them. Fortunately, early voting and the proliferation of electronic voting machines had enabled the tabulation of results far more quickly. For one thing, not having to mess around with the paper trails demanded by the paranoid few made the whole system far more efficient. It was possible to see the totals rack up for his guys even before the polls closed on the West coast.

The presidential coattails were long, and in most state and local races the maps were glowing red. With Dianne Feinstein retiring, a California Senate seat was up for grabs and the state Party was very hopeful that this was their year.

Amy Grant asked for silence and invited everyone to recite the Pledge of Allegiance together. It gave Joe goose bumps to hear them all expressing their love for God and country. Then she led them in a rousing rendition of "God Bless America."

Joe found himself feeling somewhat claustrophobic in the exuberant crowd, so he was glad to escape to the quieter, but no less jubilant, prestige events. As he stepped into the hallway to catch his breath, he saw two security guards escorting a young woman in a "Protect Our Civil Liberties" T-shirt out a side entrance. She didn't look very threatening but he assumed there must have been a disturbance he hadn't witnessed.

In the Gold Room hosted by the President's Club, Joe was handed a cocktail as he walked over to view the video wall installed at one end of the room. On different monitors were images of the various parties in the hotel, as well as the feed from the Palm Beach resort where the Bush clan was watching the returns together. The sound was tuned to a military band playing P.K. Mitchell's stirring heavy metal arrangement of "Onward Christian Soldiers."

Joe joined a conversation, already in progress, where several men were applauding the organizational skill of the FCC. "Media ownership of newspapers, magazines, TV, and radio all synergistically linked in the hands of five corporations," one fellow remarked, "it's brilliant. Terrific economies of scale. And thanks to the War on Terror, the radical left wing press is virtually extinct. An engineer buddy of mine told me that with the selective management technologies developed for the Chinese market by Cisco and Google, the FCC and Homeland Security immediately block any subversive sites on the Internet. These guys are good. I wish I had them on my IT security team."

As a waiter held out a tray of hors d'oeuvres, Jerry Rooz, a handsome man with a dark complexion, quoted a column from the *National Review*: "'American businesses, the backbone of our economy, have responded to tax incentives that sharply reduced the cost of capital.' Now they're much more productive." The others agreed enthusiastically.

It was true Joe thought. With the right technology, small executive teams could easily manage flexible operations and take advantage of the lowest labor costs anywhere in the world.

"Besides," Joe added, "it's the only way to stay competitive. Everyone else is doing it."

Joe had known Jerry for quite some time. He had come to the U.S. from Iran when he was 18 years old and had made a fortune in the semiconductor industry. The son of a leading jurist in Iran under the Shah, Jerry was a warm, big-hearted guy, very generous with his friends and family. His energy was boundless and he was one of the area's top fundraisers. Even though he and his grown children, as well as his seven siblings and their families, had all settled in the U.S., he maintained close connections with extended family who had remained in Iran. Before the Iran invasion, he had acquired property in Tehran which he now made available to defense contractors working in country. To Joe, he was living proof that America was the land of opportunity if you were willing to work hard enough.

"Minimum wage had been a noose around the neck of the American entrepreneur," Jerry said. The other men nodded. "Congress did the rational thing by eliminating it so American workers can compete in the worldwide marketplace."

A tall solid man with a ruddy face and gray hair responded with, "No doubt about it, free trade is definitely on the march" as he popped a giant prawn in his mouth. "You can see the Administration is taking the right course to incentivize Americans. Corporate taxes have been permanently eliminated. The earned income tax rate of 10% is still high but much more fair. Of course, that AMT is still a pesky business if you don't have a good accountant. Add in the tax cuts on dividends and capital gains, and many millions of equity-owning families have the option of reinvesting their new cash or spending it. The economy benefits either way. It doesn't take a genius to know which party to support."

Joe agreed, "At our company, Organic Chemical, we're seeing record profits, record cash flows, record dividends and sharebuyback capital gains, while at the same time we're investing in new plants, equipment, and technology. Executive salaries have tripled in the last two years. It's good business to reward people for doing a good job. It gives them incentive to try harder." Joe remembered arguments he'd had with his son Daniel on this topic. The lad idealistically maintained that people's dedication to their work was independent of the compensation they received, but Joe knew the opinion was distorted by a lack of real world experience.

Another man noted "When my father died last year, I inherited a couple of million which I put tax-free in my retirement account. Why should the money be taxed twice?" They grinned and toasted one another and their benevolent leaders in Washington. "Great way to protect the family farm."

Jerry leaned over and laughingly said to Joe, "Are there any left? I thought you guys pretty much cornered the market." Joe smiled, recalling childhood summers at his uncle's farm in Illinois, which had been acquired by ADM years ago, well before they merged with the Sodexho Alliance. Joe had personally handled the deal for the Sodexho ADM Alliance to acquire Organic and he was proud of the promises he'd extracted to keep most of the people at his company employed.

The local Party chairman walked up to the podium and called for their attention. The Democratic, Libertarian, and Green challengers had conceded the election and the President was ready to address the prestige events on a closed circuit satellite feed. First, he would be introduced by his spiritual advisor, the Reverend Franklin Graham, son of the late evangelist Billy Graham and president of Samaritan's Purse, a Christian relief organization that provided food, clothing and medical aid to poor people overseas.

"God has anointed his chosen representative to lead our great county. He understands that, above all else, we only want the right to raise our children in our own way. In gratitude, the President will proclaim November 7 'Jesus Day' so that people of all religions will recognize Jesus Christ as an example of love, compassion, sacrifice and service. Please join me in honoring our newly re-elected President, John Ellis Bush."

Joe saw Jerry look down at his feet and take a sip of his scotch before clapping politely. While Jerry wasn't particularly observant, his family was Muslim. Joe remembered when GW had instituted a similar proclamation in Texas in 2000 in honor of a National Jesus Day, which was supported by other governors and mayors around the country. Quite a few of the Jewish and Muslim newspapers at the time, not to mention church-state separatists, hysterically accused the politicians of insensitivity to people of non-Christian faiths and a disregard for the First Amendment. Joe was as tolerant as the next guy and he thought religion was a private matter but he hoped separatists would recognize that Christianity was simply the norm for America. Gestures like these weren't intended to make people of other faiths feel like they were second-class citizens. Joe hadn't heard about any protests recently, so maybe people had finally stopped being so PC about it and had called off the anti-Christian campaigns.

The video wall showed supporters around the country applauding and whistling enthusiastically. Then the images shifted to the Bush family arrayed around the newly re-elected President. George H.W. Bush looked a bit frail, but Barbara was her formidable self as they sat next to their son. Columba, Jeb's wife; George P., Jeb's son and current Governor of Florida; brother Neil, the Secretary of the Treasury; and other brother George W. Bush, the former President, all looked on proudly. There were few families that had made such a significant contribution to the state of the nation as the Bush clan.

Taking a deep breath, the President smiled and looked directly into the camera. "I am joyful and humble tonight as I acknowledge the honor bestowed on me by the American people. Later on tonight I will address the voters at large, but first I want to thank you, my most loyal supporters, for all your hard work. I wouldn't be here today if it weren't for you. Together we have changed the course of history. As the results from the congressional and gubernatorial races are showing, conservatism is now the guiding philosophy in the White House, the Senate, the House, in most governorships, and the majority of state legislatures. Through meticulous and persistent efforts we have solidified our firm control over the judiciary at all levels, including the Supreme Court.

"We have successfully achieved tax reform. Income tax rates are at their lowest levels in nearly a century and accordingly our economy is healthy, vigorous, and growing faster than other major industrialized nations. Government once more is restricted to what government is supposed to do—and nothing else. We are finally running government like a business, without interference from tax and spend liberals."

Joe laughed, "I'm sure that right now Grover Norquist is toasting that the government beast has finally been drowned in the bathtub."

"Yeah," one of the other men grinned, "and the New Dealers are in no position to give it mouth to mouth resuscitation."

"America is the great force for freedom and prosperity throughout the world. Our approach to market-based governance and free trade are models for all countries. As such, we will continue to focus on our core competencies: national defense, homeland security, and protecting the sanctity of life." The President paused to allow the cheers he knew were resonating in hotel suites throughout the country.

In Joe's opinion, market-based government hadn't shrunk that much in terms of actual spending but at least it was focused on the right things for the most part. He wasn't wild about the ever-expanding deficit or the continuing trade imbalance, but the economists he studied on the Hoover Institution web site were for the most part reassuring. And while the "sanctity of life" wasn't at the top of his personal agenda, he respected the sincerity of the President.

The President continued, "After reforming Social Security to reward personal responsibility, we moved on to Medicare. To reflect the longer life spans of my fellow baby boomers, the enrollment age was prudently changed to 75. By outsourcing administration to a consortium of private insurance companies we lowered medical reimbursements to reasonable levels while protecting the incentive of pharmaceutical companies to innovate. All older Americans receive a basic menu of proven cost-effective treatments supplemented with any private policies they choose. We are the healthiest people on earth."

Joe nodded and clapped. He had a premium health plan, which covered all the latest technologies and procedures as well as elective surgeries in Singapore and Bombay.

The President's voice vibrated with excitement. "But we went further than anyone dreamed was possible while maintaining our picture of a compassionate, decent, and hopeful society. Wasteful programs that encouraged fraud and dependency like welfare, Medicaid, and Head Start have been eliminated. Funding for the arts and humanities, as well as medical research has been returned to the private sector where it belongs. Delivery of social services has been streamlined through more effective, committed faith-based organizations. Vouchers let American families choose the best schools for their children based on their own personal beliefs. And in cooperation with the Republican Leadership in Congress, we cut tens of thousands of surplus government jobs that were costing taxpayers billions of dollars each year." The room was filled with energetic applause.

"Still, there remains work to be done to make government even smaller. The federal government is the largest single employer after Wal-Mart, Halliburton and Global Oil and we must continue to call into question all non-essential services. Americans should not fear our economic future, because we intend to shape it in our vision. Due to natural shifts in the private and public sector job markets, I am pleased to report that the military is able to recruit all the infantrymen we need for Operation Universal Freedom. And we've done this without a draft! For example, our Compassionate Service program allows anyone convicted of a non-violent crime or drug offense to opt for military service instead of jail. We have transformed the superior military power of the U.S. into a growth industry."

One guy who Joe knew was a lobbyist for a local defense contractor commented, "It's not public yet but the Administration is planning a new initiative for the next term. Having shown its competency with military transportation and supply infrastructure, Halliburton figured out how to restructure the combat units like a giant temp agency. You can see the implications for more cost savings since they dispense with survivor benefits, military pensions, and veteran health services. Our men and women in the armed forces know the meaning of sacrifice better than anyone else in America. They don't want welfare—they can save money from their salaries, build wealth, and join the ownership society—not the entitlement society. Ownership—that's what makes this country great."

Joe wondered if shifting defense entitlements from the public to the private sector was really legal, but the fellow had such impeccable connections he must know what he was talking about. He was part of the incredibly successful K-Street Project that convinced most corporations that formerly employed lobbyists from both parties to only hire Republicans. Spinning the story so it looked like both parties benefited equally had quelled the scandals from the previous decade.

A commercial real estate developer who had just joined their group noted that the VA hospitals were "sitting on some very valuable property and the only question was whether condo conversions or private long-term care facilities will yield a better return." After the Monterey Defense Language Institute had been relocated to South Dakota, that valuable parcel had been sold off, paying for several months of the war effort. "I'd love to have gotten that commission," he chortled. "The Lucasfilm Letterman complex they built on the old Presidio hospital site in San Francisco was another outstanding project. It showed private development on public land could be as lucrative as using eminent domain to seize blighted neighborhoods for high value development projects."

Despite Joe's firm belief in the sanctity of private property, he rationalized the practice, since the federal government no longer contributed to states and counties. Services like police and garbage pickup were appropriately financed on the local level and municipalities had to be creative in generating revenue to pay for basics. Most communities had shifted to volunteer firefighters, for example, though where he lived in Atherton few of his neighbors were willing to suffer the inconvenience or place themselves at risk. Even if they weren't on corporate jets half the time, it was amusing to imagine guys accustomed to giving the orders wielding an ax or rushing into a burning building to rescue a puppy. He smiled at the image. Rough and ready types didn't live in Atherton, so the town council was forced to maintain a paid unit. Budgeting remained a challenge because Atherton didn't have much retail activity to provide sales tax, and residents hated property taxes so much, but the thought of their own houses burning down was usually persuasive in the end.

He refocused on the speech as Jeb expanded on the challenges facing the U.S. in such a dangerous world. "As the leading champion of freedom and liberty in the world today, America is stronger and more united than ever in the global struggle against violent extremism. Together with our coalition partners, we have achieved regime change in six corrupt and evil oppressive dictatorships over the past 12 years. We have kept the struggle in the terrorists' backyard so they can never strike us at home again. When our mission of defeating terrorists abroad is complete, our men and women in uniform will return home to a proud and safer America. Our resolve is firm and unyielding. To terrorists, murderers, and all those who threaten our most vulnerable citizens—the unborn and unconscious hanging on tenaciously to the thread of life—I say to you: we will stop you dead in your tracks. We will hunt you down wherever in the world you try to hide. We stand for freedom, free enterprise, and free markets. Good night my friends—and God bless America."

The normally reserved men were stomping their feet, cheering, and clapping. They were the "have mores than anyone" and the future was bright for them and their descendents. The optimism in the room was palpable. Expensive champagne flowed on the trip home in the stretch Mercedes and Joe was grateful for the lift as he wobbled in to his silent house. He paused by the last family portrait they had all taken together before both kids had gone off to college. Good-looking family. He felt a twinge of emptiness for a moment but then the alcohol took over as he climbed into bed and drifted off to sleep.

★　　　★　　　★　　　★　　　★

On Sunday, Joe went to church as usual. The graceful structure was nestled in a grove of old oak trees and redwoods adjacent to several other churches in Los Altos. Every time he approached the building he was reassured by its tranquility and timelessness. He loved the sense of history it gave him to be a member of the Congregational Church. The denomination was originally organized when the Pilgrims of Plymouth Plantation and the Puritans of the Massachusetts Bay Colony acknowledged their essential unity in the Cambridge Platform back in the 1600s. He was very proud of his position as Deacon (as were his father and grandfather before him). In his leadership role on the charity committee, he was routinely acknowledged for his ability to summarize the issues and identify the common ground. He valued being part of something larger than himself and he believed worship of God connected him to mankind.

Joe gazed around the warm, well-appointed sanctuary, smiling at his fellow congregants. The well-scrubbed faces of the Youth Choir were rosy-cheeked as they sang hymns praising the glory of God while the ushers walked down the aisle passing the overflowing collection baskets. The minister, an intelligent and energetic fellow, gave an uplifting sermon about the role of religion in government and how it had resulted in a more positive moral climate in the country. However, quite a few people shifted in their seats when the pastor explored the appropriate boundaries of such involvement, discussing the potential impact on those who interpreted religious teachings differently. This had been one of the big divisions in their open-minded and fair congregation— those who felt religion was a private matter versus those who felt called upon by God to share Jesus Christ's message with others. Joe felt you had to respect both positions.

After the closing hymn, *Arise, Arise,* the chairwoman of the Friendship Center reminded everyone that they needed a few more volunteers to serve Thanksgiving dinner. Joe nodded encouragingly to those seated around him. He caught the eye of Sara Stokes who was sitting a few rows back with her son, Simon, and gestured to her. After the service, he caught up to Sara to ask how she was doing.

She gave him a wan smile. "It's been a little rough. Now that Simon is over 18, we don't get child support any more. His father doesn't seem interested in helping him. He took Simon off his health insurance and I can't afford to cover either of us."

Joe listened, his expression sympathetic. "That must be very upsetting. Where are you working these days?"

Sara looked down. "Well, I lost my regional sales manager's job when our company folded and all I could get was a retail position at Nordstrom's. We can get by if we're careful, but there's no money for extras like health insurance or college tuition. Simon found a job renting out portable players and movies at the airport. It doesn't pay much but he likes to talk to people and give advice about films. You remember he's always had a vivid imagination and lots of ideas."

Her son Simon, who had been speaking with the minister at the entrance to the church, came over and joined them. "How's Daniel? What's he doing? I haven't seen him since he finished high school."

Joe paused for a moment before he responded. "Well, after he graduated from Reed, he took a job in San Francisco working for a legal defense fund. I'm not exactly sure what he does as a 'street organizer,' but the group is always hitting me up for donations," Joe chuckled. "They seem a little antagonistic to me. I try to see him every few weeks. I'll tell him you asked about him."

What Joe didn't mention was that Daniel was working on behalf of gay rights, an uphill struggle now. The Supreme Court had upheld new laws in fourteen states that severely restricted special privileges like the rights of gay couples to adopt children or to joint legal rights if the child was conceived through artificial insemination. When Daniel came out to his parents in his last year in high school, Susan had blithely accepted and supported their son's announcement while Joe was more realistic. He dreaded what would happen if too many of his friends and colleagues found out about it, not because there was anything wrong with being gay, but because the world could be so cruel. A few knew or guessed, he suspected, but most were too polite to say anything to his face and Joe was careful not to bring it up. The public's gradual acceptance of homosexuality had been undermined by those on the religious right who were unrelenting in their condemnation of it as unnatural, an abomination and a sin. Even in the supposedly liberal Bay Area, some local communities had cancelled Gay Pride days and related parades without incurring widespread protest.

Sara gave him a hug. "Thanks for listening and being concerned. So many of my former friends have dropped us now that we can't afford to join in on all the group activities the way we used to do. It's hard to have so much less than everyone you know."

As they walked away, Joe wished he could do more than just listen but he didn't think it was his place to intrude. Maybe he could see if they had any openings for sales associates or administrative staff at Organic for Sara? He didn't want to admit to Simon that his relationship with Daniel had become somewhat strained of late. Daniel acted as if Joe were personally responsible for all the laws that were stripping away gay rights. He was disappointed for Daniel's sake, of course, but it's not like *he* had a problem with it. Why was it that everyone thought he was such a kind and reassuring guy except his own family?

★　　　★　　　★　　　★　　　★

On Thursday, Joe arrived at the Friendship Center in the Church refectory around 11:00. He flashed his ID badge and went in. They asked him to carry the super-sized turkey breast meat over to the serving table. It was amazing how drastically they could modify a bird through genetic engineering. He did miss the drumsticks, though.

He looked across the room and recognized one of the former graphic designers from Organic Chemical who was laid off in 2007 when the entire creative department had been moved overseas. Joe avoided catching the man's eyes as he sat with his wife and two boys. He thought about Sara Stokes but this felt different. He was afraid it might embarrass his former colleague to be seen in these circumstances. Besides, people in that situation inevitably wanted job referrals and he didn't have any suggestions.

As he turned the other way, he practically bumped into Forrest Wilson. Forrest had owned a pharmacy in downtown Los Altos before Wal-Mart had built one of their five-acre mega stores nearby. Joe asked, surprised, "What are you doing here?"

The older man explained, "I've taken a job at the Wal-Mart that put me out of business but the pay isn't enough to cover my rent, utilities, and three meals a day. Even though I don't have health insurance, I have a long history with a few of the local physicians so as long as I avoid the hospital I'm making it. I'm lucky I can use my employee discount on my own meds since I can't afford the government authorized insurance premiums either." Joe felt sorry for the guy, but he had to admit Wal-Mart had been a great stock investment for him.

As Joe turned away, he spotted Kipp Sanders. Joe was on some committees with Kipp, but didn't care for the man. Last year when the minister encouraged the congregation to sign a cross-denominational pledge for progressive Christianity, Kipp out and out refused. "We should not 'recognize that being a follower of Jesus is costly, and entails selfless love, conscientious resistance to evil, and renunciation of privilege.' Privilege was not only their birthright but enhancing it was their duty," Kipp argued.

Joe felt that even if one believed he was better, it wasn't polite to say it out loud.

Kipp was holding forth with some of the other volunteers. He was bragging about how many converts he had scored at last Sunday's lunch in the Friendship Center. Kipp liked to remind diners that Jesus was their personal savior and this meal was a gift from God in his Son's name. Joe thought that was putting an awful lot of pressure on some overcooked meat and mashed potatoes.

Jerry Rooz called Joe to invite him to a fundraiser for the Holy Land Orphans Fund (HLOF). Jerry was on the board of the organization dedicated to helping the children left parentless by the Democracy Is On the March military campaigns of the past few years. It sounded like a good cause and Jerry was a good man, so Joe accepted the invitation and drove over to a private home in Old Palo Alto where the reception was to be held.

Joe nodded to the private security guard strolling the quiet tree-lined street as he parked the Hummer and set the alarm. His ID card was scanned against the list at the door. He picked up a glass of wine from a table and entered the large living room. It was not his usual crowd. As he scanned the room, he didn't see anyone he knew. Most of the men and women were middle-aged and he was struck by the racial diversity of the attendees. Everyone was well dressed, though the general style was one of understatement. Even the furnishings seemed unconventional to him, antiques were mixed with modern pieces and there was original artwork on every wall.

Just below the buzz of conversation he could hear classical music, something he hadn't heard at a social function in a while. A string quartet was performing in the corner of the great room. He walked over and a woman whispered to him that these were the principal string players for the San Francisco Symphony. Joe knew the Symphony had fallen on hard times these days but this woman was clearly a fanatic. She condemned the dissolution of the National Endowment for the Arts, the lost donations (charitable contributions were no longer tax deductible), and the decline in attendance of those who could afford the ticket prices. She went on, complaining that "the neighborhoods around Apple iTunes Symphony Hall are deteriorating and the construction of the special garage with an enclosed pedestrian bridge is going too slowly. Even the top artists are forced to find extra jobs, which usually involve playing standards or Boston Pops-style programs. I'm sure the musicians are thrilled to have an engagement where Mozart isn't being derided as a pawn of the cultural elite." He wasn't sure if she was being sarcastic.

"Bet it's easier to find a NASCAR rally in San Jose these days than a musical performance," he joked. "Sure it's not ideal but it does reflect market tastes and the San Jose Grand Prix does make Silicon Valley feel more inclusive."

She grimaced and said, with disdain in her voice, "It's awful that, without music and art programs in the schools for the last decade, we've raised a generation of young people who don't see the value of supporting the arts. You can't expect them to simply wake up at 40 and think it's a great way to spend an evening." By now Joe had figured out that he shouldn't admit he fell asleep the last time Susan had insisted they attend the ballet.

He was relieved to see Jerry coming to his rescue. "Joe, thank you so much for coming. Let me introduce you to Jill and Liam Weintraub of RTB Associates who are on the board with me. For Democrats, Jill and Liam are exceptionally smart and practical people." Joe recognized the name of their firm as one of the preeminent branding and communications consulting companies in the Valley. They had built up their company in the boom years of the 90's and were among the few who had survived the subsequent downturn after the dot com bubble burst.

They thanked him for attending and introduced Joe to some of their neighbors. As Joe politely inquired about their fields of expertise he was impressed by the mix of backgrounds and the variety of professions represented in the group—Stanford professors, doctors, scientists, engineers, even a published author. They were engaged in a lively debate about the latest traffic restrictions and security measures being tested in the neighborhood. So far, the city hadn't decided to cordon off the affluent area, but there were a lot of mixed feelings about how to respond to perceived threats from "outsiders." There had been an increasing number of burglaries recently and the community couldn't agree about what to do, so they weren't doing anything other than adding a few speed bumps and hiring private security companies to patrol the neighborhood 24 x 7.

The music stopped and everyone listened as Jerry introduced the guest speakers, a representative from the Fund and a physician from Doctors Without Borders. Using an oversized flat panel screen built into one end of the room, they showed images of young children playing in the bombed out ruins of Tehran, Mosul, Damascus, and other cities in the Middle East. The doctor talked about his experiences caring for children who had lost their parents. He credited the Fund as one of the few relief groups that was sensitive to local cultures, so they were being invited into more areas as the situations continued to deteriorate. The woman from the Fund then spoke about their heroic efforts to prevent the children from being taken by sex traffickers posing as potential adoptive parents. There was universal support among key members of the Administration, church groups, feminists, and human rights organizations, but there weren't government funds available to back up the emotional commitment. She was a phenomenal speaker. By the time she finished, most of the people in the room, including Joe, were discreetly wiping away the tears. Jerry called on everyone to dig deep into their pockets and show how private citizens could respond to a genuine crisis. "We have to take personal responsibility for our role in the Middle East. It's never easy to introduce democracy, and these innocent children shouldn't have to suffer needlessly because of our well-intentioned quest."

Joe now understood why he hadn't been asked for a donation when he was invited. The eyes of those children were so haunting and Jerry's call to action so compelling to him that when the volunteer came over to get his donation amount and account information, he pledged $10,000. She asked him to sign on the small touch screen of her PDA so the electronic money transfer could be processed. He was glad to be in a position to help.

★　　★　　★　　★　　★

Miranda Elkin and her husband, Marvin, had known Joe and Susan Winston through REP America, a national grass roots group of Republicans for Environmental Protection. It was the one place in his political world that Susan had seemed comfortable enough to attend. She felt a particular affinity for Miranda. Both couples had gotten divorced in the same year, though in Marvin's case it was because he wanted to marry his secretary. Miranda, about ten years older than Joe, was a finance executive. She had started as the CFO of Delphi Systems, and due to integrity differences with the CEO kept getting demoted as the company grew. Finally she resigned and started her own financial planning firm. Ironically, all the Delphi founders had her manage their holdings because she was the smartest CPA they knew, as well as the most trustworthy. She managed Joe's portfolio too, though he was sure he was among her "lesser" clients since he was only worth about $15 million or so.

One Saturday, Miranda called and invited him to go for a hike. She lived across the street from Wunderlich Park in Woodside in a four-bedroom ranch-style house that was remarkably modest for a town of oversized replicas of every grand architectural style ever created. Wunderlich had been a county park established when the town was semi-rural. Now the community—home to many of the business elite—decided there was too much risk involved allowing the public to roam in their backyards. Peter Berger, the volunteer fire marshal, had closed the park one hot summer for fire prevention and it never re-opened. The Woodside town council invoked eminent domain, making Wunderlich a private reserve open only to Woodside residents. Nearby Huddart Park had been sold to a billionaire CEO so his wife and her friends could trail ride from the adjacent 60-horse facility he had purchased for her a few years before.

There had been a huge outcry among the neighboring communities of Atherton, Portola Valley, Palo Alto, Menlo Park and Los Altos Hills that *their* citizens weren't allowed in as well, but the state courts backed the town fathers. Joe suspected the rulings had been a reflection of the appreciation for all the donations the residents had made to the 'Governator' though he was surprised that an exception hadn't been made for the Atherton folks, who were equally generous to the Party.

He checked in at the guardhouse at the corner of Portola and Sand Hill Roads. Closing-off the area solved the noise pollution associated with all those motorcycles roaring up Route 84 to Skyline Blvd, not to mention the hoards of weekend cyclists who routinely swarmed the narrow, twisting roads. Now non-residents had to go several miles north to Highway 92 to get to the ridge and the coast.

Miranda greeted him with a big hug. She was trim and athletic, with short gray hair, and dressed in tasteful green shorts, plaid shirt, and hiking boots. They walked across the street and up the trail past the historic Folger stable, which had been beautifully restored by a local community organization. It didn't look like there were any horses in the barn and the riding ring had been torn down and replaced with a lovely rose garden. He turned quizzically to Miranda.

"When the park was converted to a private preserve, the stable was restricted to Woodside residents who wanted to keep their horses here instead of at home," she began. "One day Larry Edmonton, a stock broker who made millions in private social security account management, was running in the park with his 16-year old son. They ran behind a woman on horseback walking down the hill. As they approached she asked them to please not run up to horses because it could be dangerous. Larry got really angry, told the woman to stop lecturing him, and kept running.

"They happened upon another three horses and riders further down the trail. It was at a point where the trail narrowed and there was a steep drop off on one side. One of the horses, a high-spirited Thoroughbred, spooked when the two ran up behind them and kicked Larry's son in the face. He screamed and the horse on the outside reared and fell down the slope as the edge of the trail gave way. The young woman on that horse broke her neck in the fall. The boy died of brain injuries at the hospital. It was horrible."

Joe vaguely remembered—it had been in the paper for weeks.

"Larry went on the warpath. Even though he was famous for his public tirades against trial lawyers, he sued the rider of the horse, the town council, and the family of the woman who died for failing to control her horse and contributing to his emotional distress. The judge threw the case out of court but the town council decided to close the park to horses. They figured it would be easier to put up with the complaints of the remaining horse owners in Woodside than to get the much larger population of D.E. execs to show any consideration for anyone else." She shook her head. "You'd think these guys were training for the Olympics."

What's D.E?" Joe asked.

"Divinely Entitled," Miranda laughed. "You know. The people who believe the rules don't actually apply to them. That they're too important and special."

Joe chuckled. "I know what you mean. After all, it's only truly unique people like ourselves who are entitled to special treatment."

Miranda laughed again. As they walked up the trail, Joe breathed in the rich air generated by the groves of redwood trees above and varied ferns below. The smell brought him back to the days when he and Susan hiked here quite often. He often thought their best moments were in this serene place—the kids would run ahead searching out lizards and banana slugs, he and Susan would hold hands and exchange pleasantries with the other families sharing the unruly woods. It was a lot less crowded today—they only passed one other couple and a young woman running with her bottle of water and her iPod.

As they walked around a bend, the sun broke through the mist and sent rays of light streaming through the branches of the redwood trees. If they were in a movie, the choir of angels would be singing right now. Everything was damp and clean from the previous day's rain. He stopped and smiled. "It's impossible for me to look at this and not see God."

Miranda said quietly, "It is beautiful. However, I prefer to think of it as the energy of the universe rather than in religious terms. Of course, I wouldn't admit that to just anyone. Don't tell my minister." She paused and took a deep breath. "I'm thinking about selling my house. It's too big for just me and the Woodside crowd is getting to me."

"But it's a great place." Joe protested, "Woodside is one of the safest communities in the Bay Area. You got the house in the divorce. Why would you give it up? Where would you go? Your business is here. Your clients are here. Your friends and church are here."

"I know, but I'm starting to have doubts. I've been an avid environmentalist my whole life and every time I hike to the top of Windy Hill and look out at the oil platforms being built offshore, it sticks in my throat."

"I know what you mean. It bothers me too, but you can't stand in the way of economic growth or energy security."

They walked in comfortable silence for a few minutes until they reached the Meadows and sat for a while on a picnic table looking over the valley. The storm had cleared the smog and you could actually see the detail of trees and buildings on the purple and green hills on the east side of the bay.

"Maybe if you try Palo Alto, it won't be so bad. There are a lot of folks who know they've made compromises, but decided to stay for the weather and their homes. It's a more mixed community so you'd have more people to commiserate with about the environment. Besides, I'd miss you if you left."

Miranda patted his hand. "You're a sweet man. Don't you ever have doubts about where the country is going?"

"Sometimes. I suppose I was counting on the Democrats to keep things from getting too out of hand, but for the most part, the Bush family has been leading the country well. They surround themselves with exceptionally smart people. I share their belief that if you work hard in this country, you have a great life. I know we've made some sacrifices on the environment or in the name of security, but you have to admit that you and I are better off financially than we ever were. We're dismantling the big-government spending programs and now we can make real progress. Isn't that what we wanted?"

Miranda changed the subject. "Where are you going for Christmas?"

"Skiing in Aspen with the Andersens. They have a house with a view of the slopes and a gondola stop right at the end of their street. Bill's divorced sister is coming. I'm the extra man and buffer so she won't harass Bill about having married someone younger than his kids. Christmas Eve we'll go out for dinner and then hang out and watch football games and eat takeout on Christmas Day. Bill's new wife is cute, but I don't get the sense she's much of a cook and Bill let the private chef go home to see his family for the holidays. What about you?"

"I'm going to visit my daughter and her family in Australia. I can't believe she moved out of the country," said Miranda wistfully. "I miss seeing my grandchildren grow up. She and her husband are both molecular biologists and it made them crazy to see the school science curriculum eviscerated. Teaching creationism and intelligent design as equivalent to evolution makes U.S. education a joke in the rest of the world."

"They sound like my son Daniel. He says the same thing. He's going to visit Susan for the holidays. I don't see him often enough these days. I love him, but it seems like we end up in arguments every time we get together. Everyone else tells me I'm a great listener but Daniel tells me I don't get it." Joe looked genuinely distressed. "He maintains our educational system is having an adverse impact on the stock market but I'm hoping he's wrong. We have the best schools in the world."

Miranda spoke carefully. "Not to be pessimistic, but the kids may have a point. The biotech companies in India and China are overtaking U.S. companies in a big way. The decent scientists we do manage to produce are going overseas because the option packages are so much better there. Halliburton and residential health care services seem to be the only areas that are growing. Medical devices—even surgery—are going overseas to Asia.

"Maybe I'm too fiscally conservative," she admitted, "but I saw an announcement this morning that China's central bank and major corporations are reducing investments in U.S. Treasuries and are putting their money into bonds backed by the Euro instead. It bothers me that our country, the world's largest creditor nation for over a century, has become the world's largest debtor. Our economy is straining at the seams as it imports, buys, and borrows more while it, exports, produces and saves less and less. It's like we're maxing out our credit card. The U.S. is no longer what Milton Friedman had maintained it always would be—the world's savings bank.

"China and Japan hold so much paper that they can control our economy if they choose. I hate to think what would happen if another stand-off, like the one over Taiwan erupts. We had to back down the last time there was a problem."

"The Chinese wouldn't dare pull the plug on our economy," Joe countered. "We're their biggest global customer after India. Besides, they're happy with the oil they're getting from Alaska."

"You mean the area formerly known as the Arctic National Wildlife Refuge? I still remember our email campaign on that, where we teamed up with the Democratic groups. The Energy lobbyists outmaneuvered us. Too bad it's only estimated to produce for about another five years." Joe thought Miranda sounded sad as she added, "Oh yes, Global Oil is a safe bet. How could I have forgotten to mention them?"

Joe drove through the electronic gates of the Los Altos Hills estate. His hosts had thoughtfully programmed his RFID tag into the security system. The house and grounds were beautifully lit like a Venetian palace—and about as spacious and ornate. A bit much for Joe's taste but very well done. In fact, many of the artifacts and architectural details had been rescued from Venice before the daily flooding pushed out well past St. Mark's Square. The parking attendant opened the door of the Hummer and greeted him politely.

By the time he had walked up the cobblestone path, the houseman had opened the 12-foot high double mahogany doors to reveal the three story marble atrium with a huge, ornate Murano glass chandelier. An elegantly attired young woman was waiting with an icy martini in a crystal glass. He thanked her as she directed him to the solarium.

The expansive glass conservatory was filled with thousands of exotic orchids, ferns, and unusual trees. His hostess, Carolyn Wellbetter, offered him her cool, smooth cheek to be kissed. Like most of his friends' wives, she was under 30, blond, with a killer figure well toned by many hours at the gym, spa, and Poxya studio (a combination of yoga, pilates, and kickboxing that was the latest fad). Now that Viagra and more recent equivalents were as common as vitamins among their set, the women their own age just couldn't keep up, even with a full regimen of botox, plastic surgery, and diets.

Besides, women in their 50s and 60s didn't, for the most part, have the right attitude for the current approach to family values. The feminist movement, which had pushed the notion that women were equal, had faded out amongst the younger generation. Most successful men Joe knew preferred women who saw assembling a luxurious home and being instantly available for their husbands as far more rewarding than a demanding career. Of course, the new breed of breeders—he chuckled at his own joke—could be rather boring. For a moment he tried to picture his daughter Amanda in this setting, but couldn't, and shook the image from his mind.

He stood in the corner with his back to the wall as he surveyed the 50 or so guests. His host, Troy Wellbetter, the managing partner of a multinational venture fund was laughing as he told a story, surrounded by a covey of attentive admirers. In the opposite corner, Joe observed an exceedingly attractive young wife gazing adoringly at her husband, who was in an animated exchange with two other men. All three completely ignored her repeated attempts to give her opinion. Several couples were being given a tour of the host's extensive collection of Thomas Kinkade paintings by the family's personal curator. In another room, there were landscapes on loan from the Triton Museum—in exchange for a handsome donation, of course.

Troy's twenty-something son from his first marriage was talking to a group of young people. Tim had recently moved back home after graduating from Exeter and Yale, Troy's alma mater. A lot of kids were doing that these days, with jobs so scarce and less expensive neighborhoods so dangerous. Joe made a mental note to see if their company had room for a bright, well-connected lad like Tim. Troy's fund had been the lead investor in Organic's third round and Joe knew that finding a "strategic" role for Tim could be strategic for the Company, as well as his own future plans.

He stepped nearer the lively crowd. Most he recognized as the children of his friends from earlier marriages. It was very gracious of Carolyn to encourage them all to come to the party, though he didn't see any first wives in attendance. The college students among them were lamenting the changes that had occurred at their schools in the latest round of closings. Except for the top 10 that had the *big* endowments and reputations (Harvard, Stanford, Yale, Princeton, MIT, University of Texas, Notre Dame, Oral Roberts University, Georgetown, and Universal Bible College), many universities were experiencing severe funding problems. Quite a few state public colleges and universities had simply shut down, with the properties sold off to residential care companies.

A fit-looking brunette expressed her annoyance that there weren't any women's sports at her school. Going to football games, the only athletic program remaining, wasn't as much fun as participating herself. When a tall, willowy blond girl complained that the art and literature departments had folded her junior year, the other girls gave a collective shrug and went back to bemoaning the state of the dorms. The rooms were way too small and lacked the amenities they were accustomed to having at home. Joe had to admit that since these kids had grown up with 1500 square foot suites, plus large family rooms oriented towards them, it seemed perfectly reasonable that a normal dormitory would feel claustrophobic. Spoiled, perhaps, but understandable.

Joe felt a hand on his arm and turned around. Troy's wife had a pretty friend in tow. Carolyn was introducing her and saying something about how they should get together. As Joe made small talk, he found himself distracted by similarities in the two women's voluptuous bodies and soft voices. He could see their matching bee-stung lips moving at different times but it sounded like the same person speaking. He smiled attentively and tried to focus on their words. Tiffany, her name was Tiffany. She made some joke about being born to like jewelry and he graciously chuckled as his eyes followed her gesture to the diamonds sparking on her ample chest where she pointed out a gift from "a friend." He found himself wondering if the gift was the jewelry or the other delightful enhancements. Either way it must have been a very good friend.

Why were his pals' wives always trying to fix him up? He liked living alone with the quiet and room for his own thoughts. He had enjoyed being a parent when he was younger but he wasn't interested in starting another family as so many of his friends were doing. The sex was good but it just wasn't important enough to him to put up with having someone around in the morning, and the afternoon, and into the next evening.

He held out his arm and escorted Tiffany into dinner. Joe helped her into her chair. Her dress, which didn't leave much to the imagination in the first place, gave him quite a view from this angle. They were seated at a table with eight other singles. He knew the four other men from business functions or the country club. Like him, they were 50-ish, divorced, and from the secondary executive tier—two were VPs of Human Resources, one was a Chief Marketing Officer, and one a Chief Financial Officer. None of them had broken into the ranks of the top job— those guys were sitting on the other side of the room. The women...well the women were uniformly attractive though they looked like support staff more than peers.

Tiffany said she was the manager of Carolyn's favorite spa. He asked her about the challenges of her job and what she liked best about it. She responded by saying she was a "people person" but didn't elaborate. He wished he knew what people meant when they said that.

The women shared a hungry look that was a little haunted around their eyes with fixed dazzling white smiles. Three were blond and two were oriental but otherwise they seemed pretty interchangeable. He would have liked a redhead just to mix the fantasies up a bit. They laughed at the men's jokes almost too readily and were incredibly deferential when the men moved past the introductions. Personally, he preferred women with a little more going on upstairs.

The CFO announced, "I'll be attending the inauguration galas this month." A fellow Pioneer, Joe knew his company had donated $300,000 to the event, which promised to be the most lavish ever. "Now that we've gotten rid of the death, capital gains, and corporate taxes, there's plenty to go around for festivities and security. The safety measures being instituted for this inauguration are unprecedented. Every person attending any event or watching the parade down Pennsylvania Avenue has to have a retinal scan and full background check."

One of the HR guys concurred, "They had to do something after the 2009 fiasco." Thousands of hoodlums had turned out to protest even though D.C. was effectively shut down with bridges closed, snipers on every rooftop, and helicopters and fighter jets patrolling the skies above. "I was told the organizers felt that the process was still too open and dangerous."

"Well, as one of the big shots, I'll be able to by-pass all the checkpoints. It's not necessary for those who demonstrate their loyalty to America so convincingly," boasted the CFO.

The CMO bristled, "As a Libertarian, I don't see a desire for privacy as disloyal. It's nobody's business how I spend my money or what my doctor tells me. The government needs to get its nose out of my bedroom."

"Now, now," soothed his dinner partner, the blonde Joe was still trying to imagine as a redhead. "We can talk about bedrooms later," she said with a suggestive wink. "I'm happy to make my medical and financial records open to the government. It makes me feel safer."

Tiffany agreed, "I know the lines, barricades, checkpoints, retinal scans, and electronic identity cards can be annoying, but it's just part of life—no one even thinks twice about them anymore."

Joe chimed in, suggesting, "If you feel inconvenienced, post a $100,000 bond and get your ID card encoded with an EZpass accelerator that lets you bypass most obstacles. I got one and it's great."

Joe felt satisfied after the sumptuous meal of *foie gras*, black truffle soufflé, rare prime rib, and endive and arugula salad. The waiters brought out the dessert. Generous portions of lemon sorbet with a mix of fresh out-of-season berries were served in individual ice bowls lit from within with tiny lights. It was delicious even if chocolate was your preferred sweet.

Scores of staff bustled around to fill everyone's glasses with Dom Perignon for the midnight toast. As they'd found when they sold Organic Chemical to the Sodexho ADM Alliance, the frosty relationship with the French didn't seem to be a problem where fine wines and corporate investment were concerned. As the clock struck midnight, thousands of butterflies were released into the room. After she gave him the obligatory New Year's Eve kiss, Tiffany whispered that Carolyn had purchased three different kinds of endangered silverspot varieties with her donation to a wildlife rescue group.

They went around the table sharing their New Year's resolutions. Losing weight seemed to be the universal goal among the women. The men seemed focused on improving their golf handicaps. Joe mumbled something about traveling to exotic locales and the rest cracked up. It wasn't that easy finding places that catered to Americans any longer, unless they were secure resorts on private islands. Virtually every country with a sizable Muslim population was definitely off-limits as simply too risky.

Tiffany stood up to go to the powder room with the other women, smiling seductively as she left. As the men retired to the library for cigars and cognac, Joe chose that moment to slip out, pausing briefly to thank Carolyn for a lovely evening. He knew it was cowardly but he wanted to avoid a scene.

As he waited for his car, he scanned the sky. The remotely operated planes that patrolled the California airspace buzzed serenely overhead. The cool air was hazy with the smell of wood fires burning but it was still possible to see a few stars. Down in the valley he could see the rolling blackouts hitting various neighborhoods. He was glad he hadn't offered to take Tiffany home. He just wanted to start 2013 in the tranquility and peace of his own home.

Joe walked through Organic Chemical's lobby, glancing at a group of East Indian men in well-tailored gray and blue suits gathered in one of the conference rooms. One of the secretaries was serving them coffee and tea. He didn't know about any meetings so he figured they must be from an Indian subsidiary of the Sodexho ADM Alliance. Maybe they were here for "best practices" training since Organic was such a great operation? He swung by Jay's office but the door was closed. Jay was on the telephone and didn't look up when Joe signaled to him through the glass. As Joe was getting settled and checking his email, Brian Ferguson, the HR VP, stuck his head through the door, asking if Joe had time to come by later that morning. At 10, Joe went to Brian's office at the far corner of the building. He distinctly remembered Brian describing the business rationale why the Sodexho ADM executive team had decided to offshore all their legal work to India, but he had to admit that the details escaped him as the implications sunk in.

Joe was incredulous, "How could that bunch of guys downstairs understand the subtleties of the American market and legal system? It will take forever to explain the details on every contract. Half of them don't even look like they were old enough to shave for God's sake. My team is outstanding and many have been with me for years." Dear God, what would he say to them?

Brian noticed that Joe wasn't registering his recommendations for how to communicate the news to the rest of the legal staff without causing chaos in the ranks. Brian paused and went out to get Joe a glass of water. Joe gulped it down without breathing. He didn't know how long he sat there without speaking. Finally, he looked at Brian.

"If we're just trying to lower headcount for the analysts, can't we move the group to our outside counsel locally? I'm sure Frank will take on the team. It's going to be hell trying to manage this long distance."

Brian cleared his throat. "I guess I wasn't clear enough. When I said 'offshoring ALL the legal work,' I meant ALL. You and Frank are both out too. It's not Jay's call. The guys in Europe are insisting we make drastic cuts. Finance is going too, I'll be talking to the CFO next."

Joe couldn't believe his ears. He had been the one who negotiated the sale to Sodexho ADM. How could they fire him? How could *he* be superfluous? Why was Brian having this conversation with him? Why wasn't Jay telling him the news personally? He had to get a grip.

Right…Joe regained his composure as Brian went through the terms of his settlement. "You'll still collect the $250,000 bonus for closing the deal and get a year's severance. The employees on your team will get two weeks pay for every year they've worked for the Company, and, of course, the contractors won't get anything beyond what they've earned today. You can keep the Hummer for another 30 days, which should give you plenty of time to get another position and a new car lease.

"As you know—since you were on the national task force to kill the COBRA program—your health insurance will terminate along with your employment. Of course, you don't have any pre-existing conditions, so that shouldn't be a problem when you get your new job. Your executive stock package vested automatically when the company was sold, so that $2,000,000 is already in the bank.

"The legal team from India is waiting to start the transition process. You have an hour to speak with your people and listen to their concerns. Then they have to begin turning over the access codes to your department's systems and briefing your replacements about the deals and contracts in the works. I'll be busy with the finance group, but call my wireless if you run into any problems. We'd also appreciate it if you let us know if there are any inappropriate reactions. You remember, last layoff someone brought in a gun from their car and we had to get the police in with tasers."

Back in his office, Joe put in a call to the managing partner at their outside counsel, Wilson, Sonsini, Goodrich, Fenwick, West, Cooley, Goddard. Maybe he could take Frank to lunch at Spago's (last hurrah on the old expense account), break it to him gently and then ask him for a job at the same time?

Joe hated telling his team. He valued loyalty—even the contractors had worked for him before—and this group had always given him their all. They did brilliant analysis, finding every possible legal loophole, whether it was how to get around pollution restrictions (which admittedly had gotten pretty lax over the past decade), or how to play the Sarbanes-Oxley game so any control gaps could be easily explained. Saved them a ton on their outside auditing expenses! The way they had transformed a bunch of informal contracts with small organic farmers and rolled them up into a large-scale agribusiness operation was sheer genius. He knew better than to promise them that they'd all land someplace together, but he would make a couple of calls for each of them.

They took it better than he expected. There was some grumbling, some name calling, and Steve Summers, whose wife had just given birth to triplets after three years of infertility treatments, was sitting in the corner stunned, holding his head in his hands and groaning. His wife had given up her job three months before and they had a big mortgage in a new development, Page Mill Ranch, built on former Stanford open space. Joe asked Jane Andrews, the paralegal contractor, to handle the turnover of Steve's files—it didn't look like Steve was going to make it through the day. He debated whether to send Brian an email warning about Steve. Nah, it would serve them right if Steve went postal on them.

Joe reminded his staff how proud he was of them, what a tremendous job they'd done, and how as professionals, he knew they would make the handoff as smooth as possible. They agreed to meet for a drink later—without the Indians, of course.

The valet at Spago's took the Hummer and Joe caught up with Frank Lerner. He had reserved a table in a quiet corner. Frank raised an eyebrow as Joe ordered a bottle of La Jota Cabernet Sauvignon "Howell Mountain" ($250) before they had even heard the specials. They both chose the truffle stuffed quail with wild rice and *haricots verts*. Over lunch, they talked about golf, the weather, and Frank's family. Frank's wife had been giving him a hard time. The *au pair* she had arranged from Montreal had been turned away at customs because the girl had baby sat for someone else on a previous trip to California with her family, but hadn't reported it properly. The wife had to give up her daily tennis game to take care of the kids after school and Frank was worried he was never going to hear the end of it.

Frank's face turned ashen as Joe told him the news over dessert and coffee. It was the third client he had lost to an Indian outfit this month—there was just no way to compete with companies that paid their partners and associates one tenth the amount that U.S. firms did. If things didn't improve soon they were going to have to lay off all their remaining associates. The paralegals were doing the best they could, but too many of the older partners couldn't do the online research themselves, yet didn't want to make way for younger people who could.

Joe figured now was not the time to ask about opportunities for his team and himself.

★   ★   ★   ★   ★

Joe knew he was awake but he couldn't open his eyes. His head hurt too much and he was sure sunlight wouldn't help. He vaguely recalled making his way home after the all-night drinking session with his team. Guess that was one advantage of having so few cops on the roads. Turning over the files to the Indians had been unbearable. It was humiliating. Nonetheless, they had all been good soldiers and done their duty (except for Steve who didn't make it out of the men's room for the better part of the afternoon).

Jay had avoided him yesterday. You'd think after recruiting Joe for the company and working side by side for four years that the guy would want to say goodbye, but not Jay apparently. He overheard Jay's secretary on the phone suggesting that Jay stop by Joe's office, but the well-intended arrow had fallen short of its target. Most people in the office had avoided looking at him entirely, except for the finance team. Many of them were in tears, especially the ones who had been with the company since the beginning.

Joe put the pillow over his head to make the transition easier. He peered out, and then closed his eyes again. He didn't actually have to get up at all. It's not like he had to be anywhere today. The emptiness of the entire day loomed in front of him. His mouth was dry. Was it the alcohol or the thought that his schedule wasn't full?

It was afternoon when Joe awoke next. He turned on the flat panel in his bedroom. They were showing scenes of some battle someplace. Once you bombed the hell out of ratty old cities surrounded by deserts, these wars all kind of looked alike. With over 800,000 troops deployed in six countries, it was hard to keep track of what was going on in any of them. The war news was so carefully edited that you couldn't always tell what was what, only that America was winning the War on Terror. He walked into the bathroom and stood at the double sinks. His reflection in the mirror was decidedly unappetizing. Better not to look. He turned on the heater to get the steam room going, then sat down on the marble bench. It felt good just to sweat.

After his shower he debated whether to shave. One day wouldn't kill him. He took something out of the freezer and heated it up, opened a bottle of wine, and sat down to eat in the family room while he watched a bunch of overweight, ugly people argue about who had slept with whose underage child. The studio audience was roaring with approval and blood lust as one woman beat some scuzzball to a pulp. The guy deserved it. He flipped through the channels: soap operas, reality interventions for those with drug and alcohol problems, celebrity interview shows, or the War on Terrorism channel. It almost made you long for the days of domination by the Jewish media conspiracy, not that there was anything wrong with being Jewish.

He shut off the 80-inch flat panel, popped a few pills and climbed back into bed even though it was only 5:30. Joe slept a lot that week. He went to his regular golf games and tennis matches at the club—going at his normal times so no one would know what had happened. Sunday, he went to church as usual. No one asked him about work and he didn't volunteer anything. He thought about calling Daniel but he didn't really want to ask his son for sympathy (or hear the inevitable tirade about corporate insensitivity). On Monday, after he woke up around 10, he showered, shaved, and decided he had babied himself enough. Time to get moving again.

Joe was nothing if not thorough and meticulous. Setting a pot of coffee beside him, he sat down at his computer and checked his email (not much except for the usual SPAM offering $50 child brides from third world countries). Joe started going through his contact list, making a note of everyone who either owed him a favor or could be a lead. In a few hours he had a neatly organized list: church contacts, other attorneys from the bar association, executives he knew from his political fundraising activities, former colleagues, and associates who were currently employed.

Next he reviewed and updated his resume. Looked pretty impressive if he did say so himself. Four years at Organic Chemical supporting the turnaround and selling them to Sodexho ADM. Eight years at the Ghirardelli Scharffen Berger Chocolate Company going through an IPO and three major acquisitions. Eight years at HP. Six years at Brobeck, Phleger & Harrison (too bad he hadn't made partner before they went under in the dot-com bust). J.D. from Stanford Law and a B.S. in Economics from the University of Michigan.

He felt pretty damn good. Mixed himself a drink. Defrosted something for dinner. Put his feet up and watched a movie in his home theatre, *Shame of the Magdalene*, the Mel Gibson film that proved definitively that Mary Magdalene *was* a whore after all, *DaVinci Code* speculation not withstanding. One of the Olsen twins (he couldn't tell them apart) starred and it was among the top grossing films in years. He fell asleep before it was over and woke up to the flashing menu of the DVX (the technology that replaced DVDs in 2010, forcing him to get all new equipment and replace the movies in his collection).

The next morning Joe showered, shaved, and dressed in business casual so he'd have the right mindset as he made his first round of calls. He had a good breakfast, plenty of coffee, and donned his wireless headset for the phone in his study. He mostly reached people's voice mails where he left upbeat messages. A few numbers had been disconnected or had messages saying the person was out of town. The second day, he repeated the routine and got through the remainder of his list.

By Friday, only four people had called him back. Two accepted his invitations for coffee, and one invited him in to the office. The fourth just said he was too busy with layoffs. Undaunted, he started emailing likely people on his list, attaching his resume after confirming they were still at those companies. A disquieting number had apparently moved on or had unlisted numbers according to the Google National People Registry and Database. For a fee, he could have them tracked down by E-Detectives, but he decided to hold off on that for now.

The next week Joe met with a friend at VISA-MasterCard. Fred welcomed Joe into his office. Mahogany paneling, antique furniture, soft lighting and two original Norman Rockwells on the wall. Joe sat on the leather couch; on the other side of the Oriental rug Fred sat in a wingback chair. His secretary brought them coffee in a silver carafe.

They chatted about their golf handicaps, Fred's trip to the Whistler ski area last week, and his wife's plans for their daughter's wedding this June. She wanted to rent the Ahwanee Hotel at Yosemite and put up all the guests. Her best friend had rented the Sonoma Mission Inn and Laura thought it lacked the right ambiance, even though the guest rooms were nicer. "Still, your daughter only gets married for the first time once," Fred chuckled indulgently. "So what brings you in today, need a new platinum card?"

Joe cleared his throat. He hated having to ask outright. He'd thought Fred understood his casually dropped hints when they made the appointment. He explained how after the acquisition, Sodexho ADM had decided to offshore the legal and financial activities to India. It seemed like a good time to switch industries and he was hoping that Fred might have some openings coming up.

Fred smiled "Joe, we go back a long way. I'd love to help you out but the truth is, we're cutting costs ourselves. Confidentially, we're eliminating 3,000 positions next quarter. With so many people losing their jobs and their health insurance, our number of personal bankruptcies is skyrocketing. With the personal responsibility laws passed in '05 we were protected in the short run but it's hard to get folks back in the game after they've lost everything. Our ad agency misjudged how aggressively to pitch new cardholders and we're getting hammered. While people are buying more large ticket items due to rising burglaries and car jackings, they're not able to pay it back, even with our long-term 30% financing strategies. I'm sorry, but my hands are tied. If I hear of anything, I'll be sure to let you know. Let's try to have lunch in a few weeks."

The coffee meetings weren't much better. He'd managed to score only three. Everyone was very pleasant but no one had any good suggestions. Most chief counsels who had jobs were staying put. None of the general managers or CFOs had anything at the division level, and the big firms weren't taking on any new partners. There were a few lower level legal spots open here and there but no one imagined that he'd be willing to take one of those jobs. Not with all his experience.

He even thought about trying for something in the California Attorney General's Office, but when he called his contact in the governor's office, the guy actually laughed out loud. There had been a hiring freeze for the past three years.

He was feeling a little discouraged but then something came into his email in-box that brightened his spirits. The Stanford Law School Alumni Group was hosting a cocktail party to honor Supreme Court Chief Justice Roberts. Jointly sponsored by the Hoover Institution, the event was scheduled in two weeks. Joe emailed his RSVP, attaching his security bona fides, and made a reservation for a golfing week in Palm Springs. He might as well enjoy himself in the interim. He had a nice nest egg in the bank, a great C.V., lots of contacts, and plenty of drive. The right job would turn up. He had faith in himself, in the system, and in God.

Joe returned from Palm Springs refreshed and ready to tackle the job search anew. The Stanford event was a week away so he decided to focus his energies researching his law school alumni contacts in the Bay Area who were likely to be in attendance. He perused the alumni directory and did online searches, gathering background on their political donations, corporate affiliations, athletic results, and charitable activities. He wanted to be ready with topics of conversation for everyone who might be attending and he put together short profiles he could scan on his mobile communicator at the reception.

He was concentrating so hard on the task at hand that he didn't stop to eat lunch nor did he hear the initial knock at the front door. The knocking persisted. It finally pierced his consciousness, and he wondered who it could be. It was the middle of the afternoon. Kids were at school. People were at work. It wasn't like he was on the social calendar of the neighborhood trophy wives and stay-at-home moms. Since the front gate office hadn't called, it couldn't be a visitor.

Before he could reach the door, it was kicked in. Five men in helmets, black flack jackets, and very large automatic weapons burst in yelling. It must be a home invasion, how could those hooligans have gotten into Lindenwood? Then he saw their jackets were marked with the Homeland Security Logo and SWAT TEAM in large letters.

It was amazing how still you could stand when five big guys with guns were pointing them at you. His mouth was totally dry, though he realized with increasing discomfort that his jeans were not. One guy gave a signal to three of the officers to start searching the house, the other two kept their automatic rifles trained on him.

He started to say that there must be some mistake but was told to shut up. Two men emerged from his study carrying his computer, his job hunting files, all the notes he had been making in preparation for the Roberts reception, and his financial records. Another fellow came out of his bedroom with his passport, some books and magazines, and the materials from the Holy Land fundraiser that he had left on his nightstand.

He was handed a card and they all left, without even giving him a receipt. Joe decided it was prudent not to say anything. He looked at the card: Terrence Mackelwhite, Terrorist Funds Auditor, Department of Homeland Security. 202-555-5068 x1934.

This had to be a misunderstanding. He was a person of means and importance, a loyal American. Joe grabbed the phone and dialed the number. A pleasant recorded voice answered suggesting he leave a message. In an outraged tone, Joe relayed what had happened, adding that he was an attorney and a GOP Pioneer. He closed by saying he expected to have his property returned that day. Tomorrow at the latest.

Next he dialed his personal lawyer and told the receptionist it was an emergency. Jack Swenson had handled his divorce and his estate planning. He told Jack what had just happened. Jack told him to sit tight while he made a few calls.

The next three hours were interminable. Joe took a shower and changed into dry clothes. He paced the house, turned all the TVs on and off at least a dozen times. He couldn't read, watch a movie, or eat. He drove downtown to get a doppio at Starbucks and his credit card was rejected. That was strange. He pulled out some cash and paid. He was so annoyed he only left a quarter tip.

His mobile communicator warbled. It was Jack. He walked out of the cafe and stood on the sidewalk. Jack had called a contact at Homeland Security. Apparently, the agency had determined that Orphans of the Holy Land had financial ties to

Al Qaeda. With Osama still on the loose, the group was still widely acknowledged as the scourge of the universe, even though there were now over 40 groups engaged in *jihad*—and they owed nothing to Osama but token respect. Joe's $10,000 donation had triggered an investigation. Joe explained how he had been invited to the fundraiser in the first place. Jack suggested that Joe come in to the office in the morning. He'd tell his secretary to move his other appointments.

Still no word from Terrence Mackelwhite. It was infuriating. What were we paying these guys for anyway? On his home voice mail, there was a message. "Joe, it's Miranda. I tried to execute that stock trade we discussed but something was wrong with my access code to your account. Would you please call me in the morning to give me the new code? Thanks. Bye." He thought about calling her to see if she wanted to have dinner but didn't know what he'd say. Better to just wait till he talked to Jack.

The next morning, Jack's secretary ushered him in to the office. Jack didn't waste time with pleasantries. "This is not looking good. As far as I can tell, they've frozen all your bank and brokerage accounts and put a hold on your credit cards while they trace all your transactions for the last three years. Mackelwhite is out of the office for a week so I couldn't speak to him. The good news is my contact says they haven't started criminal proceedings yet."

"This is ridiculous." Joe was practically foaming at the mouth. "I'm not a terrorist. Call Jerry Rooz. He'll tell you that he invited me to the fundraiser."

"I'm sorry to say Jerry's been detained. I spoke to his wife last evening and she doesn't know where they're holding him. She's scared that he's going to be subjected to extraordinary rendition."

"What's that?" Joe asked.

"I'm surprised you haven't heard about it. The government made it standard policy years ago. It's a technique to let our allies who are less squeamish use more persuasive interrogation methods on suspected terrorists. Lots of countries do it. As Iranians, they knew it could happen at any time so she's going to visit her sister in Vancouver to see if they can get the Canadian government to help. They've been willing to intercede in other situations where innocent people have been picked up. If anything, you actually might want to play down your connection to Jerry. In Washington, they're probably tearing up all the 'click' photos of politicians shaking hands with him as we speak.

"Unfortunately right now there's nothing you can do to help the situation. It would be a good idea to liquidate some assets quickly. Furniture, paintings, that sort of thing. My wife and her friends have started a new business that might interest you. It's sort of like a reverse Tupperware party. They bring over a small group of women who they feel would appreciate the furnishings in your home and then they discreetly purchase items they like. The gals get a bargain and it's a great way to get some cash under the table. Wendy takes a small cut of 30% and you can clear enough to keep you going until we can clean this mess up."

"What about my house? My mortgage payments are due on the 15th. If I can't access my capital, I can't pay my bills. It's my money. I earned it—well, most of it anyway. On top of that my company laid me off so there's no new income coming in right now."

"That's a shame, though they'd probably just garnish your wages if you did have a job. Well, you might want to talk to the bank that holds the mortgage. Maybe they'll cut you some slack for a couple of months. I know it's not your style, but don't pay your bills for a while. Except mine, of course." Jack grinned, but Joe's normally good sense of humor had abandoned him.

"A couple of months?" Joe's voice rose. "It's going to take that long to fix this? They took my computer. I'm actively looking for a new job and I was getting ready to network at the Chief Justice reception at Stanford next week."

"You'd better forget that one. I don't think you're getting past security." Jack grinned and shook his head. "As I said, just be thankful that they haven't launched a criminal investigation yet. Stay below the radar and don't do anything foolish to call attention to yourself. I'll have Wendy call you to set up a time to come over to your house."

Jack took out his wallet and pulled out some bills. "Here's 200 bucks. Hang in there. It'll be ok."

Joe stared at the money in his hand. This could not possibly be happening to him.

★　　★　　★　　★　　★

Joe was almost out of cash. It hadn't occurred to him how dependent he was on his credit cards and the ATM. I mean, you wanted it and the money was there. Anyone willing to work hard could have a good life. He walked around the house and garage to figure out what he could sell quickly. Joe glanced at the pile of stuff he had left in the hallway when he returned from Palm Springs. He had just bought a brand new set of Callaway clubs: driver, irons, hybrids, even a new high-tech laser putter. Everything state of the art, the latest materials. Set him back about $5,000 and he had only played with them a few times. It killed him to think of selling them, especially the putter—$600 for that alone. At least he had his old set in the garage.

Since he had just a few days left before he had to turn in the Hummer and his membership was paid up for the quarter, he decided to pay a visit to the pro shop at the Club. He drove up Page Mill Road to the Country Club. The Hummer was a bit wide for the narrow, winding road, but the only thing he had to worry about was another Hummer coming down the other way.

On the way up, he rehearsed the conversation in his head. OK, he wanted to sell the clubs because…he wasn't totally happy with them. Why wouldn't he just replace the individual clubs he didn't like? He liked to have a matching set. Oh for crying out loud, that sounds like something a woman would say. How about he heard about a new technology when he was in the Springs and he just had to have them? That was better. Sanjay would buy that.

Why would he want cash instead of a credit? Think, think! A guy he knew had access to next year's models but he'd only take cash. Hmm…that made them sound like something that had fallen off the truck. What would be another reason you'd want cash? Oh, how about he could get a better discount if he paid him cash? Better leave the golf bag carrier in the car, how could he explain why he couldn't simply use that for the new set?

The guard checked his membership card and ID at the gate. Joe parked in front of the Pro Shop. The parking lot had been re-striped for the new wider models most of the members drove, and the handicapped parking spaces painted over so he was able to park right next to the entrance. He rehearsed his talking points again, took a deep breath, threw his shoulders back, and strode into the pro shop with his clubs, beaming a big, confident smile. A couple of people looked up, which made his step falter a bit and his mouth harden into a forced grin.

Sanjay was at the counter going over the schedule with one of the caddies. Later after he'd returned home, Joe realized he had interrupted them but he'd been concentrating so hard that he hadn't noticed at the time. The conversation had gone pretty much the way he had planned except for the amount of money he'd gotten for the clubs. He'd only been able to get $1800 for the lot—even with that custom-made leather carry bag. Still, it was better than nothing and he needed the money now. Besides, it would have been too demeaning to bargain that hard.

He made a dozen or so calls to see about freelance work but he wasn't having any luck. The problem was that everyone thought the lower level jobs would be beneath him. He'd been in senior corporate positions so long that no one thought of him for the few mid-level jobs that were still available. He hadn't drawn up a will, real estate contract, or liability release since school, and that piddly stuff was the only work that was being done locally, assuming you didn't want to use an online template and do it yourself.

Joe knew he was a resourceful guy. Good manager, his people liked him. He got on well with his colleagues. Loyal, always supported the CEO. Thoughtful, thorough, planned carefully, good at the behind-the-scenes work. Didn't require the spotlight, which a lot of his bosses appreciated. Worked hard. At 50, he was knowledgeable and experienced, so he knew exactly what to do and didn't waste time on petty distractions. His degrees were from two of the top universities in the country. His work with political fundraising and his leadership position in the church had given him a solid network in the community. He was gracious, articulate, and even had good table manners (not something you could say for everyone he knew). And while his hair was graying at the temples, he was more fit and trim than most guys in their thirties, not to mention tall enough to be authoritative.

There was absolutely no reason in the world why he shouldn't be able to land another good job quickly. And when doubts and fears bubbled up, Joe shoved them down into a box at the back of his mind.

For the rest of the week, Joe forced himself to make phone calls. He'd found an older printout of his list and did his research at a local FedEx Kinko's UPS computer center. The Feds had overlooked his backup files on a micro flash drive. No surprise to him, the government was still incompetent.

He came up with a good, short pitch to leave as a message. It let people know that he was looking for new opportunities beyond his legal background. He wanted to apply his legal experience in technology and food service industries to a) emerging markets or to b) mature industries in transition or to c) professional education (depending on what the person did).

It was exhausting. On the rare occasion, when someone actually called him back they either didn't have anything or told him he didn't have precisely the experience they wanted. It didn't matter if it was a job he could do blindfolded—no one was willing to even give him a chance. A couple of people gave him referrals, but those weren't proving any more satisfactory.

Joe remembered the scramble when Brobeck collapsed in 2003. He'd been able to find another job immediately, even though the dot com bust had impacted a lot of his colleagues. He knew someone at HP and had been hired on in time to get some great experience working on the Compaq merger. It was a shame that after Carly Fiorina had pushed that through so forcefully, she didn't survive herself. Of course, with the multi-million dollar compensation deal she cut on the way in, her $65 million option package, and the $21 million severance package on the way out (plus a pension worth several hundred thousand dollars a year), no one felt too sorry for her. Eventually, she landed a senior level position in government and was now the Secretary of Commerce.

He'd tried the online job directories to broaden his search out of the area but he didn't get so much as an acknowledgement email from the hundred or so resumes he submitted. He wasn't too surprised by that. After all, while his companies had posted jobs in the old days to meet legal requirements (that were no longer enforced), they'd never actually selected anyone whose resume came in that way. They always hired a candidate who had a personal referral or was found by a headhunter. He remembered Brian telling him the last time he had made a hire that they got over 3,000 resumes for every job they posted online. They laughed about playing "suckers' roulette" as they extended the offer to the nephew of one of Jay's friends from the Young Presidents Organization.

Brian was a good man. Although, like most people in Human Resources, he couldn't afford to let personal sympathy interfere with corporate responsibility, in this case he cut Joe a little slack. He let Joe keep the Hummer a few extra weeks and even arranged to have the vehicle picked up by the dealership so Joe wouldn't have to go through the humiliation of turning it in personally. When Security called to tell him the fellows from the dealer were on their way in, Joe left the keys on the hood and went into the garage to spruce up his old SUV.

The Expedition was a little battered since it had been his "projects" car when he needed to carry lumber or plants for something Susan wanted to do in the garden. He'd only kept it because Susan didn't want it when she left (she called it the "gas hog") and there was plenty of room in the 3-car garage. Joe opened the garage door and started up the engine. It ran a little rough. He couldn't remember the last time he had taken it out since they'd terminated annual smog checks. He drove the Expedition to the car wash, filled up the two 20-gallon tanks at the Global Oil Station, and took it to the Jiffy Lube for an oil change, new wipers, and an air filter. Funny how when you paid cash, these things added up so quickly. Just like that he was down $300 and when you're husbanding your last $1800, that's quite a hit.

When he got home, he immediately called Wendy Swenson to arrange a meeting.

★   ★   ★   ★   ★

Nothing in his life had prepared him for this. It was two days before he could even process what had happened. Wendy Swenson, with her perfectly groomed, hot—if remanufactured—body, and expressionless face, was the picture of efficiency. She blew through his house, making notes on her inventory list, stopping occasionally to examine a piece of furniture or appliance. He was sure she would have frowned or raised an eyebrow had that expression been physically possible. She opened cabinets, peered in closets, and pulled out the dresser drawers to examine the cabinetry work. It was so physically invasive that Joe went numb.

Other than the frequent refrain asking him what individual items had cost, she didn't say much or give any indication of her impressions. The one exception was his king sized bed. As she pulled back the 1,000 thread count Egyptian cotton sheets to look at the mattress label, her breath drew in sharply. "A Bedmaster, imported from the U.K. Hand nested, 1500 pocketed springs in a standard king size. Loose, hand teased, white curled horsehair. Overlaid with pure cotton. Loose, luxury Mohair." The woman knew her stuff. "Overlaid with loose British lambs wool, blended with silk. Super soft layers of non-allergenic polyester. Triple rows of traditional hand side stitching. Hand tufted with pure wool tufts. Pure Brass vents, flag stitched handles. Finest quality Belgian Damask cover." She folded her arms, nodded, and then wrote furiously.

He'd bought the bed after Susan and he split up, on the advice of one of the women he dated a few times. Susan would never have let him spend $20,000 on a mattress and box spring but Samantha (or was her name Ariel?) had assured him that women would jump in his bed just to jump onto *this* bed. The bed *was* comfortable but he'd come to realize that he didn't really want anyone to hang around long enough to get used to his mattress.

As Wendy was looking through his luggage she suggested, "The leather Hermes bags will command a good price. Why don't you purchase something more... suitable... for your current situation? Put your clothes and anything else you want to hang onto either into your car or consolidate into a single room with a lock on it."

She sniffed as she observed it was obvious that he had let his gardener and housekeeper go. Apparently his housekeeping standards were woefully inadequate. "My staff will be over at 8 A.M. sharp and please don't be home to disturb them. In fact, stay away all day while the sale is going on. It makes the clients uncomfortable. You can come home at 5:30. I'll take 45% of the proceeds and pay you in cash. Better get a money belt while you're at it, if you're going to be carrying around that much," she advised.

As he thought about it later, Joe felt like he'd been totally exposed and peeled open. At the time, he'd been in shock. This could not be happening. This was not his life.

Somehow, he'd managed to pick up three suitcases on wheels. Initially, he'd gone into his usual source, Edwards Luggage in Stanford Shopping Center, but when he realized that three bags would wipe out his entire bankroll he just bought an undercover silk waist money belt and a leg safe and left. He figured they might not have those at Wal-Mart.

Joe had seen the ads on TV but he had never personally shopped at Wal-Mart. It was overwhelming. Elderly people in blue aprons accosted you with over eager smiles as soon as you walked through the electronic doors. The aisles were filled with unkempt people fighting over bargain merchandise at the end of multi-tiered aisles. Fortunately, he stumbled on the luggage section quickly and bought some inexpensive pieces made in Uganda, the newest low cost manufacturing center. This was only temporary, he reminded himself. Jack would clear everything up and his life would be back to normal soon. He repeated this mantra as he stood in the cash checkout line for two hours. He looked wistfully at the self-service checkout that required credit cards.

At home, he packed his clothes carefully in the new suitcases and boxed up the overflow in some plastic storage boxes. He moved all the furniture out of the second guest room and put in the clothes along with the few items that meant something to him: a small landscape painting that was the first artwork he and Susan ever bought together, a few small rugs and keepsakes from his parents' house, a couple of photo albums Susan had left. He also figured he'd need his shaving kit, camping gear, the iPod with his music collection, a couple of cases of wine, an air mattress, some bedding and towels, and a supply of toilet paper and soap. He secured the room with a heavy lock, which was a good thing because when he returned after the sale, it was clear from the marks on the doorframe, someone had tried to force their way into the room. Guess the girls wanted a few more bargains.

There were still trucks and moving vans in the circular driveway when he returned at 5:30. Wendy was checking items off her list and directing the men who were handling his belongings. A couple of the neighbors were watching and Joe had never been so mortified in his life. He drove past the house, parked around the corner and walked back nonchalantly, using the shrubs to screen him from the view of Wendy and her staff.

He waited until the trucks pulled out. It was now about 6:45. Wendy was standing on the steps, tapping her foot impatiently. She handed him an envelope with a tight smile and climbed into her armored Mercedes. Still too stunned to say anything to her, he couldn't remember what, if anything, she had said to him.

He walked into the house. It had been picked clean except for the books in his study and some mismatched dishes and silverware in an open kitchen cabinet. There were a few old towels and tools left in the garage. There were gaping holes all over the house where his HDTVs, audio equipment, and media center had been. They had left his frozen dinners in the freezer but unfortunately the microwave wasn't a built-in so it was gone too. The Calphalon pots and pans were history but there was one battered old baking dish. He pried out the entrée and heated it up in the oven. Thankfully, he'd remembered to keep a corkscrew so he opened a bottle of wine, poured it into a juice glass, and had his dinner before he counted the money.

The sale had cleared $30,000. Wendy had thoughtfully given him a mix of large and small bills so it could fit into the money belts. Jack had told him that Wendy would take 30% not 45% but he couldn't even find the reserve to argue with the last minute change in terms on the deal. Besides, he didn't want to piss off Jack, since he was handling his case with Homeland Security, and hadn't asked for anything up front.

After several bottles of wine and two days of sleeping on the air mattress in his bedroom, he was ready to consider his next move. He thought again about trying to contact friends and acquaintances but what could he say? (And, for that matter, what on earth would he tell his son)? He had been part of too many conversations over the years with friends and colleagues that put down people who couldn't get work. If he admitted how desperate he was, they'd have no respect for him; and if he pretended everything was fine, it wouldn't even occur to them to try to do something to help. And that was without even factoring in the stain on his reputation. He was going to have to find a way out of this mess on his own.

Joe showered, shaved, and got dressed. It was a beautiful spring day. He decided to go out for a real breakfast. Unfortunately Ann's, his old favorite, had closed, a casualty of the skyrocketing rents that had decimated most of the small businesses in town. You'd think with the unemployment rates so high, commercial real estate prices would have decreased but it hadn't worked out that way. He debated among Starbucks, McFriendly's, and Denny's, finally settling on the last because it was cheap and the portions were big.

As he chewed away at his eggs, sausage, bacon, ham and pancakes, Joe pondered what to do next. Jack had said the hearing with the Homeland Security people to unfreeze his assets couldn't be scheduled for at least 18 months—they had a backlog and no amount of yelling, string pulling, or cajoling had seemed to do the trick. Joe tried calling some of his contacts from the Party organization but no one was returning his calls. He couldn't sell the house, but he couldn't pay the $8,000 a month mortgage either. He figured he had a couple of months before any foreclosure proceedings would be complete, but his utility bills were pretty steep, about $1,000 a month and the annual association fee of $10,000 was coming due next month. Maybe he should invest some of his $31,000 nest egg to pay the utilities and phone so he could continue to look for work from home?

He stopped by his bank to talk to Todd Williams to make sure there was a way to protect his equity in the house. While Joe did manage to get in to see Todd, it wasn't a very encouraging meeting. Todd was sympathetic and polite but it was clear that taking on Homeland Security was not something Todd or the bank were prepared to do. "I'm sorry. The government has issued strict rules. There isn't anything that is within our discretion. You know, like mandatory sentencing for judges. You should consider yourself lucky that no formal charges have been brought against you. It might help to think of your equity in the house as a sunk cost. If you do manage to clear up your situation in time, it won't be any problem. Home foreclosures have happened to a significant number of our clients. One just has to get over it quickly and move on."

Joe was furious but tried not to show it as he strode out of the building. It wasn't going to change anything and it's not like Todd could affect the outcome. It pissed him off to have no recourse. Who *could* do something? he fumed. He should get a gun and go visit the Homeland Security office and demand his money back. He pictured himself wielding the revolver and Terrence Mackelwhite cowering in terror, like in the movies. Then he imagined the guards shooting him in the head while his body crumpled to the floor in a pool of blood. Maybe it wasn't the best idea after all.

For the next few weeks, Joe camped out in the empty house. For the first time in his entire adult life, he didn't pay his bills. The notion of being a deadbeat bothered him. It made him feel unclean. Without a job he didn't have anywhere to go. It was so depressing to make so little progress with his job search—no matter how hard he tried—he stopped playing golf and going to church. It was feeling too hard to keep up the pretense that everything was normal. Even the most casual inquiries that were part of routine conversation felt intrusive and overbearing. He thought about calling Miranda but he didn't know what to say. What if she thought it really was his fault that this had happened? It was better to fantasize that she would help him if she had a chance than to test it and find out she'd slam the door in his face.

After a sleepless night during which he debated his limited options, he decided to get out of the Bay Area for a while and look for a cheap place and some kind of work to tide him over until the market picked up. A break would do him good and let him clear his head. Then he could resume the job search with renewed energy and vigor.

It made Joe feel better to carefully make a list of everything he needed to do. He called Daniel and left him a message that he was taking off for a while. He went to the store and bought a supply of energy bars, ready-to-eat food, and bottled water. He divided the cash between the leg safe and the waist money belt, taking out $500 and hiding it under the floor mats in the SUV. Then Joe packed up the Expedition with all his belongings, unplugged the appliances, emptied the fridge, and locked the door. He tried not to look back, but couldn't help glancing in his rearview mirror. What if he never saw his house again? What if he couldn't get it back? How the hell could this be happening? What was wrong with those idiots at Homeland Security? Why weren't they concentrating on real terrorists instead of respectable citizens? Having an orderly, secure, predictable life had been his anchor, and it terrified him to not know what was going to happen next.

Joe drove north on 280. Now a protected toll road, it was the safest route. Electrified fences with concertina wire were tastefully hidden in the foliage along the highway. Exits and entrances were constantly monitored and patrolled by armed security personnel.

The view of the Crystal Springs watershed never failed to thrill him. The wooded hills framed the chain of small lakes in one of the Bay Area's many microclimates. The play of light between the sky and water was dramatic, whether it was a sparkling sunny day or threatening with stormy-looking clouds. He could see the tile roofs and redwood decks of the 25,000 sq. ft. luxury homes that had been tucked into the dense trees over the past few years. Since the area was already gated and secure, it was ideal for private development when the county was looking for new revenues.

When he came to 19th Avenue going through San Francisco, the open fence changed to a solid wall. One block of residential housing on each side had been demolished so the roadway could be widened and secured. Periodically there were crossing areas and checkpoints, especially when inviting drivers into the Stonestown Galleria Shopping Mall.

As Joe approached the Golden Gate Bridge, the traffic slowed. Even though it was late in the morning, there was a line of cars and trucks waiting for clearance to cross. He was afraid to use the EZpass and took out his regular ID card. The National Guardsman held the card up to the RFID scanner and punched in the license plate number.

The guard looked at the monitor, frowned and picked up the phone, turning his back to Joe. He tried to stay calm. OK, he reminded himself, Jack had assured him that even though the asset freeze was in place there still weren't any charges filed against him. He just had to remain calm and unobtrusive. Joe deliberately quelled both his rising sense of panic and his feelings of impatience at the delay. The guard turned back, asked him to remove his sunglasses, and passed a retinal scan wand across his face. The computer beeped and the guard waved him on. He could finally breathe.

The sun glinted on the waves as he drove across the Golden Gate. Gunboats guarding the bridge bounced jauntily on the whitecaps. Other than the massive guard posts on the Marin side of the bridge, it looked as spectacular as ever. This was such a beautiful place to live. As he passed the upscale Marin communities, the density of the housing developments adjacent to 101 increased. He saw acres and acres of identical subdivisions—each with the requisite shopping mall containing Starbucks, Applebee's, BKFC, McFriendly's, Home Depot, and Wal-Mart at every exit.

At Smith Ranch Road, he turned off 101 and followed the signs to Point Reyes Station where Don Collins, a former colleague, was running a B&B with his wife, Mary. Don had been Organic Chemical's VP of Marketing. He was talented and creative. His people loved him. Under his watch, the company's visibility had increased and sales had doubled. When layoffs grew more frequent, Don objected. At one discussion, he offered to take a pay cut and suggested that his peers do the same. Joe recalled the stony silence that followed that remark. It was unrealistic to think people would volunteer to cut their own pay. Jay wouldn't look at Don for the rest of the meeting.

After the company renegotiated the contracts with the local farmers who were part of the original co-op that formed the nucleus of Organic—unfortunately most of the farmers subsequently went under—Don quit in protest. Joe tried to talk him out of it, but Don had had enough. Don and Mary bought the Lighthouse Inn, hired local labor to remodel it, and kept on the former innkeeper and staff.

When Joe arrived, he was disappointed to see a SOLD sign. Boxes were being packed. Several people were crying. He found Don comforting Mary. They both embraced him warmly despite the circumstances. Don, clearly frustrated said, "If you'd shown up a week later, we would have been gone. We couldn't make a go of it. The foreign tourism business to the Bay Area died completely a few years ago. Europeans and Asians got disgusted with the fingerprinting, eye scans, and full body searches at the borders so they stopped coming. Our domestic business picked up for a while, since Americans aren't being welcomed with open arms abroad, but that tapered off too."

That made sense to Joe since most of his friends preferred high-end luxury resorts to the simple charms of a B&B. Don continued, "The economy has taken its toll on our traditional customers, so we decided to sell the place and move to Ireland. A number of other families we knew left the U.S., and it seemed like the right moment to follow.

"You're welcome to camp out in one of the rooms for a few days. The new owners aren't closing for a week and our innkeeper is staying on as a caretaker. We had an offer from the CFO of a wealth management firm who wanted the eight-acre property and 18-room inn for a weekend retreat, but we decided to take a lesser offer from a guy who wanted the property as a compound for his extended family and friends who had lost their homes. We liked the idea that the place would be in good hands." Joe thought it sounded dumb and sentimental, but if Don wanted to act like a communist, that was his business.

Don paused. "We've seen Susan. She's living in a small community up near Willits." The wives had met at a company party when Joe joined and they really hit it off. "Susan and Mary stayed in touch, and when Susan moved north, she stopped by the

71

Inn to visit. We go up to see her every now and then and it seems like she's very happy."

Joe admitted, "I've heard occasional news from Daniel but I haven't spoken to her directly in quite a while. I'm glad to hear she is doing well."

Joe hung around for a few days. The National Park had been leased to an oil refinery to support the new drilling up the coast so Point Reyes wasn't quite as nice as he remembered. He took Don and Mary to the Tomales Bay Oyster Company for dinner and was horrified at the price of oysters—increased pollution and human activity had affected the supply. At the inn, he pitched in to help with various projects, repairing out buildings, weeding the garden, and painting the fences. He wasn't a skilled worker, but Don was patient and the room and food were free.

★　　　★　　　★　　　★　　　★

Joe followed the directions Don had written out for him, winding through the back roads. His curiosity about Susan piqued, he figured he might as well stop by since he was in the neighborhood. He didn't imagine he'd be coming back this way any time soon. He passed through Willits, which consisted of one traffic light and a few buildings and storefronts along the two-lane highway. Only a few people were visible on the street. Now that's a major metropolis, he laughed to himself and promptly missed the turnoff. Arrrghh. He had a tough time turning the SUV around on the narrow road. The shoulder hadn't been maintained too well, so he almost got stuck in a ditch.

When he finally found the village of Aquamarine, the light was the golden color of twilight. The houses were small, mainly Craftsman bungalows, wooden cottages, and single story shacks. He noticed a few that looked like straw bale/adobe houses. There were primitive solar panels on many of the roofs. Are these folks here totally off the grid or do they have underground power lines?

A small general store that looked like something out of an old Western was open, so he stopped. He vaguely wondered where people got their coffee as he noticed there weren't any Starbucks that he could see. He locked the SUV. Inside, when Joe inquired about how to find Susan's place, the man narrowed his eyes. There was a young boy helping stock shelves at the back of the store. The man whispered in the boy's ear and he slipped out the back door. Joe studied him—he looked about 45, tanned, his hair and clothes definitely out of style—the guy could use a good makeover. He handed Joe a glass of cold lemonade, which Joe gratefully accepted.

Before he had finished, he heard Susan's voice behind him. She had lost weight, her hair was longer and loose, and she was wearing an old shapeless sundress that he remembered from the back of her closet. He always hated that dress but he had to admit that it looked pretty good on her now. She was smiling and her face had lost that drawn look and the dark circles she'd had the last time he'd seen her.

Susan introduced him to Dean, the guy who ran the store. Dean's face had relaxed as he watched Susan welcome her former husband. It had been three years since the divorce had been finalized and they'd only had limited contact since then. She had asked for a lump sum settlement instead of alimony (so she wouldn't have to deal with him he suspected) but she had to be fixed pretty well living in a place like this. What was there to spend your money on anyway?

"Mary gave me a call before she left so I was expecting you. Daniel will be glad to hear you're alright—he was worried when you left Atherton." Susan's voice was warmer than he remembered. "Come to the house for dinner and you can tell me about your plans. Just leave the car here."

As they walked down the narrow shady street, he studied her. He hadn't seen that energy and bounce in her walk for years, not since the kids were little and before he started getting all those promotions. Her house was a creamy pale yellow with white trim and an inviting front porch. Bent willow rockers with print cushions beckoned you to sit and relax. The front yard was filled with ferns and wildflowers and a rock fountain. There were bird feeders and colorful sculptures.

Inside, the walls were painted in bright colors and there were books and artwork everywhere. Susan would never win prizes for her housekeeping. It was all slightly erratic and jumbled and, like Susan, cheerful and welcoming. It occurred to him that he hadn't really said anything yet, though Susan had acted as if she hadn't expected an explanation. It disconcerted him to see how well she still knew him. Was he really that predictable?

"Joe, this is Stan." A handsome, silver haired man of about 60 reached out to shake his hand. He had always hated it when Susan introduced someone without giving him some background information. How was he supposed to know how to treat them?

"Would you like a glass of wine?"

Joe nodded and Susan handed him a handmade goblet, kind of heavy. "Those paintings on the wall next to the doors to the garden, those are Stan's." He walked over to admire them. He didn't understand what all the different colors meant but he wanted to be polite. "Very interesting. Have you been an artist long? Where have you shown?"

Stan smiled. "I was a heart surgeon and cardiologist. When the insurance companies stopped letting me practice real medicine, I decided it was time for a change. I didn't have much of a taste for a practice that was confined exclusively to wealthy patients with premium health plans and the hospitals weren't exactly encouraging pro bono surgeries. I moved here a few years ago, hung out my shingle as a family doctor and started painting. I'd never had the time before."

Susan added another place setting. He noticed that all three plates were different patterns and the silverware was mixed from a variety of designs. There were colorful bowls of salad and peas. The roast chicken was covered in herbs and smelled delicious. She lit some candles and invited them both to sit down.

Joe appreciated that they weren't asking him any questions. He wasn't sure that he had any answers. Susan and Stan chatted about what had happened during the day. She was laughing about something the kids in her class had done. Stan told her about a Mrs. Greenstein who was using acupuncture to deal with her arthritis. Joe didn't think people were doing that weird stuff anymore. Hadn't the AMA outlawed those needles? After a great dessert of tiny strawberries and fresh whipped cream, they had tea in the living room. Susan was inordinately proud that the mint came from her garden (along with the berries and vegetables). The chicken and cream came from a neighbor's small farm.

Stan rested his arm along the back of the sofa, his hand touching Susan's shoulder. When she looked at him, her eyes sparkled and Joe felt a twinge. He recalled when Susan used to look at him that way, but he quickly brushed the thought aside. Stan got up to make the bed in the guest room, leaving Joe and Susan to walk to the car and get his bag. "Why don't you plan on staying for a few days? You can relax at the house tomorrow and walk around town. We can talk after school about what's going on."

Joe slept late, took a long shower (fortunately the day was warm because the hot water ran out before he was done). He made a cup of tea and straightened up. It was clear that Susan didn't have help in the house and it bugged him how untidy everything was—that hadn't changed.

By the time Susan came home from school, Joe was planning to tell her everything, but somehow he just told her that he was thinking about moving out of the Bay Area. Every time he started to say something, it didn't seem like the right moment. During the day he'd wander around the village or drive into Willits. After a week, Susan told him, "One of my neighbors has a cottage to rent. Would you be interested? We don't really need any lawyers in town, but we are building a new community center and you're welcome to put in some time in exchange for meals. The rent is reasonable and the cottage is clean, if a bit smaller than you're used to."

It was the best offer Joe had received since losing his job and he couldn't think of a good reason to leave.

no [handwritten annotation]

Joe settled into a routine. He was surprised that he didn't miss his house or electronics (though he did wish they had a golf course nearby). The only thing that bothered him were the conversations over meals and while people worked. He tried to tune them out, but these people were obsessed with the government, business, and religion. They talked about politics obsessively. It was like breathing to them. At least, when they weren't smoking pot, meditating, or practicing yoga.

A typical episode took place one day when the crew building the community center was taking a lunch break. One guy claimed over a cheese sandwich that, "the terrorist anthrax attack that occurred during the 2008 Democratic convention was related to the 2001 anthrax incidents after 9/11. How come the supposed terrorists only targeted Senate Democrats and mainstream media personalities?"

Another fellow agreed, "Based on the DNA, everyone knew the strain was from a U.S. government lab at Fort Dietrich. I've always suspected it was an inside job."

A woman chimed in, "I never understood why they were never investigated. With all the fixation on terrorists, shouldn't they at least have tried to figure out what happened? Was it incompetence or collusion?"

He's brainwashed [handwritten annotation in left margin]

He wanted to tell these paranoid fools to shut up. They were wrong. They didn't know what they were talking about. They were brainwashed. Why did they think that everyone who didn't agree with them was stupid? It was great now that taxes were low and we weren't paying for all those expensive social programs to support lazy welfare cheats. The country was much safer. Because of Susan he guessed they put up with him even when his contempt for their misguided principles leaked out.

When he expressed too strong an opinion, someone would want to debate him, so he generally tried to avoid confrontations. Once when they were ranting about the Republicans giving the lion's share of the benefits to the top 1%, he made the mistake of trying to explain to them that Middle American conservatives might be a little puritanical but they were egalitarian too. "All the major populist movements came out of that culture, not the wealthy elitists on the coasts," Joe said, hoping to educate them.

"But that's my point," a young woman responded intensely. "I don't understand why so many millions of these people vote against their own economic interests."

Another guy sneered, "The rich guys buy the poor slobs' votes with a conservative social agenda that distracts them. Evil liberals want to take away your guns. Religion as public policy. Gay marriage. Rights of the unborn—what about the rights of the actually born?" He turned to Joe.

"Don't you believe the actually born should be free to vote their consciences?" Joe said defiantly, "It's clear the Administration understands the economy and international dynamics better than the opposition."

"Yeah right. That's why they ignored legitimate concerns of Senators on both sides of the aisle and sent John Bolton in to dismantle the U.N. back in '05—and now our distinguished Secretary of State Cheney is going to put the last nail in the coffin. They dismissed millions of antiwar protesters around the world as 'focus groups.' The peace movement was right about the exaggerations on WMDs and the non-link between Saddam and Osama. And the economy? I don't know about you, but my business was going great guns during the Clinton years and tanked after you guys took charge."

"That's old news. Besides the recession started under Clinton and the economy rebounded under Bush," Joe maintained. "Both Jeb and GW are deeply religious men. They believe in the morality of their policies. You have to respect their spirituality. Isn't that what I hear you people saying all the time?"

"I can respect their religious sincerity but I wonder if its use in the political arena is more cynical than that," the woman countered. "They take advantage of the genuine loyalty people feel for God and their country and repeatedly tell them that they are being good patriots by following along, and that it's only the disloyal people who are asking the questions. I mean these guys don't even take care of their own. Look at how returning soldiers get treated. They can't even get adequate health services and counseling much less a good job. We have thousands of veterans with PTSD and no work. And let's not get started on the incompetence they demonstrated when Hurricane Katrina destroyed New Orleans and the Gulf Coast. It only got slightly better with the storms the next year and the years after that. How much proof for climate change do these guys need?"

It was pointless to argue with these people. Joe didn't try to reconcile his experience with their comments. It was easier for him to think of his situation as an aberration. He instinctively knew that if he told any of them what had happened to him, it would be natural for them to use it to support their own opinions at his expense. When anyone asked why he had left the Bay Area, he said he needed a break between jobs. Since most residents had lost their primary livelihoods for one reason or another, no one questioned him further.

Susan asked him to help her with one of the boys at the community's school who had a reading disability. After school a few days a week, he would read with the kid. He had to admit he got a kick out of seeing the youngster improve. With his nest egg and this low-key lifestyle, Joe felt pretty good about his survival. Sure, it wasn't intellectually challenging, and no doubt his golf swing had suffered, but all in all it was a passable way to spend the summer. He was in good shape. He was healthy and he had as much human contact as he wanted. Susan and Stan invited him over for dinner a couple of times a week and he'd started to get to know some of the other folks, many of whom had a gentle, earnest quality that he found restful, though naïve. He had to admit that even the strident ones only got worked up when it came to the welfare of other people or the environment.

He and Susan talked about Daniel and how their son was doing. Daniel had been pleased to learn that Joe was staying in Aquamarine, and told Susan he'd try to make it up there later in the summer. The one time they tried to talk about their daughter Mandy, Susan started crying. Joe couldn't deal with her tears, so he left and they avoided the subject after that. Their truce wasn't ready to survive that kind of exploration.

He inadvertently found himself playing an odd role in the community. Several people perceived him as a fairly benign representative of the corporate power structure and asked him lots of questions. They always prefaced their inquiry with "But you seem like such a nice guy, how can you believe or support…?" Fill in the topic. He did his best to provide them with insightful analogies to explain administration policies or corporate practices but it was frustrating when they didn't understand the basics.

At the dinner celebrating the completion of the community center, Joe found himself at a table with Susan, Stan, and some of his fellow workers. Everyone was thrilled with how the building had turned out. The children's chorus sang songs, several musical groups performed, and one of the oldest residents read a poem in a quavering voice. Susan teased Joe that after all these years of living in the abstract he had finally "made something concrete."

He was pleased by her reference to their shared history. He was embarrassed to admit that he shared her pride that he had made something with his hands that was more substantial than a contract or a legal brief. The main room wasn't fancy but it had a clean, simple look and the proportions were very satisfying. Good team effort and all that.

He realized someone was sounding him out on yet another concern. "You're a decent guy who fits in well here. Why do you think successful business people feel like they need so many possessions to be happy? I mean, I think it's great to have a comfortable, affluent lifestyle, but some folks seem to go overboard. What is it about a more equitable system that feels so threatening?"

Stan was laughing. He bent sideways to whisper to Joe, "Starting to feel like a 'credit to your race' about now?"

"Something wrong with that?" Joe retorted, and then turned to answer his questioner. It felt strange to be treated like an oracle by people who had such a fundamentally different view of the world. It was like visiting a primitive society when you came from the modern world.

"It's about personal responsibility. If I make the effort to get a good job and earn lots of money, I should be able to spend it the way I want. Why should I be forced to give it away to someone else who's too lazy to work themselves?" Joe argued. "I knew this guy who was offered three jobs and he turned them all down so he could stay on welfare and play music."

"I'm curious, why do you assume people without jobs are lazy?" a young woman asked softly. "Aren't there are lots of reasons why people aren't working? I know plenty of people who would love to have jobs and be self-sufficient, but either the jobs aren't there or the few that are pay so little that they can't feed their families." Joe felt guilty. He knew she had a valid argument, but he was not prepared to concede the point.

"But that's just it," Joe continued, falling back into the familiar rhetoric. "We all can talk about people we know who have had different experiences. Who's to say what's right? Aren't your beliefs a reflection of people you know? Successful people invest in the community. The more they consume, the more chances there are for jobs for people who make, sell, and service the products."

Susan was looking amused. "Don't bother to try to get him to admit there's a problem out there. He's a lawyer. You'll never pin him down. Let's listen to the music." She shook her head.

★ ★ ★ ★ ★

On July 4th, it was a beautiful day. Sunny, hot, the bees were buzzing. Everyone had gathered at the community center. Musicians were playing bluegrass and tables were set up for a holiday picnic. Children were running and playing. Mothers were dancing with babies in their arms. The older residents had joined in too, even the ones who had to be carried out to sit in the shade. Joe could see Susan laughing with Stan and he found himself to be very pleased for her.

He heard a rumbling sound in the distance. A few people looked up. As the noise came closer, he could hear engines roaring. The next thing he knew a dozen motorcycles rolled through, upsetting tables, knocking kids over. The nearest adults ran to protect the children while a group of young men and women tried to confront the unwelcome visitors armed with only firewood and tools that were nearby. It was not a fair fight; the bikers were heavily armed and the few hunting rifles in the community were kept locked up to protect against accidents. Screaming, "You bastards want to take away our guns, do you?" the visitors shot several residents at point blank range.

A huge pickup truck pulled up and three muscular youths with heavy chains and crowbars jumped out of the back and started chasing a group of teenagers who had been sitting under a tree playing music. "Faggots. Homos. Perverts. Stay away from our little brothers." As an intruder caught one boy, he laughed,

"Let's see how this smashes a guitar compared to a head" and made good on his experiments. A kid from the community tried to stop him by jumping on his back, but the two other brutes pulled the smaller youngster off and punched and kicked him bloody.

Joe stood frozen. Watching violence on TV didn't prepare you for being center stage in the real thing. Then he saw three men shoving a pretty redhead down behind a tree calling her a "hippie slut" while they tugged at their belts. The sight galvanized him—he couldn't bear to imagine what was going to happen next. Joe ran towards them, and with a fury he didn't know he possessed, he grabbed a fallen branch and began hitting the man closest to the girl. When more people from the community joined him to free the girl, the other bikers scattered, abandoning their buddy whose face was barely recognizable. Joe stepped back shaking as the others tied the fellow up.

Joe could hear more shots being fired. People were screaming and bleeding and Susan was trying to round up the other kids and bring them into the center building. Joe ran back and helped some of the men move two women who had been shot into the center, where Stan had set up a makeshift triage area. He asked Joe to go to his office and pick up his bag and supplies.

As Joe surveyed the picnic area, he was astounded at the carnage. It looked like a war zone. The place was a wreck. Several houses had been torched. There were bodies of dead and wounded everywhere. Why had this happened? These people weren't hurting anyone. They might be annoying but they certainly weren't dangerous. Why would a gang of thugs attack a place way out in the middle of nowhere?

Joe brought Stan his bag and went over to the store to get ice, bandages, hydrogen peroxide, and rubbing alcohol. It had been ravaged. Everything that wasn't broken was in scattered across the floor. Dean's face was covered with blood and his mouth was filled with the wreckage of broken teeth. He had gone back to check on his store when the commotion started and they had beaten him severely. Joe knelt down.

"They said a talk show host told them it was the duty of all good Americans to hunt down the liberal scum that want to ruin this country. " Joe could barely make out Dean's words. "To show true patriotism on the 4th of July, every gun owner should take a shot at radicals who hate Christianity, teach evolution, and sympathize with terrorists."

Dean looked at him. "What's happened to us? This is not what America is supposed to be. How can…" The words stopped as Dean lost consciousness. Joe ran to get help. Stan and Susan were trying to remove a bullet from a teenage girl's back. She was screaming. Joe got his SUV and drove down to the store. He lifted Dean into the back. As he carried the man's limp body into the center, he realized that Dean was dead. Joe went outside and shivered even though it was so warm. Looking down and seeing his own clothes covered in blood, he went back to his cottage to clean up. Fortunately, they had spared his place though several nearby houses were still burning. He threw the ruined garments in the trash and sat down on the bed to catch his breath. He suddenly noticed tears were rolling down his cheeks. For a long time he remained in a state of shock. His mind simply could not take in what he had just experienced. He had watched his share of violent movies, including those about war, and was thrilled when the good guys inevitably won in the end. But like many who ran the country and had carried out threats of preemptive war, Joe Winston had never *been* to war, had never seen *real* violence, up close and personal. Until today. Finally, he pulled himself together and began to think about his situation.

What would happen if the sheriffs' department came to investigate the incident and he was found here in a questionable community? He'd never get his house, savings, and life back.

Besides, they would need his cottage for the community he reasoned and he didn't want to take up resources that were better used for someone else. Impulsively, he packed up and put everything in the Expedition. He stopped at Susan and Stan's house and left $5,000 on the kitchen table with a note saying he hoped this could help the community rebuild. He reassured himself that this was best for everyone.

★   ★   ★   ★   ★

It was good to be on the road. Joe concentrated on his driving and eventually his heart rate slowed down. He tried to make sense out of what had just happened. These people weren't bothering anyone. They weren't taking anything away from anyone. Just minding their own business. Sure their ideas were a little wacky, but it's not like they were in a position to impose them on anyone else. They weren't the ones in charge. All they had were their opinions.

Joe kept hearing Dean's dying words. He used to listen to Savage, Limbaugh, Barbara Simpson, Sean Hannity, and the local guys. They were entertaining. Sure they used extreme language but that didn't mean that people should go out and act on those rants. When they said to "go string someone up" or "get rid of liberal scum," he was sure that they didn't expect a bunch of hooligans would take them literally. And when that blond conservative woman—he couldn't remember her name—published a book called *TREASON* and accused liberals, people like those who had taken him in (and been kind to him), of betraying the United States, he had shrugged it off as mere rhetoric. As a lawyer, he didn't know that he'd argue the case on the basis of free speech—that had taken kind of a beating lately. However, he was positive there weren't many judges left who would see this kind of media raving as meeting the legal standard of incitement to riot.

He had left in kind of a hurry. Oh shit, he just remembered that he had left his sheets and blankets on the bed and he had a load of laundry being washed and ironed by one of the young women in the community. It was kind of foolish to have given them the five grand, he regretted that now, but he had about $25K left. That should be enough to get him resettled and get his case resolved. And life in Aquamarine had taught him that he didn't really need that much stuff anyway.

He stopped for supplies in Cloverdale and camped near Lake Sonoma on the way down. It was quiet and peaceful and spending time in the woods recharged his batteries. As he listened to the water and the birds, he felt comforted, but he missed his church services. The Aquamarine Spiritual Center held ecumenical, non-denominational prayer meetings extolling the virtues of love, kindness, tolerance, and peace, but the readings gave just as much weight to Gaia, the earth goddess, and the Dalai Lama as to Jesus. They didn't say anything that he disagreed with but he missed the structure of the familiar Congregational services. He thought momentarily about going to his church for help but the notion passed quickly. It would be too awkward. How could he go from being one of the church leaders offering help to being a loser who needed charity? Not that he thought he was a loser, but it might look that way if someone didn't have all the facts and couldn't see how grossly unfair his situation was. He recalled Sara Stokes and her dilemma. What if they treated him the way they had others who had failed?

The more he considered what happened in Aquamarine, the more confused he got. He had always believed the conventional wisdom that the left, particularly during the turbulent 1960s, used vicious and ridiculous debating tactics to make their points—like attacking the messenger, or calling people names, or questioning the oppositions' motives. Conservatives had only been forced to resort to similar methods to hold their own and protect their property from socialists who wanted to impoverish everyone. Maybe liberals were adopting new techniques, but the people he'd met there didn't seem all that aggressive. When they did get upset, it was usually on behalf of random families who did not have enough to eat or children not being adequately protected and educated, or protesting the government's getting involved in private matters. Well, actually both sides wanted that. At some point, he wasn't exactly sure when, disagreement with the government became downright unpatriotic. Of course Joe believed that families should have enough to live decent lives, and that government ought to be reasonably protective of civil liberties, but he didn't agree with the ideas of those in Aquamarine about how to achieve such goals. Still, he was having trouble seeing what was so scary about them that would warrant such a vicious attack. Thinking about it made his head hurt, so he decided to start driving again.

The holiday weekend traffic was heavy and while it took about 90 minutes each to be processed at the checkpoints in Santa Rosa and San Francisco, he moved through without incident. That was a good sign that no criminal charges had been filed while he was gone. His communicator hadn't worked up north and when it couldn't get a signal driving through Marin, he suspected that his account had been shut off for non-payment. He cut over to 101 at 380. The walls that shielded residents from traffic noise had been extended so it was like traveling through a concrete chute.

Joe thought his best bet was to check into a hotel near the airport and call Jack. He parked in the lot of the SF Airport Hilton and was getting his bags out of the car when a security guard stopped him. He saw the man eyeing his somewhat rustic attire. To be honest, he hadn't paid that much attention to his clothes that morning. Before he could say more, the guy was demanding he get back in his vehicle and go elsewhere.

OK, now what? He needed gas so he stopped at a Global Oil station. Near the airport it was $6 a gallon. A refill would be at least $250. That was more than he had in his wallet so he surreptitiously sat in the car and pulled up his pants leg to get to the leg safe. He noticed the sign that said "Restrooms for customers only," and realized that he could change into a suit there.

He deposited a wad of bills with the bullet-proof-glass protected cashier, filled up the SUV, got his change, and drove over to the restrooms so he could park and lock the car. He took out a pair of suit trousers, a shirt, dress socks, and shoes. The suit was a little rumpled from the hasty packing job but he figured he looked like someone who had slept on the plane. He showed his receipt to the restroom attendant and was admitted to a dank, dim toilet. It was disgusting. You'd think that with a customers-only facility it would at least be decent. He tried not to let anything touch the floor but in the process of putting on his trousers, he dropped his dress shirt. Damn, there was a smudge on the clean white pocket. Hopefully, his suit jacket would cover it.

Back at the car, he combed his hair, put on a tie, and debated whether to put on his jacket or not. Better put it on so it was clear to the next parking lot guard that he was a person of means. He drove down the access road and pulled into the lot of the Hyatt.

This time he and his bags made it through the parking lot and past the security guard at the entrance. Because he didn't have a prior reservation, he was directed to a special desk adjacent to the main check-in counter. The young clerk appraised his rumpled suit and cheap luggage and Joe found himself self-consciously smoothing down the jacket. He mumbled something about the long plane trip from the east coast. She invited him to sit and fill out a form on an electronic tablet. "Please provide your home address and phone, the flight number you flew in on—you can show me the proof of the return ticket if appropriate—your travel plans in the Bay Area, two local references with phone numbers, and your social security number. I also need to see proof of identity and two credit cards."

After he obediently filled in the information (taking liberties as needed), Joe cleared his throat. "I'd like to pay cash and I'm happy to pay in advance." The young woman frowned as she scanned his entries and noted his ID and home address were local. "Why are you staying in a hotel, sir, when you live in the area?"

He thought quickly. "I'm getting back into town early from a long business trip and my caretaker hasn't opened the house yet." She did not look like she believed him. "This is highly irregular. I have to check with my supervisor."

Not sure whether they'd actually validate the flight number with the airline to see if he had indeed traveled or try to verify the credit cards, he decided it was prudent to make a leisurely exit while she was away from the desk. He got up and tried to look nonchalant as he rolled his bags out the door.

Back in the SUV, he decided to go to his house. It was still *his* after all. When he got to the Lindenwood gatehouse on Middlefield Road, the card reader at the residents' entrance didn't respond to his key card. He tried several times, growing increasingly frustrated. Stupid machines. He smacked it a few times. He didn't recognize the guard on duty who came up to see if he could be of assistance. Joe gave his name and address and when the man entered the information into his handheld computer, he turned to Joe, "I'm sorry. You're not listed here."

"There must be some mistake. I've lived here for years. Look, I just got back from a long trip and I'm exhausted. Here's my ID card. See the address? I have the keys," he dangled them in front of the young man. "Can't I give you my mother's maiden name or the name of my first pet to prove I am who I say I am?" Joe insisted.

"I believe you are who you say you are, sir. I simply don't have any way to prove that you still own a home here." He punched in some other data. "I see a different name at this address. I'm sorry."

"That's ridiculous. Who's living in my house? They're not authorized. What's their name?"

"I'm not at liberty to say, sir. Perhaps you'd like to speak to someone at the homeowners' association office? They're open Tuesday and Wednesday from 11 AM to 4 PM."

"But I want to go home now," Joe was horrified to hear the pleading note in his voice. If he weren't careful, he'd be crying for his Mommy soon.

"I'm sorry sir. I wish I could be of more help," the young guard seemed genuinely sympathetic. Joe realized he must sound like a con artist or a lunatic.

He drove recklessly over to Jack's office in downtown Menlo Park and bounded up the stairs of the stylish building. Jack's secretary looked startled and apprehensive when Joe burst into the reception area. "May I help you?"

"I'm Joe Winston. I'm a client. I need to see Jack, now."

"I'm afraid he's left for the day but I'll be glad to tell him you stopped by. Is there a number where he can reach you?"

"No, there isn't a number!" Joe knew he sounded nasty and slightly off balance but he couldn't help himself. "I can't get into my own house and my wireless phone doesn't work." He realized the woman was edging towards the side of her desk, looking quite panicked. "Look, I'm not going to hurt you." His frustration pushed the volume of his voice louder. She bolted out the door and the next thing he knew, two security guards were dragging him out of the office. While one was calling the police, Joe managed to wrench himself free and run off. His suit was rumpled, his tie was askew and his shirt was a sweaty mess. His brain wasn't doing much better. He wasn't cut out for this.

He drove north on El Camino Real looking for a cheap motel where they wouldn't ask so many questions or demand the details of his life. Most that he passed were just too depressing looking. In San Carlos or San Mateo, he could never remember, it all just looked the same, with chain stores, fast food restaurants, and the occasional car repair or oil change shop; he found one that didn't look too bad. It was two-story and if he got a room on the first floor, he could park right in front of the room, so he could keep an eye on his car and his belongings.

The check-in desk was behind a scratched, plexi-glass protective shield. The clerk, an older man who looked like he could use a shave, glared suspiciously at Joe and his expensive suit. He apparently overlooked the wrinkles. "You a Fed?" he spat out.

"Hardly," said Joe, wishing that he had at least thought to take off the silk tie. "I'd like a room, preferably on the first floor. I'd like to pay cash and make it a non-smoking room if you have it." "Eighty dollars a night or $500 for the week," he said laughing as if Joe had been wildly amusing. Joe placed four twenties in the plexi-drawer that the guy slid out to give him the key. As he walked away, Joe could hear him still laughing about the "no-smoking room."

Fortunately there was a parking space right in front of room 102. He approached the room cautiously. He could honestly say he had never been in a hotel room like this in his entire life. It smelled like stale cigarettes and beer. The curtains were dusty as he pulled them back to let in some light. The rest of the room seemed relatively clean but everything was threadbare and mismatched. He pulled back the bedspread and felt the rough sheets. They weren't pressed. How did he know someone else hadn't used them already? Maybe he'd just bring in his sleeping bag. There was a TV welded to a metal frame set in the wall, and the remote control was fixed permanently to the nightstand.

He rolled his bags inside and carried in his storage boxes. He tried to leave as little as possible that might attract attention visible in the SUV. Fortunately it had tinted windows so you couldn't see the outline of his camping gear. He weighed whether it was safer to leave his belongings locked in the car or unguarded in the room while he went out for a bite to eat. Neither felt very secure. He used the bathroom with its rust stained sink, shower, and toilet. There weren't the usual shampoo and other complimentary toiletries. Fortunately, he had soap in his toilet kit and dried his hands on the thin towel.

There was a bar across the street that indicated they had food, as well, so he decided to grab a burger and a beer. He closed the blinds, changed into some casual clothes so he'd be more unobtrusive, and locked up the room. He thought about putting a Do Not Disturb sign on the door but there wasn't one that he could see. Either the usual clientele didn't mind being disturbed or they didn't have a choice.

He sat in the smoky bar and watched the news on Fox as he ate. Former Senators McCain, Snow, Hagel, Collins, Specter, Graham, and Chafee, who had all been Swift-boated when they protested the trend towards unlimited executive powers during an unending state of war, were holding a news conference on the steps of the Capitol. Before they could finish airing their concerns and recommendations, the gathering was broken up by security forces which escorted them away from the cameras. When the reporter referred to the group as "angry rogue Republicans who had been discredited by the Party," Joe felt a chill go up his spine. He drained his glass and left quickly, feeling like he needed a shower.

As he walked back to the motel, he saw three teenage boys peering into the windows of his SUV trying to examine the contents. Joe yelled at them to get away from the car but they approached him threateningly. Instinctively, Joe made an aggressive gesture and raised his voice. One of the teenagers spotted the gold Rolex on Joe's arm, whispered into the ear of another, and they dropped back and slunk away. He checked the doors of the Expedition to make sure they were locked and nothing was missing. The doorframe of his room had screwdriver marks near the knob but it was hard to tell if they were recent.

He didn't get a lot of sleep that night. The air conditioner was very loud, but didn't put out much in the way of cool air. Not only could he hear the couple next door fighting through the thin walls, but he woke up every time he heard someone walking past, especially if the footsteps paused near his car and the door. At one point he thought he saw the shadows of the three teenagers silhouetted against the curtain, and his body tensed, ready to fight them off if necessary. By the time the sun came up, he was exhausted.

After a hasty breakfast at McFriendly's, he decided to take inventory of his belongings. He set his stuff out on the bed and pulled everything from the suitcases and boxes. In one pile, he put all the items he figured he wouldn't need for a while: tuxedo, white linen suit, ski clothes and boots, wetsuit. In the second pile he put the clothes he'd need for working: business suits, dress shirts, ties, nice business casual slacks and shirts, cashmere sweaters and raincoat. In the last pile, he put everyday attire like underwear, t-shirts, swimsuits, oxford and polo shirts, jeans, khakis, pajamas, fleece jackets, and his down vest. He was a little short on his third pile after his mad dash from Aquamarine so he made a mental note to replenish his supply. He also had one set of sheets and four towels, a few pots and plates, and a sleeping bag, two-man tent, camp stove, some odds and ends, and the box of sentimental junk he'd left in the SUV. Fortunately, he'd never unpacked them.

He took out one of the picture albums and sat on the edge of the bed. Other than the gray in her hair, he thought Susan looked as good now as she had when the kids were small. Mandy was such a sweet child and Daniel was such a sturdy little guy. He had to say the 90's were a great time for them. The economy was booming. Everyone was optimistic about the future. The schools were good both for the kids and Susan. Of course as his salary increased so did his taxes, which marred the happy picture. He couldn't figure out why the people in Aquamarine didn't see the problem the same way. Maybe they had never earned enough for it to be an issue?

He decided to look for an inexpensive apartment. He needed to call Jack to see what was happening. Hopefully, the secretary had calmed down by now. It wouldn't hurt to check in with his accountant, Tom, either for that matter, as well as Miranda. The communicator seemed to be out of order, so he'd have to fix that so they could call him back if necessary. The phone in the room cost $2 a minute so it probably was worth getting the wireless phone first. Then he'd call Jack and the others, find out what happened to the house in Atherton, and have a number available if he needed a rental.

Making sure the curtains were closed, Joe unwrapped the money belt from his waist and the safe from his leg. He took the money from his wallet as well. His stay in Aquamarine had been quite cost-effective, except for his ridiculous parting gift. What was he thinking? After the camping, gas, motel, and meals, he had about $25 in his wallet. The rest yielded a little over $20,000, divided between the two hiding places, and there was still the $500 under the floor mat in the SUV.

Joe estimated that to make the money last until he could resolve the misunderstanding with Homeland Security, he needed to find a rental under $1,000. Of course, he'd offset the expenses by working, and when he landed a real job, he could trade up to a better place. Maybe a month-to-month situation would be better.

It had been many years since Joe had rented, so he wasn't exactly sure what the going rate was these days or how long it would take. Maybe he should keep the room another night so he didn't have to cart everything around with him. Then again, what was the guarantee that everything would be here when he returned?

Checkout wasn't until noon so he compromised with the committee debating in his brain and deferred the decision till later. He stopped in to ask the clerk where the best place was to get a pre-paid wireless phone. The clerk yawned and directed Joe to the Guardian Angel Cash Advance Boutique down El Camino. As he climbed into the SUV, he thought he spotted two of his pals from the night before standing on the corner across the street.

The Guardian Angel Boutique was another new world for Joe. They carried a full-line of services and products for the financially short-changed. "Heaven's answers to your prayers" and "End-to-end cash management solutions," read the banners. In addition to paid-in-advance wireless phones in a variety of designer colors and animal print patterns, you could get an advance on your paycheck for only a 25% fee, buy a pre-paid utility card, or pawn your more desirable belongings.

The image of the teens eyeballing his Rolex flashed through Joe's mind. Maybe walking around town with an $18,000 watch wasn't such a hot idea. And if he was so stressed about protecting his clothing, was it really worth trying to beat off kids for a watch? He asked the guy behind the counter what he could get for it. It was 18K gold Joe assured him and he'd paid the full retail price at the Rolex store in Stanford Shopping Center. Joe could tell he didn't believe him. The idiot had probably never even seen a real Rolex. "A thousand bucks," the guy offered, turning it over. Joe snatched the watch back. Clearly, this was not a seller's market. He was about to tell the guy he was a thief when he realized that he still hadn't bought the phone.

Trying to hide his anger with a gulp of air, he asked about the wireless plan. Joe started to argue about the price, each minute cost triple of his normal plan, but the dark look on the clerk's face stopped him. Clearly, this was not a buyer's market either. Whose market was it? He shoved $100 across the counter. "Uh, the sales tax? 20%." Joe forked over another bill and stalked over to the car. He shoved the watch in his pocket.

The spaces directly opposite his room were taken, so Joe had to park a little further away. He saw the boys walking towards him but managed to get to the door before they did. His hand fumbled getting the key in the lock but he got the door open and slammed it in their faces. They banged on the door but he ignored them. Suddenly they laughed and left. He would have pushed a piece of furniture against the door if everything weren't nailed to the floor.

When his heart rate came back to normal, he dialed Jack's number. Fortunately Jack's assistant answered the phone instead of the secretary. He said Jack was in a meeting and would call him back. Joe left the number. He repeated the routine with Tom's office. OK, he had to get out of here. He'd try Miranda later. Check out time was in 20 minutes so Joe packed everything up checking the room three times to make sure he hadn't left anything behind this time. He was still sweating but there wasn't time to take a shower, so he called the front desk to request a late check out. "Sure, the hourly rate is 20 bucks." Deciding it was a rational investment, he opted for the extra hour.

Despite his aversion to seeming like a girly-man, Joe couldn't decide what to wear. If he dressed too well, people would be suspicious of his desire to rent a cheap apartment. If he looked too sloppy, they probably wouldn't rent to him at all. In the end he went with khakis and an oxford shirt with the cuffs rolled up. It was too warm for a sports coat. No tie, but he'd keep one handy. Out of habit, he went to put his watch on. Where was it? Oh my God…he couldn't find it. He checked the pockets of the trousers he'd been wearing earlier and realized the right pocket lining was torn. He traced his steps in the room. Nothing. What if he'd dropped it outside the door when he was struggling with the key? Maybe that was why they had left so suddenly? Absurdly, he thought "well they'll only get a $1000 if they hock it." He felt sick to his stomach and his head was pounding.

Joe pulled back the curtains, looked out, then opened the door quickly, and rolled his bags into the car. He thought about walking away without paying the extra $20 but decided to go into the office to file a complaint about the theft. The same geezer from yesterday was there and when Joe started to explain he merely shrugged. "You've got to be kidding mister. You think anyone is protecting this crumby neighborhood? You're just lucky they didn't slit your throat to get the watch."

★　　　★　　　★　　　★　　　★

Driving down El Camino into Menlo Park, Joe recognized the sign for Afterwards, a luxury consignment boutique. He had taken a lot of his old wardrobe there when he upgraded. It had yielded a few bucks and this might be a good strategy to lighten his load a bit.

Afterwards had been started by a couple who previously managed the Ralph Lauren Polo store at Stanford Shopping Center, and they had built up a thriving business taking surplus possessions off the hands of wealthy people who liked to frequently change styles in clothing and furniture, merchandising the goods with flair, and offering them to those who liked quality at a bargain. With a large segment of the population affected by downturns in the economy, Afterwards had turned into a real entrepreneurial success story, expanding into bigger spaces and more cities around the country after it went public on the NYSE. Joe wished he had invested when he had had the chance.

Location was always a delicate issue. The stores had to be safe enough so the affluent would leave their cocoons of security to drop items off (though Joe had heard they had started a pick up service). It had to be accessible enough so shoppers of more limited means would feel comfortable coming to the store, yet intimidating enough that the homeless wouldn't be tempted to come in and browse. Fortunately, Keplers Bookstore, one of the last big independent booksellers in the area, had gone out of business and their big corner space was available. Joe thought it a shame that Keplers had been unable to survive the convergence of factors, since he liked the celebrity book readings they hosted. They had gone under at one point years before, but local residents banded together and invested in the operation to keep it going. In the end, market forces prevailed: price pressure from Amazon.com and the big chains, the demise of smaller publishing houses, a popular culture that ridiculed people who read books for knowledge, and a faltering public school system that focused on standardized testing more than reading literature. Free markets meant sometimes you got outcomes you didn't like, he supposed.

Joe pulled into the lot, gave $5 to the attendant, removed the bag that contained the tux and other non-essential items, and grabbed a lightweight sports coat from the garment bag to slip on. He smoothed his hair back, straightened his shoulders, and rolled on in.

Sandy, the pretty brunette who had helped him the last time, was seated at a desk in the private drop-off area. She remembered him and greeted him warmly. Boy, it felt good to be treated like his former self. His whole body relaxed and he had to hold back an unexpected urge to cry.

He took the items out of the bag. Sandy's brow furrowed. "We're a little slow on formal wear and white suits right now," she said gently. "The people who need tuxedos on a regular basis usually prefer to buy their own new. The wedding market rents.

Let me give you some estimates and we'll see what we can do. Should I credit the sales to the same bank account as last time? You're still at the Atherton address right?"

Joe cleared his throat. "Um, is there any way that I could get cash instead upfront?" That was the problem of coming in on impulse. He didn't have his story straight. "I've had some complications lately from…" Think. Think… "identity theft and it's made everything a real mess. I'm actually in the process of moving." Hey, that was pretty good he told himself. Sandy was watching his face.

"I'll tell you what. You've been a very good client in the past and you referred several good sources of both clothing and home furnishings." She pointed to a new lot that had just come in. Joe recognized, to his horror, a few pieces that must have come from his house. He looked quickly back at Sandy. She smiled. "It's not our customary policy, but I can either give you $200 cash or $350 of merchandise from some odd lots we just picked up. They've got all the tags on them and I haven't even put them out on the floor yet."

"Sure, that would be great. I needed to pick up some shorts, jeans, and shirts anyway. This will save me the time of going over to Neiman Marcus." Sandy helped him find the right sizes, made some color recommendations, and talked to him in a way that made him feel normal again.

As she was putting everything into shopping bags, she asked, "Are you sure you're ok? I know that identity theft can be very stressful. It happened to my cousin last year and it caused him a lot of problems. Not to scare you, but he lost his house and it destroyed his credit for the next millennium. Thirty-eight years old and he's back living with my aunt and uncle."

In the warmth of her concern, Joe was tempted to tell Sandy what was happening to him but decided it was too dangerous. He didn't want to risk having the first person who had treated him like a real human being, since this nightmare started, look at him with suspicion.

"When I settle down in my new place, I'll stop by and say hello. Thanks very much for your help." Joe didn't want to leave but he couldn't think of any logical excuse to stay and besides, he had to find a temporary place to live, or at the very least, sleep that night.

★ ★ ★ ★ ★

Joe checked in with Jack's office again. "Jack still isn't available," his assistant said. "There is no word on an earlier hearing date. And I'm afraid there is some bad news—the bank foreclosed on your house and the new owner has already moved in. I'm so sorry. I'm sure it's very upsetting. Please call in with your new address as soon as possible." Joe was about to raise his voice and argue when he realized that he'd better not alienate the assistant too. Then he'd never get to talk to Jack again. So he only said goodbye and disconnected.

The last time Joe had rented an apartment was in 1985. He and Susan had recently gotten married, and she was supporting them while he was in law school. When he joined Brobeck in '87, they bought their first house in Menlo Park and then moved to the Lindenwood area of Atherton when his company went public. He had a feeling that the best way to find a place might have changed, since there were so few local papers any more.

He went to an Internet café on University Avenue in Palo Alto, which unfortunately had acquired the air of Telegraph Avenue in Berkeley. Lots of high-end shops and restaurants yet a substantial number of rather dubious looking characters wandering the streets. The City Council had passed several anti-loitering laws to support the merchants, but the number of homeless people had overwhelmed the understaffed police force.

He googled "apartments Silicon Valley." As a corporate attorney, he found it hilarious that the Silicon Valley legend had gone the way of kleenex and xerox and their trademark had become a generic term for Internet search. He found a good link to craigslist.org, which seemed to have a fair number of options.

There were quite a few in his price range but as he read through the ads, there were some other snags:

> **$990 / 1br - Furnished HOUSE with Garden in Silicon Valley (housesitting)**
> Reply to: 59871535@craigslist.org
> Date: 2012-07-15, 12:32PM PST
> Why stay in a crowded apartment when you can live in a sunny, safe HOUSE? (housesitting while we are out of town) Available for 4 months minimum. NO SMOKING, DRUGS, or DRAMA!!
> House includes 1 bedroom, living room, bath, kitchen (about 800 SF interior), front and back yard, patio, garden with fruit trees, safe driveway parking. Basic furniture included. All utilities are connected and are lowest cost in the area. Energy-efficient appliances. We pay for telephone (local), water, garbage, recycling and gardening.
> Looking for a (one) clean, quiet and responsible employed professional (no work at home or self-employed), with MINIMUM baggage (possessions). Mature adult NONSMOKER without pets please. Green thumbs welcome.
> Ideal for someone new in the area who needs temporary place, or a commuter who needs a home away from home (lower rent if here only on weekdays).
> PLEASE send info about yourself and your situation and requirements (where do you live now, when and why do you need a place, for how long, etc.) Please include local phone number. Will not respond to e-mail without information above.

He wasn't sure his story would pass the "no drama test" and while he certainly was a clean, quiet, professional with minimum baggage in all senses of the phrase, he didn't meet the "employed" standard at the moment. Here was another one that looked good:

> **$900 / 1br - Unfurnished COTTAGE**
> Reply to: anon-59835@craigslist.org
> Date: 2013-07-15, 12:32PM PST

I have a nice cottage behind my main house, which will be
available as of 8/1/2013. The address is 592 St.Cloud Ave., Palo
Alto, CA 94306. My cell phone is 650-555-7460. My name is
Rashid. The cottage is newly remodeled with marble shower
and skylights and tile floor. It is a lovely place for a single
professional. Please call me if you are interested. No pets, no
smoking. Thanks.

Maybe someone with a foreign sounding name would be
sympathetic? Then again, maybe bunking with a possible Arab
wasn't the smartest move at the moment. He kept going.

$1090 / 1br – APARTMENT on great property
Reply to: anon-59X3735@craigslist.org
Date: 2013-07-17, 12:32AM PST
This great 1 bedroom apartment is set on a stunning 5-acre property
filled with trees, lawns and gardens. It has a spacious private patio,
plenty of storage space and much more. Fresh paint, clean and
sparkling. Covered parking and bike storage are also included. Come
see for yourself. Call 650-555-2244

Now this sounded terrific. He called. A man answered and
told him about the place in more detail. They had a great conversation and Joe's spirits lifted. "Sure, you can come and see the
apartment this afternoon. Fax over your bank information and we
can do the credit check before you come over. I'll have the lease
ready for you to sign. You can move in as soon as you want."
Crestfallen Joe said, "I have another appointment today but I'll
call you back tomorrow."

OK, here was another that appealed to him. The "Flex Cash"
special sounded particularly good.

$1000 / 1br and 2br APARTMENTS
Reply to: anon-598235@craigslist.org
Date: 2013-07-10, 3:32PM PST
Large Floorplans / 1 Bedroom for under $1100.00 Stanford Villa...a
prestigious apartment community designed to complement your
individual style of living. The collection of spacious apartment homes
is situated around uniquely landscaped courtyards and three sparkling

pools. We offer spacious Studios starting at $945.00, 1 & 2
bedroom/2 bath apartment homes starting at $1045.00. Other
conveniences include a state-of-the-art fitness center and relaxing
sauna. Enjoy easy access to highways 280 and 101 as well as fine
dining and entertainment.
Come and tour the community and ask about our current
"Flex Cash" special
- 24-hour emergency service and armed security guards
- Near Stanford Shopping Center
Stop by your new home at 3375 Alma Street in Palo Alto:

He decided to drive down. It was close by, and maybe if they
saw him in person, they'd relax some of the requirements. He
found the manager's office without any problem. They went on
the tour of the facility. It wouldn't have been his taste a few
months ago but considering the prospect of another night at a
motel that accepted cash, it was fantastic. There was a one-
bedroom available, which would suit his needs just fine, so they
went back to the office. The manager handed him an application.
"Just the usual stuff: employment and personal references, security
status, plus bank accounts so we can do an automatic deduction
for the 'FlexCash' special."

"I'd like to pay actual cash, if you don't mind," offered Joe
casually. "It's no problem for me to pay first, last, deposit, and a
few extra months if you'd prefer. I think the complex is exactly
what I'm looking for."

It was clear that the manager thought this was a very odd
request. "You seem like a nice guy and I'd like to help you out, but
we're not set up for processing cash." He thought for a moment
and scribbled a name and address on a piece of paper. "Someone
I know might be willing to rent you a room. Stop by around 6
PM. I'll give him a call and let him know you're coming."

Joe thanked the man and left. By now perpetual
embarrassment was beginning to seem routine.

★　　　★　　　★　　　★　　　★

Joe went to the address on the paper promptly at 6 PM. It was a nondescript house on Alma Street, and the middle-aged man who answered the door was equally undistinguished. You'd be hard pressed to pick this guy out of a crowd. He welcomed Joe into his living room, which smelled of stale cigarettes and scorched coffee. Joe sat perched on the edge of the worn sofa. He was not living here. He was not that desperate.

The man, Warren, was telling Joe about some alternative housing situations he could arrange. Thank God. He wouldn't be rooming with this fellow. It would cost Joe about $250 to be taken to these various accommodations, which didn't require any bank accounts or proof of employment, and they took cash. If Joe made a deal, then he'd owe Warren another $250.

$250 just to look? How did Joe even know that he'd be interested? "What sort of places? What was the rent? What were the facilities and amenities like?" He fired out the questions.

Warren rubbed his chin and gave Joe a wry smile. "Maybe you haven't been looking very long, and my guess is that this is a new experience for you…but how far do you think you're going to get without a bank account or a job? People who only pay cash look suspicious. My associates don't care if you're a drug dealer or a fugitive or whatever, as long as you pay your rent on time."

Joe started to bluster that he was *not* a criminal and then caught himself. It wasn't going to do any good to pick a fight with Warren, and besides, what he was or had been didn't seem to matter much. How was he going to be able to get a job if he didn't have an address, or a shower for that matter? Trying to find a place to live was taking so much of his time he didn't even have the bandwidth to look for a job.

"Sleep on it. If you're interested, come back tomorrow around 9 and I'll take you to some properties in Palo Alto." He held the door open for Joe. No anger, no animosity, just a kind of take it or leave it attitude that let both of them know who was holding all the cards here.

Joe walked into the cool evening air and realized that he didn't have 'a place to sleep on it.' Did he want to try to find another motel that didn't require credit cards? It was probably easier to sleep in the SUV tonight. Since it was early, he decided to go back to the Internet café and do another search. He stuck his toothbrush and toothpaste in his jacket pocket. It would probably be too weird to try to shave in the restroom. Maybe he could find a room in a house where they didn't need to ask so many questions? He paid for an hour on the computer in advance and picked one ad at random.

$600 / ROOM FOR RENT
Reply to: anon-5944499235@craigslist.org
Date: 2013-07-11, 8:32PM PST
Hello,
Looking for a roommate again. My present roommate can't afford to pay rent any more and will have to go to a shelter. (If anyone knows of any trade for board opportunities, or can otherwise help her and her two-year old girl in some way, please drop me a line. She is 25, organic vegan, and can do Raiki.)
(OK, back to me :)
I am looking for a non-smoking, environmentally conscious person, to share a beautiful 2 BR/2 Bath townhouse in Campbell close to Whole Foods, Trader Joes, farmer's market, Santana Row, library, and many coffee shops. I am about 1.5 miles from 280 and 17 and 2 to 5 miles from San Jose City College, Santa Clara University, DeAnza College and San Jose State University.
I am looking for a housemate who is piscatarian, vegetarian, or vegan. I am 29, clean, respectful, fun, spiritual, open, and easy-going. I am a professional working in the information technology industry, have lived in my home for almost ten years, and enjoy going to the beach, dancing, and hiking, and other outdoor activities.
Seeking a housemate who enjoys living in a clean, easy going home, appreciates nature, and who is both responsible and fun.
The room is 130 square feet, including the sliding door closet, and is a beautiful lavender with a purple ceiling. I have a futon available. The place has wall-to-wall carpeting.
Rent is $600 plus half utilities.
Lease term is flexible depending on your needs. Rent includes use of

much of the house, all common furnishings, washer and dryer, dishwasher, private patio / garden, fully staffed kitchen, a common swimming pool, and the company of a very nice cat. Plus: Super-high-speed Wired and Wireless Internet Access! Available Now. Female preferred. Gay/Leather/Kink-friendly.

This was horrible. How had this happened? He had always worked hard, done the right things, gone to church, been kind to children and old people. He was a good person. How had he come to a position where he had to beg some kink-friendly (whatever that was) weirdo to live in 130 square feet? His walk-in closet was bigger than that. He was willing to work. He even had money. It's not like he had to be a charity case.

He kept looking. Unfortunately, there were not many ads seeking an unemployed 50-year old heterosexual male roommate facing a potential terrorism investigation.

He left at closing time, climbed in the Expedition and tried to find an unobtrusive place to park. Most of the residential streets had "no overnight parking without a permit" signs and all the commercial parking lots seemed to be chained off. He noticed there were a number of cars parked in the old railroad station parking lot. The trains had stopped running after the government subsidies had gone away. The station itself had been turned into a Starbucks and the lot seemed to be one of the few that weren't secured. At least he could get a cup of coffee in the morning.

He pulled into a spot and rearranged his belongings to make a comfortable bed. OK, maybe comfortable wasn't the right word. He had forgotten to get the air mattress filled and he didn't want to call attention to himself by getting out the bicycle pump and standing in the parking lot. If he hadn't been so tired from the previous night, he wouldn't have slept at all.

There was lots of noise. Cars kept coming by and he could hear people laughing and talking as they returned to their cars from an evening out. He tried to find a tolerable position. At one point someone pointed a flashlight in the driver's side window. He held his breath and tried not to move. They rattled the doors and then moved on when they found them locked. It seemed like forever before he fell asleep again.

He felt like hell in the morning. Everything was stiff. His neck ached like someone had been standing on it with heavy boots. Every athletic injury he had ever suffered in his entire life was present and accounted for. He needed to take a leak.

Joe pulled on a clean sweatshirt, smoothed his hair—hoping his beard wasn't too scuzzy looking—and tried to stroll nonchalantly into the Starbucks. He seriously doubted he was making a favorable first impression on the well-pierced youth behind the counter. He ordered a doppio and a scone. $3.50 for a scone? It was highway robbery. However, it was worth it to be able to use the single person rest room. He took off his shirt and washed under his armpits, drying them with the paper towel. Only a slight improvement. He tried not to look at his face in the mirror. It was too depressing. He wished he had remembered to bring his razor with him.

As he ate his scone, Joe debated whether he should go see Warren. It was still summer, he could find a place to camp. But if he did, how would he look for a job? No-tell motels didn't seem like a very good bet, and sleeping in his car wasn't really an option. He desperately wanted a hot shower. How bad could it be? It was temporary. He'd find a job and get his life back on track. He had to. He fought back the inner voices that said it wouldn't get better.

As he walked back to his car, he saw two policemen examining his vehicle, peering in the tinted windows. The police had always been on his side, so naturally he walked up and asked them if there was a problem. They looked at him like he was some kind of derelict.

"This your vehicle, fella?"

Joe was used to being addressed by young guys like these as "sir" and he started to bristle, but something in the cops' faces stopped him. "Yes, officer. It's my car. I assume that it's parked legally."

"We got a report that this was parked here overnight. You living in your car, buddy?" he said, eyeing Joe's unshaven face. Joe started to sweat. What should he say? Should he admit he'd been here? What if he lied and they had proof from a surveillance camera? That would make him look guilty of something worse. OK, if he had to admit he was there what would be a good excuse? He knew he couldn't risk getting arrested for vagrancy. What if Jack's secretary or the security company had filed a complaint? At least it didn't look like they were running his plates. Stay calm. Be polite.

"Of course not officer. I came back into town after backpacking for a few weeks up north. I got in really late and my new apartment isn't going to be available until later today. I figured I'd grab a snooze and a cup of coffee before I went over. It wasn't worth getting a hotel room for a couple of hours."

The cop who didn't look like he believed Joe was fingering his handcuffs when a call came in on the radio. His partner nudged him. "This is more important. Let's not worry about this old guy."

Joe tried to maintain his composure, nor let his relief show on his face. "The rental agent should be ready for me now. I'll be on my way then."

★   ★   ★   ★   ★

Warren didn't seem surprised to see him, nor did he comment on Joe's rumpled look. He simply accepted the money and told Joe to follow him. They drove to one of the office parks on Page Mill Road. With so many businesses going under and most non-executive operations being outsourced overseas, there was a lot of excess office space. Some buildings had been vacant for a decade and were looking a little worse for wear. Apparently some enterprising souls had "repurposed" some of the less desirable office buildings into an innovative living arrangement. Nobody was enforcing zoning ordinances any more, and it created a new source of revenue for the real estate developers.

Warren pointed out the various options. Joe could rent, on a month-to-month basis, a former conference room or private office for $1,000 to $1,500, depending on size and whether there were outside windows. He had a couple available now. These had the advantage that you could lock up your belongings when you left the building. For $500 a month, you could get a cube. Joe could see that some were decorated in a festive manner reminding him of his high tech days. Posters of exotic locations and colorful beach accessories seemed to be popular themes.

Warren gave him the run down. "Everyone shares the kitchenettes. They're equipped with small microwaves and refrigerators. It's best to mark your food, although there are no guarantees. If you keep food in your space, then it has to be in a metal, sealed, container so it doesn't attract bugs or rodents. The rest rooms are cleaned twice a week, and the handicapped stalls have been retrofitted with prefab showers. There is electricity available, though the data and phone lines in the building are dead. The living areas are heated to 58 degrees in the winter and cooled to 80 degrees in the summer. You can't open any windows, so we keep the fans running for circulation 24 x 7. You get used to the sound. Wireless phone reception varies depending on where in the building you are. Residents take turns vacuuming and mopping the common areas and hallways, depending on how much the dirt bothers them.

"Parents are responsible for monitoring their own children. Some do a better job than others. A lot of the families here can't afford private schools, even with vouchers. The public schools are so broke they're pretty run down and dangerous, so many of the parents home school their kids. The good news is that means there's always someone around during the day. Pets are definitely discouraged since people do such a lousy job of cleaning up after them. We're not heartless, so we look the other way for the odd goldfish or turtle.

"Rent is due on the first of the month. If you're late, you get charged an extra $20 a day and after a week you're evicted. No exceptions."

Warren pointed out the fire extinguishers. "We ask people not to smoke but it's not like we're here to police them. Same for alcohol and drug use. People have to exercise personal responsibility. The front door is locked at night but again, it's up to the residents to watch out for strangers and deal with any suspicious characters. This building hasn't had too many problems, but with 600 or so people on three floors, you can't expect perfection."

Joe briefly considered a large corner office overlooking the courtyard for $1,500 but decided a smaller room for $1,000 was a better way to conserve cash. It faced the new Stanford Executive Homes Park III under construction. The former open space had been developed by the Stanford Land Development Corporation, but at least you could see the Santa Cruz Mountains in the distance —if you stood at the window and looked sideways. As Joe counted out the money, he consoled himself that this was temporary, and the location offered great highway access.

★   ★   ★   ★   ★

It took Joe about half an hour to get moved into his new place. He didn't know exactly what to call this "alternative living arrangement." There was one chair that had been left in the office. Warren hadn't known what happened to the desk or the couch. Probably someone had snagged it when the last person moved out. Joe vaguely wondered what had happened to *him*—did he get a real apartment or was he now camping in a cube? Warren hadn't known, or cared for that matter.

He pumped up the air mattress and opened the sleeping bag. He'd get a new blanket tomorrow. He unpacked the box of treasures and hung the small painting on a hook that was left in the wall. There were some built-in book cases so he folded his clothes neatly on the shelves and hung his suits on the hook on the back of the door. He left his winter coats and heavy sweaters in the large suitcase. There was a glass panel facing the area with the cubicles, signifying the original occupant of the office hadn't been important enough to rate a set of blinds for privacy. For the moment, he stacked up the suitcases so they blocked the view. He'd pick up an extra sheet or a curtain and some tacks too.

He tried the wireless phone. It had a signal. He called Jack's office. Unfortunately, the secretary answered. He disguised his voice and asked for the assistant, to whom he provided his address. He tried reaching Miranda. A recording said that she had closed the office and moved. Her accounts were all being handled by Kim Whitfield of KPMG-GrantThornton-Schwab and gave Kim's number. Oh great. Now he had to explain what was happening to someone whom he didn't even know.

Joe called the number and reached Kim. "Oh, Joe Winston. I remember your portfolio. The one where everything was frozen. We couldn't make the transfer."

"What do you mean 'you couldn't make the transfer'? There was over $15,000,000. What the hell happened to my money? You've got to be kidding. This is completely unacceptable."

"Don't yell at me. It's not my problem you got mixed up with terrorists. You're not even my client." She hung up on him. He tried calling back and got her voice mail. Struggling to keep his voice calm, he left a message asking her to call him back so he could track down his portfolio. He called Jack's office and left word with the assistant as to this latest development. The assistant didn't know when Jack would be free to call him. He left another message with the accountant.

He tried taking a nap, but the afternoon sun was too bright. The kids were outside playing and hollering. That didn't bother him; at least it sounded commonplace and he could forget where he was. He dozed off and dreamed of Mandy and Daniel playing in the backyard. Susan was laughing. Suddenly, thunderous clouds darkened the sky and Susan was running around frantically. Mandy was missing. She and Daniel had looked everywhere. She was pounding on Joe's chest, crying. Joe woke up bathed in sweat. It was dark outside.

Maybe now would be a good time to take a shower and shave. No one would be in the bathroom and it would be quiet. He took off the money belt and leg safe. They were dingy and grimy and gave off an unpleasant odor. He looked around for a place to hide them and donned a pair of jeans and a T-shirt. Grabbing his key, a towel, and toiletry bag, he walked to the men's room, past sleeping families and a few quiet conversations.

Other than a tired looking man washing his face, there wasn't anyone there. Joe avoided the man's eyes and stepped into the handicapped stall. The water wasn't very hot but it felt good as he scrubbed his hair and shaved his face. He tried not to look at the floor of the shower and made another mental note to get a pair of flip-flops. Too bad he had given away the pair he'd received at the 2004 Republican National Convention in NYC. They'd make quite a statement.

The next few weeks took on a rhythm of their own. He'd get up early, find someplace beautiful to walk—there still were a few parks open to the public—and then he'd get breakfast and hit the Internet café for the morning. He'd look for any new job postings and send in his resume, always tailoring his cover letter to explain why he'd be perfect for the position. He was starting to wonder if there really was anyone on the other end, because he never received a single reply. It took all his self-determination to keep trying in the face of complete rejection.

Then Joe would grab lunch and seek out work that might not have made it to the web. He tried local merchants and retailers and walked into as many offices as he could. If he could actually get someone to speak to him, they all pretty much told him the same thing: he was over qualified. Even when he lied and didn't tell them he was a lawyer, it was still obvious that he was a college graduate, not to mention too old. They said they were worried he'd get bored or wouldn't have enough passion for the position. It didn't seem like something he would aspire to. (Of course not, but that didn't mean he wouldn't do a great job.) They didn't want to invest the time in training him only to have him leave when something more appropriate came along. Telling them he needed the job didn't seem to have the slightest effect. They'd just laugh and tell him it wasn't their problem, or remind him that there were other people who needed the job more.

He'd pick up something to eat for dinner and a bottle of wine and head back to the… place. In his own mind he nicknamed it the "Page Mill Astrodome" due to its communal similarity to the shelter used during the Hurricane Katrina disaster of '05. At least it was better than the hellhole of the New Orleans Superdome or the squalor of an underprivileged neighborhood.

Inevitably, there'd be some other poor slob sitting outside, and they'd share a bench, a glass of something, and their stories.

★　　　★　　　★　　　★　　　★

Martin Berman had been a successful photographer specializing in product "hero shots" for high tech companies. He'd had his own business for years until the dot com bust when his business plummeted. He'd been keeping his head above water thanks to savings and a sporadic, though less profitable, sideline in family portraits. Unfortunately, his wife suffered a massive stroke. It was a long and costly illness and he was required by "The Culture of Life Act" to keep her going on life support even after it was clear all brain functions were gone. The doctors inserted a feeding tube, hooked her up to a respirator, and kept a defibrillator next to the bed, even though Martin knew his wife wouldn't have wanted to be kept alive that way. Then his insurance carrier dropped them, and as an independent consultant he didn't have any clout to fight the decision.

By the time she died from a staph infection accidentally brought in by one of the health workers, he'd lost his house and studio, and his savings had been wiped out. Martin rented one of the cubicles and a janitor's closet to store his photography equipment, since the portrait work was too uncertain to qualify for a lease. Plus, even though his clients were wealthy, they often didn't pay their bills for months, and it was tough to get past their handlers to collect when there was an issue. He finally shifted to a cash up-front model that reduced the number of clients, but at least weeded out the problem cases.

Margot and Mike Smith were younger. They'd both had good jobs and health insurance and their kids were in parochial schools. When Mike was laid off, they cut back on everything and Margot carried them while Mike looked for something else. His job hunting experience had been similar to Joe's. Either he was overqualified or there were hundreds of applicants and he didn't have the precise experience they wanted. The twenty-something hiring managers didn't seem to understand that if you had similar experience you could apply the same skills in a different context. Mike felt the problem with a generation trained to obediently memorize facts was they didn't value imagination, much less understand how to apply it.

When Margot's company moved out of the area and didn't bother to offer her a position in the new location, they simply couldn't make ends meet. They maxed out the credit cards and got deeper and deeper into debt. Eventually, the bank foreclosed on their house. Now they were living on the proceeds from the sale of Mike's BMW. They were lucky—the school gave the kids a scholarship so they could stay enrolled. If Margot's car needed a big repair or one of them became seriously ill, they'd be on the streets.

It made Joe feel a little better to know he wasn't alone, but it didn't mean that he felt good about himself. As much as he hated to admit it, maybe there was something wrong with him. What if it was hopeless? What if it didn't matter that he could do a job when no one would give him a chance to try? What if this was all the money he was ever going to have? He drank the rest of the bottle and went to sleep. Fortunately, he didn't have any dreams he could remember.

Summer cooled into autumn without Joe really noticing. The place wasn't that bad. Most of the people were solidly middle and upper middle class, if you defined class as a sensibility rather than current income level. They all had been productive, hardworking, contributing members of society, not shiftless types who had chosen poverty. They had fallen on hard times, or a piece of bad luck, and had spiraled out of control. Like him, they were caught up in circumstances that weren't their fault.

At the end of September, the Mervin family, who occupied a large conference room on the second floor, moved out. The kids were crying. They had made lots of friends and the parents looked stricken. Joe had spoken to them quite often and they were a lovely couple—the sort of people he liked—quiet, modest, well mannered, and kind. They were packing up whatever they could carry with them and selling the rest. Joe traded them one of his big rolling suitcases and a backpack for a futon on a wooden frame. He gave them the name of the coordinator for the Friendship Center at his old church and suggested they look her up. It was so sad to see people he knew personally face a life on the street.

Warren paid one of the women $5 to vacuum out the conference room. All that was left was the original credenza, which was too heavy to lift. A new family was moving in. People hovered around, trying to appear casual and not too nosy, but the new residents were hard to miss. For one thing, they had more stuff: boxes, suitcases, even some furniture and art. More surprisingly, they were louder and more talkative. Most people here seemed to operate at just above a whisper; it was as if their vocal cords had been surgically altered. The husband looked familiar to Joe. He was agitated and his wife was trying to calm him down.

The three kids, who looked to be between the ages of 6 and 10, were clinging to each other and looking at the surroundings as if they had been transported to another planet.

Suddenly, it hit Joe how he knew the guy. They had been in the local bar association together. Of course, they ran in different circles. Ben Stern—that was his name—was a litigator. He was big in medical malpractice and class action suits against pharmaceutical companies. Gave a lot of money to the Democrats and was always writing guest opinion pieces for the local papers. Served him right to be here. Proof positive that tort reform had worked.

The next day, he ran into Ben and his wife in the kitchen. "Say, don't I know you?" Ben inquired, "It's Joe Winsome...wait Winston, right?" Without waiting for an answer, he shook Joe's hand and continued, "What are you doing here? Last time I saw you, you were working at some high flying company. Win some, lose some, eh?" Joe just smiled and made a slight grimace at the bad joke. The wife stepped forward, "I'm Betsy Stern. How do you do? You'll have to forgive Ben. I'm sure this is a little unsettling for all of us."

Joe stuffed a couple of bills in the coffee kitty and got them each a cup. They walked back to the Stern's room and sat down on the folding chairs the Sterns had brought with them. Betsy explained that she had been a program manager for Children's Mental Health Services of Santa Clara County. In the series of budget cuts that had slashed their funding, the agency had finally collapsed and everyone had been laid off. "I still don't completely understand it. We had a great program called 'Wraparound' that treated emotionally troubled kids by supporting the whole family. It was not only effective, it cost less than letting situations deteriorate. It was pioneered in southern California by a Republican state legislator and it eventually became a success nationally."

Ben started to rant about the rampant stupidity of this kind of move as Joe listened impassively, hoping that Ben didn't remember that Joe had led the Silicon Valley Bar group that had favored eliminating non-essential government jobs and cutting social service programs. Ben and Betsy had both gone into private practice in their respective fields. With more conservative judges on the bench, and the federal and state restrictions capping settlements, even the most egregious cases were receiving very small judgments, if anything. And, while more people probably needed mental health support than ever before, the only places that paid decently were private clinics for the very wealthy. Betsy had landed a job at one such facility, but after their youngest child's leukemia ceased to be in remission, she resigned to care for him.

"During our 'professional transitions,' we had been forced to change health plans, causing Sammy's illness to be regarded as a pre-existing condition," Ben explained. "I suspected that it gave the execs at the insurance company a real thrill to deny our claim and appeals, since I had kicked their butts in several cases. Anyway, we had to pay for all treatment out of our own pockets at the non-negotiated rates, which meant that everything cost at least three times as much. The doctors tried chemo, bone marrow transplants, and an experimental procedure using stem cells retrieved from umbilical cords. We even applied to go to Europe for an embryonic stem cell treatment that is proving successful but isn't legal here. We went through our savings, sold the house and Betsy's jewelry, and moved into an apartment."

Betsy took up the story, "Ben's parents were in an assisted living complex—his mother had dementia and his dad couldn't care for her without help—and we were paying for that too. Unfortunately, the reduced social security benefits didn't cover a reasonable facility."

She started to break down and Joe gathered that Sammy didn't make it. Ben said bitterly, "Between the incredible bills and the need to keep subsidizing my parents' care until they passed away, we ended up here." Privately, Joe thought the Sterns were foolish not to have accepted the inevitable. I mean, for all their heroic efforts and willingness to try every experimental treatment, the child died anyway. But he knew it would seem unfeeling if he pointed it out. He was also somewhat surprised that they would share the details of their story with him on such short acquaintance, but it was clear that these people were different on some fundamental plane. They let everything hang out, and didn't seem embarrassed by their own emotional excesses. Ben struck Joe as a very angry guy.

He saw that disparity illuminated further the following week. Joe walked past Ben when he was berating another resident for not voting. Apparently, the object of his harangue, a woman in her thirties who lived in one of the cubicles, had admitted in passing that she wasn't very interested in politics. When she said that it really didn't concern her, and that all politicians were the same, Ben went ballistic. Joe didn't see how telling the woman she was naïve and shortsighted was going to persuade her that Ben was right. No one wanted to believe any of this was their own fault, and they all felt crappy enough as it was. It wasn't helpful to make them feel worse, or tell them they had been duped by people they trusted and put into office.

In his earlier life, Joe might have enjoyed debating Ben, but this wasn't the time or the place. Most residents avoided talking about politics altogether. Joe wasn't sure that he'd find a lot of kindred spirits among this crowd, until one day he ran into Simon Stokes. Despite the circumstances, Simon exhibited his usual high-spirited energy and was eager to get Joe's opinion on his inventive ways to earn money. He was sure that Simon was as glad as he was to find a familiar face here.

When Joe asked about his mother Sara, Simon looked at his feet and didn't say anything for a couple of minutes. Joe waited for him to speak. "We were doing OK you know. Most of the time. My mom was always, like, kind of depressed around the holidays, since she and my dad split up, you know. Last year, right before Christmas, they had like a big sale at the store she was working at. This woman got into a fight with her over the price of some stupid coat, or something, that wasn't even Mom's fault. The customer made such a stink that they fired her and didn't bother to give her the last paycheck. The timing was really bad. We were already behind on the rent and the landlord was bugging us. She cried for three days.

"One day when I came home from seeing some friends, there was a cop at the door telling me she'd been in an accident and hadn't made it. The landlord felt bad so he let me stay through the holidays since my dad didn't want me to be part of his new family." The very thought astounded Joe. How could a father abandon his own child this way? He didn't understand.

Simon continued, "The insurance company questioned whether it really was an accident so I didn't get the money from her policy. They said she killed herself on purpose." His voice cracked. "I got extra hours at my job so at least I have a roof over my head," he said looking everywhere but into Joe's eyes. "Even if it's not much." He stuck his jaw out, "I'm making it and I have plans."

After that Joe made it a point to seek out Simon and listen to him or buy him a meal. If his son were in a similar position, he'd want someone to take Daniel under his wing. Besides, it was sort of like having family around again, which was kind of nice. But he avoided asking himself the obvious question—why had he failed to get in touch with his own son for months?

$\star$ $\star$ $\star$ $\star$ $\star$

One overcast afternoon, Joe was sitting in the laundromat waiting for the rinse cycle to finish. He hadn't done his own laundry since freshman year in college. Even as an upper classman, his fraternity had laundry service, and then Susan had done it when they moved in together. After the divorce, he'd always hired someone else to do it, even in Aquamarine. He lost one batch of clothes by going out for coffee instead of waiting and wrecked another by putting in a sweater that apparently wasn't designed to be washed. He did have a certain feeling of satisfaction when he folded his clean clothes.

An older man of about 70 sitting next to him struck up a conversation. He was quite distinguished looking, which made him appear incongruous in these surroundings, but Joe hoped he looked a little out of place himself. The man introduced himself as Robert. They talked a little about the weather as the first rain of the season was being eagerly predicted.

Robert paused and asked Joe what field he was in. Joe explained that he was a corporate attorney and was presently looking for a new position. Robert took this in without surprise. "I had been the head of R&D for a biotech company when the board and the investors decided it was too expensive to actually try to discover new types of drug compounds. I was laid off in 2006 with a nice package but who's going to hire a 62 year old Ph.D., even one who was one of the leading experts in the field? No one is funding innovative research anymore, and there are plenty of young minds available who are capable of running bioinformatic analyses 18 hours a day to reevaluate existing drug compounds. The venture capital community is only interested in backing 'specialty pharma' companies that acquire or license compounds already in clinical trials, because they want a five to seven year payback. While it can be rewarding, the supply of available compounds is drying up. To maintain our leadership position in the world market, I believe we need to work on early stage preclinical compounds, but the money guys see it as too risky." Joe found himself nodding as Robert described his fruitless search for another position, even something menial. The number of talented, experienced professionals who couldn't get jobs was astounding—what a waste it was!

"The wife and I sold our large place and moved into a small rental—we don't have children to keep us here, but we like the area, so we didn't really want to move.

"After we lost our health insurance, my wife learned she had breast cancer. While she was in the hospital for a mastectomy, we discussed our options. The hospital stay and surgery alone were going to be over $100,000, and the chemotherapy would easily come to another $50,000 to $75,000, plus doctor's visits and tests. If she did the whole course of treatment and then one of us got sick with something else we'd be wiped out. She was more afraid she'd end up cured but destitute. There was no way that I could just allow her to give up so easily so she did the first course of chemo.

"Unfortunately, the treatments had horrible side effects. She wanted to stop, and I was trying to respect that, but some well-meaning nurse turned us in to Focus on the Family's 'Fight for Life' Campaign." Robert's voice grew darker, "She was forced to go through every possible treatment even though none of them changed the outcome and they left her violently ill all the time. Finally, I was able to find a judge and four doctors who would declare her case hopeless so she could be allowed into Hospice.

"As an attorney, you might know this, but the more aggressive laws aimed at prohibiting addiction mean that hospice isn't allowed to use morphine or medical marijuana anymore. Luckily, we found some Native American remedies that haven't yet been outlawed. I'm with her most of the time, so it's the little trips like these that qualify as my respite time. I figure that when my time comes, I can die quickly because there won't be any money left to do anything and there aren't any children who could be held accountable to pay my bills. Ironic, isn't it?"

Joe was at a loss for words. He couldn't think of anything to say to comfort this man, who was about to lose the person he obviously loved most in the world. His eyes filled with tears as he sat with Robert in empathic silence. When the buzzer went off on the washing machine, Joe moved his clothes to the dryer and went outside for a breath of fresh air. He was leaning against the doorway looking off into the distance when he heard a cheery "Joe, whatever are you doing here?"

Marianne Craver, one of his old neighbors and a gardening enthusiast like Susan, was coming out of Common Ground, the organic nursery across the street, her arms filled with paper bags. "I was just picking up some bulbs and a new trowel. Checking out the laundromat?" She was obviously surprised, and amused, at the absurd image of Joe washing clothes, much less at a place like this.

Before Joe could think of an answer, Robert was beside him, introducing himself to Marianne. "Joe's here to keep me company. Our machine broke at home and my wife asked me to make an emergency trip because we're going out of town tomorrow. Joe didn't tell me he had friends who were so attractive and handy."

Marianne laughed again. "Well, it's nice to run into you. We see the young couple that bought your house all the time. You know? Jack Swenson's daughter and her husband. Are you living in Palo Alto now?" Joe nodded in the affirmative, forcing himself to smile. He couldn't trust himself to speak. Just wait till he got hold of that double crossing bastard. Marianne smiled and climbed into her bright yellow Hummer. She waved as she drove off.

"It seemed like you stopped breathing when she mentioned those folks living in your house. I take it you know them but didn't know they were there."

Joe spoke slowly. He wasn't sure how much he wanted to divulge. "It's complicated but let's just say that Jack's my attorney and I trusted him to look after my interests in a less self-serving manner."

Robert gave a wry smile. "In my lifetime, I've seen that it's common for people to look after their own interests ahead of the other guy's and certainly ahead of their principles. Take me for example. In 2004, I voted for Bush even though I was a lifelong Democrat. I believed at the time that he'd be better for my bottom line, better for Israel, and better for business. Besides, Kerry didn't do much for me. I was more of a Lieberman supporter.

"But the point is, when I cast my vote for what I thought were *my* interests, I never dreamed things would turn out this way for the country. I figured Michael Moore and the Deaniacs were paranoid and the moderate Republicans and Democrats in Congress would keep things from getting out of hand. Look at what's actually happened."

Joe cleared his throat. He wasn't sure he should express a common disappointment with Robert. Instead he said, "I confess I don't agree with the entire government agenda, but I've believed in the values of the Republican Party my entire life: small government, personal accountability, low taxes. Keep government out of private life and let the market correct itself. My parents were Republicans. Almost everyone in the town where I grew up in Illinois was Republican. I still consider myself a Republican."

"So it doesn't trouble you that there are some inconsistencies, shall we say, with the actual policies and the specific principles that you believe in?" Robert's cordial tone didn't seem challenging or hostile, merely curious, so Joe didn't feel on the defensive.

"The market is self-regulating and people have the opportunity to experience personal responsibility without becoming dependent on the government. After all, moving all those jobs overseas and consolidating distribution has meant lower prices to the consumer," Joe declared, but somehow the words of his life-long credo sounded a bit unconvincing.

"One could argue, what good are lower prices, if people don't have jobs or the money to buy the products," Robert asked, and then gave Joe an ironic smile.

Joe countered, "Well, it's really the Clinton policies of the 90's and the tax and spend crowd that caused the problems in the first place." He stopped himself. It was getting a bit stale to blame Clinton for everything, especially now that Clinton was the first family's favorite golfing buddy. 41 and 42 had really bonded over the Tsunami relief and Katrina fundraising efforts, and as long as Clinton was kept away from Barbara, they were fine. 43 had teamed up with 42 for one of the celebrity pro-am tournaments, because all the best caddies liked Clinton.

"Well, think about what I've said. I've got to get back to my wife. It's been a pleasure talking to you. This is my usual time to do laundry so maybe I'll see you here next week." Robert left with his neatly folded laundry and left Joe with his conundrum.

★   ★   ★   ★   ★

Joe was furious when he learned Jack's family was living in his house. He called Jack's office again. When they tried to give him the run-around, he told them he was going to keep calling back every hour until he spoke to Jack. Finally they put him through.

"What the hell do you think you're doing, stealing my house," he yelled at Jack. "You're supposed to be representing me. You're not trying to do anything to resolve my case, are you?"

"Think of it as my fee. You should consider yourself fortunate that I didn't call Homeland Security myself after that stunt you pulled with my secretary," Jack said coolly. "The poor girl was scared for weeks. In fact, if you ever come near my office again, I'll be happy to tell them I've discovered that you were part of a terrorist cell after all. Nobody's heard from Jerry Rooz since they picked him up."

"I'll have you disbarred, you asshole." Joe was beside himself.

Jack laughed. "Knock yourself out. Who do you think they're going to believe? Oh, and since I know where you're living, just remember I can send a squad car out for you any time I choose. Don't even think about causing trouble. I will let you know if I do recover your assets, though I wouldn't count on ever seeing that money again." He hung up leaving Joe alone with his dial tone and his fury.

Joe waited for Ben to get back that evening, insisting on talking to him before the man could even take off his coat and kiss his wife and kids. Ben listened, expressionless, as Joe recounted his situation with Homeland Security.

Ben thought for a few minutes while Joe paced the room, muttering that he'd like to strangle Jack with his bare hands.

"Look, I know it feels like the most satisfying thing in a world right now would be to take a gun and blow the bastard's brains out, but that won't get you your house back and it certainly won't convince the authorities that you're innocent of all charges. Even if I were to do the case pro bono, we'd still need tens of thousands of dollars in filing fees and court costs. And if you lost, you'd have to cover Jack's expenses too.

"To be honest, I think your chances of getting your assets back are pretty slim. I'm sure this guy will figure out a way to siphon off a significant portion. Luckily, I do think your criminal case has probably fallen through the cracks if they haven't come looking for you by now."

Joe was tired of people telling him he was lucky that he hadn't been arrested, when he hadn't done anything wrong.

"If he were to make good on his threat to turn you in as a terrorist, you wouldn't be around to fight a civil suit in any case. I'd hate to see you hanging by your thumbs in Bulgaria or wherever they're rendering undesirables these days. It sucks, but I think he's got you by the short hairs, my friend. There isn't anybody left in charge who cares about the underdog and is in a position to do anything about it."

He told Betsy not to hold dinner for him and took Joe to a local bar. Joe had enough grace to thank Ben and recognize that the man didn't say "I told you so" at any point in the evening. For the first time, Joe was willing to concede that maybe there were legitimate reasons why guys like Ben were angry about the system.

★　　★　　★　　★　　★

As Thanksgiving approached, Joe tried to focus on what was right with his life. While the job hunt was thoroughly discouraging and he was down to one day a week researching and sending out resumes, he still had a cash reserve. He had a roof over his head and some pleasant neighbors despite seeing more of them than he'd like. Joe even had friends. He saw Robert at the laundromat each week and they would discuss a range of topics: scientific research, economic policy, environmental concerns, and the arts. Robert would bring him books. The area where they found the most agreement was on religion in government. Both of them believed that spirituality was a private matter, that the government had no place in religion or vice versa. From that common place of connection, Joe found his own convictions softening on some topics and discovered they were closer than he'd thought on others. Robert made very good points, and Joe realized that his recent ordeal had influenced his perspective. It was easier to be "sure" when you didn't have personal experiences to contradict your opinions.

Joe Winston had even come to appreciate the Sterns. While their edges were worn down by their new circumstances, they retained a liveliness that reminded him of earlier times. Although he didn't have enough work to support a partner, Ben had given Joe a few small legal projects that brought in a modest income.

Betsy was a kind person and made sure that Joe joined them for a meal or two each week.

Joe had grown quite fond of Simon. They had many conversations about the merits of the ownership society, and Joe felt Simon shared his values and drive. It was clear Simon was determined to get ahead. Together they evaluated Simon's entrepreneurial dreams and ideas, and Simon was very receptive to Joe's input. It seemed like the kid never slept. He had one of the cheapest cubes on the bottom floor but he was always coming up with little ways to earn a few extra bucks here and there. Joe felt like Simon was the son he wished he'd had. They could really relate to each other—Simon even wanted to learn to play golf when their situation improved, whereas Daniel had never shown the slightest interest and ranted about all the chemicals it took to maintain the courses.

Joe, Simon, Robert and the Sterns all went out to Denny's for Thanksgiving dinner. The Stern children liked it because they could order pancakes instead of turkey. Robert seemed to enjoy himself with the group, even though he had to get back early to relieve the respite caregiver. Betsy and the children hugged Robert when he left—they said it felt like having a grandfather again.

Robert wasn't at the laundromat the week after Thanksgiving. Joe was worried his wife had died, but he realized he didn't know Robert's address. He knew they lived in the nearby College Terrace neighborhood with its small bungalows and two story apartment houses, but he had no idea exactly where. Joe kept looking at the door while he did his laundry, hoping that Robert would either appear or send someone, but he never did. Joe packed up his clean clothes and walked around the nearby streets hoping that he'd run into Robert or see something that would give him a clue. When he saw a woman looking at him through her window and pick up the phone, Joe figured it was time to call off the hunt. Maybe Robert would be there next week.

Joe never made it back to the Laundromat himself.
got home that afternoon, he noticed a terrible smell ...
sound of retching and coughing. An outbreak of the flu was
sweeping through the building. None of the residents had been
able to get flu shots. With the profits so low and the quantities so
variable, there were few companies willing to make the vaccines.
The parent groups who believed that thimerosal caused their
children's autism had found sympathetic legislators that succeeded
in getting the preservative banned, which reduced the supply even
further. Most of the limited production went to private doctors
and facilities. There were no free or subsidized programs any more
for the uninsured, because the money simply wasn't there to pay
for it.

He went into the men's room to wash his hands. It was a mess.
He used water as hot as he could get it and then locked himself in
his room. Joe took every possible precaution. He bought a surgical
mask and some antiseptic soap and hand wipes. He kept his
distance from everyone and spent as much time as he could
outside. It was raining off and on so he hung out and read in his
car for much of the day.

Despite his best efforts, two mornings later he woke up with
chills and nausea. Every part of his body ached. He tried to run
for the bathroom but he wasn't moving quickly enough. When he
slipped on someone else's vomit, he crashed to the floor and didn't
make it to the stall in time. It was humiliating. He cleaned himself
up a bit and went back to the room for a towel and change of
clothes. Then he had to wait in line to use the shower. By the time
he got back to bed, he was incredibly weak.

His fever raging, Joe was getting sicker and sicker. Betsy
stopped by to bring him some broth, but he couldn't even keep
that down. She left him a bottle of juice and some aspirin, but he
could only stare at it. When she came by later, she told him, "You
still look awful. I heard the VA hospital down the street is

accepting non-military personnel who can pay, to help them cover their costs. It might make sense for you to consider that."

"You're probably right," he said. "Would you please find Simon to take me to the hospital?"

Joe struggled to pack a small suitcase with some clean underwear, socks, pajamas, T-shirts and sweat pants. He threw in an extra sweater for good measure. It looked gray and raw outside so he put on his warmest jacket. He checked for the money belt under his shirt when he remembered that he hadn't paid the rent for December yet. It was due today. Joe didn't have enough in his wallet so he took $1,000 from the leg safe. As he was tugging down his pant leg, to put on his socks and boots, Simon came into the room. He handed Simon the room and car keys and asked him to pay the rent to Warren. He knew he could count on the young man. They had become so close. Simon helped him out to the Expedition, but it took so much effort that he passed out as soon as the engine started.

It was only a short drive to the VA hospital. Someone helped him onto a gurney and put the bag across his thighs. He was shivering. The waiting room was crowded and there were a frightening number of young men and women with burn scars and missing body parts. He kept drifting in and out of consciousness. He saw a forty-ish man in a crisp white shirt, dark slacks, and a surgical mask trying to avoid accidental contact with the people sitting next to him. Two guys who looked to be about the age of Vietnam vets were in a heated exchange with two younger men about whose war was worse. This was definitely not like Stanford Hospital or the Palo Alto Medical Foundation.

He could hear someone shouting at him, "last four." He had no idea what they meant. They repeated it several times. Finally a man took pity on him and explained that they wanted the last four digits of his social security number or his VA identity card. When Joe said he wasn't a veteran but coming in on a cash basis, the clerk called for another person to wheel him to a separate admissions office to conduct the intake procedure.

It was clear that he wasn't the only one with the flu. The place was jammed to the rafters, while a few people with clipboards were trying to do triage. Joe was mortified when he puked as soon as the young woman came to take his information. She deftly sidestepped the arc and waved for an orderly, who was busily tracking the immediate path of the pandemic.

She got his information, but when she heard that he didn't have any insurance, she asked for a deposit of $1,000 to be paid before he could be admitted. He asked her to move the suitcase and reached down for the leg safe. When he realized his leg was bare, he started to panic. He felt for the other money belt on his waist. Thank God it was there, so he unbuttoned his shirt and took out a wad of bills. She counted the money, gave him a receipt and the excess, put the bag back on his legs, and asked an orderly to push him to another line.

Joe's mind was racing like a sports car on a foggy slick road—it was obviously dangerous to go too fast. He was sure that he'd been wearing the leg safe. Maybe he'd forgotten and left it in its hiding place. He'd been so groggy. Had he locked the door to the room when he'd left? Simon would take care of everything. He's a good kid. In his rush, he hadn't grabbed the wireless phone so he couldn't call Simon or Ben. OK, he just had to have faith it would be all right. It wouldn't do any good to get upset. Besides, he felt so horrible. When were they going to do something for him? He called for water. A passing nurse said, "I'm sorry sir, you're going to have to wait your turn."

"But I've been here for hours already," Joe moaned. "This just seems like it's taking forever."

"Look, I know you're not feeling well, but veterans have had to wait patiently here for decades, and now so do you. This is the worst flu epidemic in a hundred years. We're short-staffed and we're doing the best we can. We're all working double and triple shifts. You're just lucky that we're letting non-veterans in at all. If you want special treatment, get premium health insurance and go to Stanford Hospital. Otherwise, stop whining and remember there are lots of others worse off than you are." She turned her back and strode off.

Joe wasn't used to being treated this way and started to take offense. Another wave of chills came over him as he clutched his bag to his chest and curled around it. At least they'd left him on the gurney. He fell asleep feeling very sorry for himself.

★   ★   ★   ★   ★

Nine days and 16 liters of IV fluids later, Joe was feeling better. The fever had broken and while he was still woozy, the nurse announced at 5 PM that they were releasing him within the hour.

"But I haven't had a chance to make any arrangements to be picked up," he protested.

"Sorry, we need the bed," was the blunt reply.

After relieving him of a few thousand dollars more, the hospital hadn't left much in the money belt. He knew he had more in the leg safe and there was his extra stash in the Expedition.

It was already dark as Joe trudged up Foothill Expressway pulling his suitcase. Thankfully he didn't have far to go. It was scary being on the shoulder as the cars whizzed by. He'd be glad to get back to his room, take a hot (OK tepid) shower, and put on some clean clothes.

He didn't see his Expedition in its usual space. Maybe Simon had parked it in the lot on the other side. A few folks were leaving as he came in so it didn't matter that he didn't have his keys with him. He dragged the suitcase up the stairs—it felt too heavy to carry. When he got to his room, he was startled to see the door open and a couple sitting on the futon laughing.

"Who the hell are you?" Joe asked.

"Hey man, this is our place." The man was much bigger than he seemed sitting down. "We rented it yesterday. Get your ass out of here."

"There must be some mistake," Joe protested as the man shoved him towards the stairs. The other residents looked on silently. No one said a word to Joe. He couldn't believe it.

He went down to Ben and Betsy's. Betsy was there assembling dinner for the kids. She closed the door and walked with Joe into the stairwell. "How are you doing? You look much better." Betsy paused. "I don't know how to break this to you, but Simon didn't pay your rent. In fact, he sold most of your things, and took off in your SUV. It turned out that his incredible energy was fueled by a serious meth habit, and he said he was going to use your money to set up his own lab. He was laughing about the 'ownership society' as he left and didn't seem the least embarrassed by what he was doing. It wasn't only you, we all misjudged him."

"Why didn't anyone do anything to stop him?" Joe was incredulous.

She shrugged. "I suppose people don't like confrontation. Besides, the new guy who rented your room seems like someone you don't want to have mad at you. No one wanted to get off on the wrong foot with him or risk losing their own spaces for fighting."

He borrowed Betsy's wireless phone to call Warren who told him that there weren't even any cubicles available. Since he was such a nice guy, Warren said, Joe could sleep in the hallway tonight but he had to be out tomorrow morning.

Joe woke at dawn. He felt miserable. He wasn't sure if the nausea was due to the lingering effects of the flu or the realization of his situation. He'd been haunted by disturbing dreams all night, in which he was wandering in the dark, searching for a safe place, and being shunted away. He couldn't remember ever feeling so scared—everything that he had ever used to define himself was gone: no home, no job, no money, no family. He wondered if God had abandoned him.

He saw that someone had left a small pile of clean clothes, a bar of soap and a towel with some cash tucked inside. A note pinned to the towel read, "*Sorry. I wish I could do more—Betsy.*" A few tears escaped before he realized he'd better shave, take a shower quickly, and leave before everyone got up for the day. He was too embarrassed to be seen. When he had arrived here, it had seemed like the most terrible thing that had ever happened to him. Now he was feeling sad to be leaving.

Joe dressed, grateful for the extra clothes. At least he had taken his warmest jacket to the hospital with him. He tried not to make a mental inventory of all that he had lost, but it was hard to fight the images flashing in his brain—his cashmere sweaters, wool slacks, tailored suits, silk ties, crisp cotton shirts, towels, sheets, sleeping bag, camping gear. His SUV—what was he going to do without his car? The car—the one with his extra cash. He should probably call the police. Surely, they'd track that down even if his other property seemed too trivial. The wireless phone, why hadn't he taken the wireless phone to the hospital?

How could Simon have betrayed him? He had been more supportive than the boy's own father. If nothing else, why had Joe been so stupid? Why hadn't he asked Betsy to help him instead? He wasn't sure if he was more furious at Simon or himself for being such a fool. The kid was a drug addict. He should have seen it. He thought all that energy was ambition and enthusiasm for hard work. Betsy told him they found traces of a meth lab in the janitor's closet near Simon's cube. Empty cold medicine packets and cans of solvent. Now *Joe's* car was a rolling meth factory. Oh my God, what if Simon got caught or left the car somewhere and they traced it back to him! Great, then he'd have the authorities after him for being a drug dealer. How could someone like him get caught up in this sort of crap? He had done everything right—this was not supposed to happen to people like him.

He was a lawyer...with connections. He had a big house, lots of money, everything anyone could want. *He had.* Now he had nothing. Not even a crappy place like this. He was going to be on the streets. He didn't even have a car to live in. This had to be a nightmare. He'd wake up and it would all be over and he'd be back in his house. Joe realized he was becoming hysterical. Take a breath. Think. He wished his brain wasn't so fuzzy. He still wasn't feeling very well. He knew he should eat something but he really didn't feel like it.

Joe packed his remaining belongings in the small suitcase and slipped out the side door. At least the sun was shining on the construction site, and he could see the hills beyond. It was one of those crisp, clear winter days you get after a storm passes through. He trudged down Page Mill Road towards town. He had driven along this road a million times without thinking, gazing at the hills across the bay. Walking alongside the traffic, he had a sense of altered reality. The wide-open vistas were gone and he was isolated from those traveling safely in their little steel cocoons. He headed for the Laundromat. At least it was a familiar place he could sit and get his few remaining clothes clean. Maybe he'd even run into Robert. He wasn't sure if he thought that was a good thing or not. He didn't want to impose, and he didn't want Robert to see what a loser he was. He still couldn't understand what had gone wrong, how could he explain his circumstances to anyone else?

As he sat in the laundromat, he knew that he still looked normal, not affluent maybe, but like a regular guy. Assuming regular 51-year old guys did laundry in public places. No one *he* knew did, but maybe it wasn't as alien as it seemed to him. Joe took his time so he could stay as long as possible. It was warm, it was dry, and he could sit, quietly pretending to read the paper. As he was folding one of the pairs of pajamas, he stared down at the pale blue striped Egyptian cotton cloth, beautifully tailored. He must have been delirious when he'd packed them. The other three men in the room at the VA hospital had doubled up with laughter when they saw them. At least he gave them a laugh before they started puking and coughing all night.

These pajamas cost $200 a pair. Where was he going to wear them, the Ritz-Carlton Homeless Shelter? They were obviously pajamas—he wished he had the money instead, or a few more pairs of jeans. Maybe he could wear them under his sweats, as an extra layer of insulation?

After a few hours, more students and families had come in, waiting to use the machines. It was getting crowded and Joe felt conspicuous so he decided to move on. He went into the JJ&F grocery store, one of the few remaining family-owned stores in town. He bought some day old bread (on sale), a jar of peanut butter, and a couple of bananas. He looked at the aspirin and cold remedies. They were so expensive he decided to pass. Besides, a sign said you had to show ID and register to buy cold medicine to prove you weren't part of an illegal drug operation. He wondered how Simon had been able to circumvent the rules, grimly admiring the young man's ingenuity.

He lingered at the wine display but anything decent was at least $15 a bottle and he'd have to buy a corkscrew and glass too. When he got a cup of soup from the deli, he grabbed a plastic

knife along with the spoon and as many napkins and
he thought he could get away with. When asked "pap
he chose the latter, figuring it would be more vers...
longer. He sat at an outdoor table to eat, trying to decide what to
do next.

Joe had never been one to enjoy the thrill of the unknown.
He'd never backpacked in Nepal, or gone to Paris without reservations at a good hotel, and there was always a driver to meet him
when he traveled abroad on business. He thought the guys who
went heli-skiing, dropping into remote wilderness areas, had a
death wish. His life was orderly, predictable, and safe. He took
tremendous pride in his ability to plan carefully, invest wisely, and
anticipate his next move. He read maps—he didn't ask for
directions. He was self-sufficient—he didn't ask others for help.
Besides, whom could he ask? Miranda was gone. Susan probably
wouldn't speak to him again since he'd substituted money for
commitment yet one more time. Daniel would just tell him it was
his own fault. He couldn't picture having the conversation with
one of his golfing buddies or business associates. Showing up at
the church Friendship Center would be mortifying.

Maybe it was time to eat crow and try to reach his family. His
parents were both dead, but he did have siblings. His sister Brenda
was deeply involved with a fundamentalist church in the same
small town in Illinois where they had grown up. She and Susan
never got along and she couldn't understand why they hadn't tried
to "cure" Daniel of his homosexuality. When his denomination,
the United Church of Christ, made a public statement in 2005
supporting the idea of gay marriage, Brenda lost it and told him
he was going to hell. He found her opinions so extreme there
wasn't enough common ground to make family gatherings
pleasant, especially since their younger brother Edward was also
gay.

Ed was a stockbroker and had been an active member of the gay Republican Log Cabin Club. When the GOP pushed the anti-gay marriage and other repressive initiatives through, and he and his partner lost custody of their children, Edward became so enraged he broke all ties with the party. He wanted Joe to do the same, and then stopped talking to him when Joe continued to defend the administration.

Maybe there was chance one of them would see past their differences and help him. He was their brother after all, and he'd never asked them for anything before. He looked for a pay phone but there didn't seem to be one on the street. He tried going into one of the smaller office buildings to see if he could use someone's phone but nothing seemed to be open. He tried the corner Starbucks and asked the *barista* if he could use the telephone, "I'll be glad to pay for the call."

"I'm sorry," the young woman replied. "We all use our own cell phones. There isn't a phone here, just an emergency alarm if we get robbed." One of the other workers who overheard the conversation offered, "I'll let you use mine for a dollar a minute."

He dialed Brenda's number. When he heard her voice, he hesitated. The last time they'd talked it hadn't gone well. "Um, Brenda, it's me Joe."

"Yes?" Her voice was cold and guarded.

"I know it's been a while since we spoke. How are you and the family?"

"We're fine, thank the Lord. What is it you want? Have you come to your senses and accepted Jesus in your heart?"

"You know I've always believed in Jesus. I simply chose a different church than you did." He could picture her lips pressed together disapprovingly. "I'm sorry to bother you but I've been going through some difficulties lately and…," God it was hard to ask for help. "Maybe I could come and visit you for a while?" Did he really want to do that? How would he get there?

"You must be desperate," she said grimly. "Do you rea'
I could forget everything you said to me? About how su..._ₗ
minded I am? You're being punished for your profligate ways. You
had a chance to save your children and you didn't do it. God is
right to call you to judgment." She hung up. Joe dropped his hand
and stared at the phone. The boy who owned the phone nodded
sympathetically. "My folks didn't want to have anything to do
with me after I ran away. It's tough."

"Wait, I want to try another number," Joe said dialing Ed's
house. A voice answered. It was Craig, his brother's partner,
"Hello?"

"Hello Craig, this is Joe. Is Ed there, please?"

There was a long pause. Joe wondered if they had been
disconnected. "I don't think your brother wants to talk to you. In
fact, neither one of us wants anything to do with you." Craig's
anger was mixed with tears. "He's not here and I'm not sure when
he'll be back."

"Well, please tell him that I called." He clearly couldn't count
on Craig and Ed to come to his rescue. He had to face the fact that
no one he knew was going fix this. Joe liked to think he was a
realist and he was worried that he had neither the talent nor
imagination for what was immediately before him.

Joe left the coffee shop and started walking. Where could you
go pulling a rolling suitcase and not look like a vagrant? The sun
was starting to go down and it was getting colder. He decided to
walk down El Camino as if he was headed towards one of the
motels along the road. Maybe something would occur to him.

As he walked, the lights of the on-coming traffic made him
dizzy. He still wasn't feeling well and he envied those hurrying
home to nice, warm houses. Hell, he envied people checking into
cheap, cheesy motels at this point. He'd walk into a store every
now and then, but the clerks looked at him with such suspicion
when he said he was just looking, that he soon gave up on that.

Finally, Joe simply had to sit down. There was an alleyway between two buildings that looked like it might afford some protection from the wind. Some construction debris could make a bit of a seat so Joe rearranged the wood and concrete blocks so he wouldn't be directly on the ground. The clear sky meant the temperature was dropping quickly now that the sun had gone down, so he slid on another sweatshirt under the jacket and sweat pants over his trousers. He wished he had a blanket. At least the towel was dry he thought, as he draped it and an extra sweater over his legs. For a while Joe shivered as he huddled against the building but, mercifully, he passed out.

He dreamt he heard a little boy's voice calling and giggling when he decided that he might actually be awake. He was warm. A scratchy but thick gray wool blanket was tucked around his neck. He opened his eyes, squinting at the sun that had peeked between the buildings. A woman dressed in shapeless clothes had her back to him as she spoke to the child. As he moved, she turned and smiled. "Oh, you're finally up. Here, drink this, it's nice and warm." She handed him a cup of soup, and as he sat up and reached out, he realized there were woolen mittens on his hands and a knitted cap on his head. "I'm Maria and this is Miguel. We've been starting to worry. We found you the day before yesterday and you've been sleeping all this time. Drink the soup, you'll feel better." Joe obediently complied. It was fragrant with ginger, spicy and soothing at the same time.

While he drank, he peered over the rim of the cup and studied his benefactress. She was young, with soft light brown skin. He couldn't see what color her hair was since it was tucked under a hat, but her eyebrows were dark. The little boy looked like her, with eyes that sparkled and tipped up at the corners. When she turned the other cheek, he could see a thin but pronounced scar that ran from her ear to the corner of her mouth.

When Joe finished the soup and stood up, somewhat unsteadily, she discreetly took the boy for a walk so Joe could relieve himself. He found the most remote corner, which smelled like it had served this function before, and then made his way back to his perch. When they returned, he introduced himself and was entranced when Miguel came over to sit beside him. "Thank you so much," he said to Maria. "I probably would have frozen to death without your help."

"It didn't seem like you knew how to survive on the street from the looks of it," she offered by way of observation.

"I'm not feeling well and I have to admit I'm a bit of a novice when it comes to this," Joe conceded. He usually disliked admitting that he didn't know something, but Maria's manner seemed very non-judgmental. Besides why should someone like him know anything about living on the street? Maybe because that's what you have to do, his other inner voice reminded him.

Maria used a plastic tarp and rigged up a small shelter. Miguel played quietly while Joe slept. When he woke, Maria gave him small meals—a little soup, a burrito, a piece of chicken. She didn't hover or ask him what he was doing there, but he knew she was taking care of him. Finally, when he was feeling better, he asked her why.

She looked faintly surprised by the question. "You clearly needed help," as if that explained everything. He was a tad suspicious and checked his pockets. The money he had was still there. "What do I owe you? For the food and everything."

Maria smiled, "Don't worry about it now. It will all work out." She changed the subject. "Why don't you see if you can stand up and walk a little? You've been sleeping for quite a few days so it's going to take a while before your legs are steady." She helped him stand. She was right, he did feel unbalanced but it was good to move around. They would practice walking, then he'd sit down and rest, and then they'd go again. She did take some money to buy them all some meals, mostly from a burrito stand and a Chinese fast food place nearby.

Joe really enjoyed Miguel's company. The little boy was shy but happy. After his initial reserve, when he saw that Joe was kind, he warmed up to his newfound friend. As the boy was sleeping, Maria stroking his dark curls, Joe asked how old her son was. "He's actually my nephew. His dad was in the military and was killed overseas. My sister was having trouble making ends meet after he died. She got desperate and was caught shoplifting some shoes and a coat for Miguel, so she was sent to the county jail." Maria paused. "The infirmary was run by a private contractor who ignored her requests for her diabetes and heart medicine. They said she was just faking her symptoms. It's still hard to believe it, but she's gone. Fortunately, I was able to take Miguel so he didn't end up in a juvenile facility."

"I'm sorry about your sister, and her husband. Weren't there survivor benefits or a military pension or something?"

"He was a new recruit. He hadn't been in the service long enough to qualify for a pension. With all the wars going on, the life insurance was just too expensive for them. He and my sister never had anything but low-paying, under-the-table jobs. Funny how you die just like a career officer but, from what I hear, their families don't get much either." Her tone wasn't bitter, just resigned, as if she knew the situation was as beyond her control as the weather.

"I'm surprised that your sister wasn't able to get her medication." He knew better than to comment on the harsh sentencing for minor crimes. He had helped raise money for the state initiatives that created strong mandatory sentencing as a deterrent against the small property crimes that were rampant these days. "I know they outsource the medical services to private companies to save money, but it's supposed to be adequate care."

She shrugged. "Depends on what you mean by 'adequate.' If you mean 'cheap,' then I suppose it is. There aren't very many doctors assigned to each facility, and the ones that are there aren't the greatest, and heaven help you if you need surgery or drugs." Maria rubbed the scar on her face as she spoke. Joe guessed she might know about this first hand and he thought it better not to press the point. He hoped she wasn't a murderer. Of course, she didn't seem like one, and if she had wanted to kill and rob him she had had ample opportunity while he was passed out. It's not like anyone would have noticed if he never came out of the alley. Joe realized Maria was talking to him. He had missed it while lost in his own thoughts. "I'm sorry. What were you saying?"

"There are better places to stay than here. Let's see if you can handle the walk and try to get you cleaned up." They packed up their belongings. Maria swept all their debris into a neat pile next to the construction waste, since the public garbage cans had all been removed so terrorists couldn't use them to plant bombs. "Keep your shaving kit and your comb handy. Here's some special shampoo that doesn't have to be washed out. Take off some of your extra layers and put on your cleanest sweater. Oh, and fold a clean T-shirt and put it in your pocket."

As they approached a small two-story office building, Maria stopped. "Hand me your suitcase and tuck your shaving kit under your jacket. They don't lock the front door or the men's room in that building. Walk in like you have an appointment. If the men's room is empty you can shave, if someone is coming in, then go into one of the stalls." It was clear she knew the drill. "Just look like you are supposed to be there. Smile but don't talk to anyone."

Over the next several days, Joe found that Maria was an able guide. She knew where public restrooms were located, and which you could sneak into if you looked fairly pulled together. Sometimes she had him wait with Miguel so she could slip in. In others, they would use Miguel to gain access—people were often kind to a young mother (or grandfather) needing facilities for a cute little boy. And Joe learned how to take frequent sponge baths, using the basin in restrooms. Even short tepid showers were becoming a distant memory.

Staying clean and presentable was a major effort, but it was worth it because people treated you better if you didn't smell or look disheveled. A lot of people on the street drank to numb the pain but Maria cautioned him against that tempting fix. The telltale odor of alcohol oozing out your pores worked against you.

She knew how to forage for food with the savvy of a skilled hunter-gatherer. Which restaurants would give out the remnants of the last sitting's offerings. What time to pick up a spare bag of rolls or loaf of bread as deliveries were being made. Which farmers at the farmers' market would give away unsold produce. She was a walking timetable of all the soup kitchens in the area.

She took him to the Ravenswood Episcopal Church one Sunday afternoon. While it was much less upscale than his congregation's Friendship Center, he found himself amazed at how ordinary most of the people appeared. Some looked vaguely familiar, but he wasn't sure if it was because he had seen them around town or knew them from some former life. It was best not to ask. Sure, there were some scary looking street people with obviously untreated mental illness, but the majority looked like anyone else. Most were polite and grateful for the meal. Maria knew how to time it so they came early enough to be sure of a full portion and to stay late enough to collect any leftovers. She even had her own containers hidden in her belongings, since the volunteers weren't allowed to wrap up any food to go.

Maria was also a master of how to navigate the limited universe of warm, dry public spaces—shopping malls, the lobby at City Hall, waiting rooms in hospitals, lines of people waiting to pay utility bills or register a car at the DMV. Joe had always hated waiting in long lines; now lines were his friends. You just had to pretend you had forgotten something in your car before your turn came.

They frequently took Miguel to the children's section of Palo Alto's one remaining public library or to the junior museum. Those activities elicited warm looks of approval instead of the usual icy stares. Joe reciprocated by using the library to teach her about subjects that interested her—ecology, history, and literature. Because they didn't have an address, they couldn't get a library card and take out books, but they'd hide books in unlikely corners and out-of-the-way shelves so they could come back and be sure to find them the next day. He was amazed what an avid student she was. She asked challenging questions and he found himself paging through the books trying to search for the answers. Her vocabulary and grammar improved just by mimicking him. She probably would have made a great lawyer. Maria was even more ecstatic by the progress Miguel was making in his reading and arithmetic with Joe's help, and Joe found himself incredibly proud every time the boy mastered a new word or concept.

They posed as a family going to educational and cultural venues, hiding their bags behind dumpsters or retaining walls. Most had the occasional free day or evening and Maria had a myriad of tricks for getting past the guards at the doors when there was an admission fee. The rest rooms were generally pretty good, too. Joe was impressed how adept one could get at controlling one's bodily functions, though he made friends with his fair share of shrubs as well.

On nice days they could go to parks or the Baylands. They recognized others doing the same things, striking the same poses; and they honored each other's illusions through polite, casual conversation that avoided acknowledging the obvious. Often, they found themselves in the same places at night along the creeks, vacant lots, or in groves of trees in semi-public areas. Maria was particularly skilled at making shelters from discards and junk.

She was generous about helping people erect temporary shelters and, as a result, others would share their materials with her.

They didn't discuss whether they should continue the arrangement, but Maria didn't ask him to leave, so Joe stayed. He admired her energy and enthusiasm and he was growing fonder and fonder of Miguel. It wasn't the sort of existence that invited a romantic relationship so Joe chose to close off that possibility in his own mind.

Christmas was coming up, and, while the child was sleeping, Maria showed him the present she had found, a child's quilt, left among the donations at the back door of the Bargain Box, a second hand shop run by the Stanford Hospital Women's Auxiliary. "People never seem to read the sign NOT to leave stuff there at night—they must think that notice is for someone else," she laughed as she described the place. Her comment made Joe recall his "Divinely Entitled" conversation with Miranda during their hike, a million years ago, when he was still D.E. himself.

The next day, he took some of his remaining cash and bought the boy a brand new stuffed tiger. He was terribly pleased as the sales clerk wrapped the toy. For Maria, he bought a used copy of *Incidents in the Life of a Slave Girl,* her favorite book, which she said always gave her the courage to keep going no matter what. He flipped through it. He had never read a slave narrative in his years of studying American history and law. It appeared to be the autobiography of a slave woman who ran away from her owners and escaped by hiding in a tiny attic space for seven years. She managed to compel her old master to sell her children to her free grandmother, who sent them north. Talk about making the ultimate sacrifices for your kids. Eventually, she made her way to Boston. Seemed a little intense for his tastes, but it looked like an exciting read.

They went to Christmas Eve services at one of the nearby churches (which also had a little party with food afterwards).

Miguel sang all the familiar Christmas carols loudly. It seemed to Joe that the same 12 songs were replayed endlessly. When the minister told the story of Mary and Joseph looking for an inn and being turned away, Miguel commented, "just like us!" Fortunately, only a few congregants turned around to stare.

Joe's pleasure was even greater when Miguel ripped the paper off and squealed in delight on Christmas morning. Wrapped in his new quilt and clutching the tiger, he and Maria sang more Christmas songs. They had camped that night in a patch of redwoods in Rinconada Park, tucked in the shadow of the swimming pool pumps. Maria grinned as he opened his present—a slightly used swimsuit, towel, and a pair of goggles. He looked at her quizzically. She explained, "Now, when you need a shower you can go to lap swimming." She pulled a handful of tickets out of her pocket, "I didn't want to spoil the surprise. You do know how to swim don't you?" She suddenly looked worried and Joe reassured her that he did.

Maria loved the book. Her old copy had become tattered and the cover had fallen off long ago. She kept smoothing the hard cover with her hands. She opened it to a favorite passage, where the author is reunited with her children, and read to Miguel, who snuggled up against her. Joe smiled at the site of them, his spirit feeling very light. They were going to Christmas lunch in the Paly High School cafeteria, sponsored by a local synagogue and catered by a Chinese restaurant. As they walked over, Joe and Maria both held hands with Miguel who was happily singing his twentieth rendition of *White Christmas*.

At lunch, sitting with several other families, the man sitting next to Joe told him about an opening for an orderly on the graveyard shift at the Classic Residence Continuing Care Retirement Community where he worked. Would Joe be interested? It didn't pay much but it was enough to keep him in food and some extra clothing. He wrote down the name and address and told Joe to be there in the morning at 7 AM. He'd introduce Joe to the hiring supervisor at the skilled nursing facility.

Joe turned to tell Maria the good news but she was deep in conversation with the saddest looking woman Joe had ever seen. He listened in as he helped Miguel cut his food.

"Next week is the anniversary of my son's execution. It helps me to talk about him. Do you mind? " She looked at Maria. "I ran away from my sixth foster home when I was a kid. The only way I could make it was to start hooking. He was my first baby. I was only 15," she said shifting her gaze to Miguel.

"You understand. I wanted someone who would love me. After the second one was born, a judge made me get a birth control implant in my arm. By the time it stopped working they weren't giving those away anymore. I couldn't get any protection except rubbers and sometimes the johns wouldn't use 'em. I got pregnant again and didn't have any money for a doctor and I maybe didn't do the right things. Anyway, my youngest was born too soon. He weighed less than two pounds and even though the doctor suggested I might want to let him die because he was going to have horrible health problems, I couldn't do it. It wouldn't have been right.

"I got help from a local church's 'Keep Hope Alive' fund. They paid for the medical treatments, which were big time expensive, but after he got out of the hospital the church handouts didn't amount to much. Our public assistance ran out a few years ago, and we never had enough to eat, much less money for everything else he needed. The doctor was right—that baby had a lot wrong with him. You could tell just by looking at him. My daughter got so sick of his crying all the time, she ran away. My older son was sweet but not too bright so he took care of the little one while I was working. School didn't do much for him and at 13 he fell in with some rough kids. I mean I couldn't watch them all the time."

Joe didn't think these were justifiable excuses for neglecting your children. However, he had to concede that he saw her circumstances didn't leave a lot of options.

"One day he had the baby with him when there was a drug deal going down. Some rich kid who was buying started making fun of the baby and calling him all kinds of names like 'sewer rat' and 'mud slug.' My older son kinda went crazy and punched him. There were guns and in the fight both my baby and the smart ass were killed. My boy was tried as an adult and got the death penalty. You don't get automatic appeals anymore, you know, so he was dead at 14. I don't know where my daughter's gone to. I'm all alone now—and I wish I was dead too."

Maria hugged the woman as she cried miserably. Joe couldn't keep himself from wishing that the rule of law looked out for the actually born as much as it did embryos. God, he was thinking like those freaks in Aquamarine!

Later Joe told Maria about the job. She was sad at the idea of being away from him during an eight-hour shift, but enthusiastic about the possibilities. Would he be willing to take care of Miguel in the afternoons so she could look for something too? Then maybe they could afford to get a room somewhere. The shelters were all full and there was a huge waiting list so two incomes could make the vital difference.

★　　★　　★　　★　　★

Joe was waiting at the facility early. It was a lovely complex, exquisitely landscaped, luxuriously appointed. It reminded him of the Ahwahnee Hotel in Yosemite with its stone façade and striking details. He walked up the palm-lined driveway opposite Neiman Marcus at Stanford Shopping Center. The sign indicated the valet parking staff hadn't come on duty yet. When he walked into the elegant lobby, it looked like a four-star resort. Beautiful woodwork and art, obviously custom carpeting, uniformed clerks standing behind the front desk. Tasteful signage indicated the locations of the various restaurant style dining rooms or the elevators for the four levels of apartments and public rooms. A small sign on the desk indicated that the complex was fully subscribed, but it was possible to be put on the waiting list for the multi-million dollar units. He'd be happy to live here himself.

The thought brought him crashing down. He could have afforded this place in his golden years, if the government and Jack hadn't wrecked his life. While he would have liked to indulge himself in a wave of depression, he knew that Miguel and Maria were counting on him. He didn't want to disappoint them. He had to pull himself together.

At that hour there weren't too many residents visible, mostly staff cleaning the public areas. The concierge directed him to an attractive one-story building further down Sand Hill Road, past the assisted living facility. The receptionist at the front desk used the intercom to call Arthur, the man from Christmas dinner, who took him back to a quiet office at the rear of the building. The graveyard shift was getting off as Arthur introduced Joe to his supervisor, Milton Weinstein. It seemed to Joe that both men looked more like doctors than orderlies in their gray scrubs.

Milton sized him up and asked, "Have you ever done anything like this before?"

Joe shook his head, "I'm willing to learn. I was an attorney in my former life."

"I was an engineer. Just don't sue, OK?" Milton chuckled darkly. "Be here tonight at 11 PM. Here's the employee rulebook. It tells you what's expected and how to behave with the residents and their families. You can fill out the paperwork when you get here, and for the first night you'll follow Arthur around. After that you'll be on your own. The families here prefer help with a profes-

sional demeanor. The toughest part is acting like you k
place."

He knew it was pathetic in a way, but Joe was so del
the prospect of earning money again that he studied the
handbook as if it were an annual report of a company whose stock
he wanted to buy.

That night, Arthur gave Joe the nickel or should he say, $50
tour. This particular facility had been opened by Hyatt Hotels in
2005 and was now a joint venture among an insurance company,
pharmaceutical house, and concierge doctors' practice. It was an
extremely lucrative business and one of the major growth
industries in the U.S. Despite the restrictions on Medicare, the
abolition of Medicaid, and an accelerating shift of medical care
to the for-profit sector, healthcare still took up a staggering
percentage of America's GDP. Of course, the lion's share of
services went to those who could afford to pay for it, and those in
the last few years of life. This facility was a shining example. Most
of the residents were either parents of successful Silicon Valley
executives, retired Stanford University administrators and
professors who'd liquidated their large Palo Alto homes, or aging
superstar entrepreneurs featured in the Computer History
Museum. Several shelves in the community library were reserved
for resident authors.

Most had large apartments with costly furnishings from their
own homes. All had premium medical insurance that covered the
best care, treatments, and medication. The clients preferred the
term "Retirement Community," so even though this particular
building was a skilled nursing facility, the staff was instructed to
avoid the use of the term "nursing home" which made people
uncomfortable.

Again he was reminded that a place like this would no longer
be his own destiny. He couldn't even be sure he'd end up in a
standard nursing home that required you to turn over the assets of

a middle class existence. Far too many were dismal places—minimally regulated, under-staffed, and overcrowded—yet still superior to the dank Dickensian squalor of charity wards that were the final rest stop for people of modest means. The indigent merely died in their rooms or on the street, often from treatable diseases like diabetes, heart ailments and routine cancers, providentially exempt from the laws that safeguarded against assisted suicide and discouraged Do Not Resuscitate orders.

But here, all was bright and beautiful; things like physical decline, senility, and death were tastefully screened by the amenities of gracious living. As an orderly, Joe would be assisting the certified nurses aides with lifting patients during bathing or changing, cleaning up soiled linens, and generally fostering the illusion that theirs was a meaningful existence. Rules were very strict to avoid even the appearance of euthanasia, and residents were given every conceivable (and costly) drug and treatment to keep them going.

The food was excellent—pureed for those who could no longer chew. Rooms were cleaned daily so that if families came to visit, everything looked perfect. Many residents existed in a state of suspended animation for years.

Joe found it fairly easy to disconnect his brain from the unpleasant aspects of the work he was doing. At first he was worried about running into an acquaintance, since he recognized a lot of names among the families, but he soon found it wasn't an issue. Even when an ex-church member or business associate walked by, Joe learned he was invisible. It didn't occur to the "Divinely Entitled" inhabitants of his former world that they would know the person who was wiping their parent's bottom.

Milton had been willing to pay him in cash—for a minor discount, of course. Initially, it was the look of glee on Maria's face when they could buy a collapsible tent or ice cream cones for Miguel and his friends that motivated him. Her open hearted generosity had rubbed off on him, and he discovered he really delighted in helping his fellow homeless find a good spot for the evening or scoring enough food for a communal meal. The little favors he did for the residents, bringing someone an extra cookie or rubbing their feet with lotion, gave him a satisfaction previously reserved for closing a big deal. He'd worked out an arrangement to put in a few extra hours cleaning toilets and floors in exchange for blankets and towels that were unacceptably worn for the facility's residents, but a treasure for people on the street.

Maria found a part-time job cutting vegetables and washing pots in a restaurant kitchen. She was able to bring back leftover food after her shift, so their tent quickly became a gathering spot. It was funny but when they all fed each other, there was always enough to go around. Although it was a harder life than he could have ever imagined for himself, Joe was surprised to find he felt more at peace than he had in a long time. He cherished the time with Miguel, realizing how much he had missed in Daniel and Amanda's lives when they were small. He regretted that he had been so cross with Susan when she asked him to spend more time with the kids. But back then, work came first.

With their focus on survival relaxing a bit, Joe and Maria started to open up to each other about their lives. He told her about growing up in the Midwest in a small town. It was amazing to her that you could have parents who stayed together, who didn't beat or abuse you, where you always had enough to eat and your own room. "You mean you always knew you were going to college?" she asked incredulously, "and your brother and sister too? Where are they now?"

He admitted he had lost touch with them. "My sister Brenda is born again and thinks we Congregationalists are a bunch of heathens. She and my ex-wife didn't like each other and she objected to my son's 'lifestyle' as she put it. She wanted us to get him de-programmed. Her church even has a government-subsidized program for doing just that. It didn't go over too well with us or with our younger brother Edward, who's also gay.

"Ed is a very successful and established guy. He and his partner, Craig had adopted two mixed race infants with health problems and were wonderful parents. When the laws changed and they lost custody of the kids, Edward was furious at me that I didn't do enough to help him fight it."

"But what could you have done?" Maria looked puzzled. "The Government does stuff. It's not like regular people can do anything about it."

"At the time, we both thought I had contacts who might have been able to make an exception for him, especially since the kids weren't very adoptable, but I didn't want to call attention to my family's problems. I thought it might damage my standing in the Party organization. My son is probably still in contact with him, but I haven't spoken to him since I've lost everything."

"That's so sad. Don't you think they'd want to help you now?" Maria rested her hand on his forearm. Joe choked up.

"I think it's too late." He hated to confess that both his sister and brother had rejected him and he was too afraid to reach out to Daniel, so he shifted the topic. "What about you? What was your childhood like?"

She looked at him intently, "Are you sure you're ready for this? It's nothing like your life. I'm not sure you'll even understand." He could see she was hesitant and afraid to speak so he just looked at her encouragingly. She took a deep breath and began.

"I didn't know my father. All my four sisters had different fathers. My mother had a series of boyfriends who would stay with us for a while and then leave because she was so crazy. Most of them hit us—some did worse. Mom wanted them to stay around, so she'd look the other way if one of us tried to tell her something had happened. Eventually, we knew better than to try."

Joe's initial indignation when he heard about Maria's mother was tempered by a flash of self-awareness. He knew it was all too easy to ignore the obvious. Maybe he wasn't in the position to condemn Maria's mother.

"When I was about 16, Mom got into a fight with her current guy. He hit her so hard it broke her jaw. Then she had...I think they called it a 'psychotic breakdown.' Neighbors called to complain and the police took her off somewhere and all us kids were split up."

"Wasn't there some kind of foster program available?" Joe thought that was a standard service.

"Not anymore. Foster parents weren't paid a lot, but at least their basic expenses were covered. The younger kids were taken in by a private church group, but my older sister Sandra—she was Miguel's mom—and me were pretty much left on our own.

"Sandra moved in with her boyfriend at his parents, but there wasn't room for me. I tried staying with school friends for a while, but you wear out your welcome pretty fast when you don't have any money to buy your own food and clothes. I'd offer to do extra chores but not too many people are interested in another mouth to feed when it's not theirs." Maria didn't sound sorry for herself, just matter-of-fact, as if she was remarking on the weather.

"So, I learned pretty fast that I had to take care of myself on the streets. I did some stuff that I'm not proud of, but I survived. I tried to avoid the guys who turned their girls on to drugs, because I saw that it took all day just to get the next fix and they'd do anything, and I mean anything, to get that next high. I didn't want to be that desperate." She looked down, studying the scuffed toe of her shoe. "I admit I was tempted at times, because it would have been nice to numb out and not feel cold and hungry, but I was afraid because I saw how much pain and effort it took to be an addict."

She paused. Joe wasn't sure if he wanted her to go on. Maybe he really didn't want to know this much. If she shared her story, she might want to know about him—not the recent problems but the earlier secrets he kept buried from himself.

"I let myself get close to this guy, Derek. He protected me and helped me find food. He had been in the Marines until he got a bad head wound. It never healed properly. They kicked him out because he was too messed up mentally, and they didn't want to have to keep sending him to a shrink. He's the one who taught me how to build shelters. Anyway, one day, he was showing me how to tie a tarp to a tree so it wouldn't damage the tree or pull off in the wind, and he collapsed. Something must have burst in his brain and there was blood everywhere. It was a mess. He got blood all over the few clothes I had," she frowned.

"I didn't know what to do. I tried knocking on some houses nearby to ask someone to get help but everyone was afraid and wouldn't open their doors or even call an ambulance for me. When I went back I could see he was dead, so I took off. I couldn't stop crying, there was blood all over me, and when I collapsed in an alley behind a restaurant, someone called the police and they picked me up.

"I got tossed into jail. That's where I got this," she rubbed the scar on her face. "I saw some women beating up another girl and ran to a guard to get her to stop it. Not only did it not save the other girl, the same women beat me for snitching and made sure that I was marked so everyone else would know. They all stopped talking to me after that, except for the ones who would bother me in the shower." Maria straightened her shoulders. "Eventually, they let me go."

"Didn't you have a trial or a hearing and a lawyer?" Joe asked.

Maria looked at him with disbelief. "You're kidding, right? What world did you live in? They don't need a reason to lock you up if you scare the wrong people. And free lawyers? They don't give them to you automatically. You have to find someone who'll do it and I didn't have anyone who could go look for me."

Joe remembered doing some pro bono work many years ago, but he'd never had a case like Maria's. He also vaguely recalled that the office of public defender had been restructured and now depended heavily on voluntary representation by lawyers, who, through the bar associations, had agreed to devote a certain amount of their time to defending those unable to pay for counsel. But most of that work had been sloughed off on paralegals, who shuffled through the paperwork while lawyers made brief, if any, appearances in court. And those who could not afford counsel and got caught up in either criminal or civil proceedings had little hope of getting a shot at an appeal. Appellate reform, like bankruptcy reform, had cut out "frivolous" appeals. Seemed like a good idea at the time but now the reasoning seemed to have a few holes.

"Anyway, I kept my distance from most people after that. I got pretty good at looking out for myself. But when Sandra got arrested, a friend of hers tracked me down to ask me to take care of Miguel. It was supposed to be temporary, but then she died and he became my responsibility. You see how he is. I couldn't help but love and care for him; he's my family. None of the things that happened to him were his fault.

"Having a kid changed how people looked at me—good and bad. At the playgrounds, the mothers who noticed our suitcases would glare at me like I was a bad mother, especially when Miguel would stare at their kids when they ate their snacks. It never occurred to most of them to share with Miguel. How is a little one supposed to understand that? That's when I started taking him to educational places and figured out how to hide our stuff so we'd look like we belonged there. But other people like me, who were barely surviving, would be kinder a lot of the time. They'd give us little bits of food or a blanket or an old sweater if they could spare them.

"Then I found that certain restaurants would give us leftovers at the end of the day, and I'd share it with people who had helped us or were missing meals themselves. Their faces would light up when Miguel and I brought them food. I may have been a little hungrier than I would have been otherwise, but I felt really good, do you know what I mean? My heart would just swell up and get all warm and full. It was the best feeling I'd ever had. Except for maybe when Miguel hugs me and says he loves me." She stroked the curls of the sleeping child.

"Why did you help me?" Joe asked. It didn't make sense to him that a complete stranger would go to so much trouble.

"I saw you staggering into that alley but it didn't look like you were drunk. I try to be careful—there are homeless people on drugs, and a few are crazy or just plain vicious, but most of them are like you and me and Miguel. Still, I waited a while before I went in. When I saw you passed out, I came closer because it was so cold. You didn't smell like booze or piss. You were kind of clean for a person on the street. I figured you could die and I had the power this time to do something to prevent it, so I took a chance. Besides, Miguel asked what was wrong with you and I wanted to show him how to be a good person," she smiled. "Then you turned out to be a nice man and didn't hit on me or act weird with Miguel. I like how you teach us things. I missed a lot in school, and I want Miguel to have a chance at a better life."

Joe's eyes filled with tears. He'd forgotten what it was like to be admired, especially for something that wasn't related to work or a significant financial contribution.

She asked him, "What happened to your wife and son? Do you have any other children?"

"Susan and I divorced a few years ago. She's living up north. My son lives in San Francisco. We'd been having some problems.

I don't actually see him much any more." Joe changed the subject. He was enjoying the reflection of her opinion of him and he didn't want it to dissipate just yet, so he chose to ignore her second question. It would have made him bring up dark memories that were increasingly lurking in the back of his mind.

★　　　★　　　★　　　★　　　★

That night he dreamt about Mandy again. Normally he tried to avoid thinking about her and the dreams stayed away, but sometimes they crept back in and he couldn't control it. In his dream, he was back in his house and there was a pounding on the door. He was afraid it was the SWAT team again, but then he heard sobbing. When he opened the door, Mandy fell through and he caught her. She told him that she needed to be with him. He woke up disoriented, thinking about her and crying quietly.

That may have been the reason that, on the following morning, Joe surprised himself and told Maria about his second child as they watched Miguel play with some other children at a park. "She was the greatest kid you could have. Smart, pretty, sunny, athletic. She excelled at every sport she tried, charmed even the dourest old coots, and baked the best chocolate chip cookies. Mandy had lots of friends and never gave us a moment of worry.

"Her teachers loved her and the other students always looked up to her. I truly believed that if there were ever to be a woman president, my little girl could grow into that role. In high school she was always president of her class, earned top marks, and was a leader in the Young Republican Club. Her high school boyfriend was a superb young man, captain of the football team, son of a CEO. They both took flying lessons and even though it terrified me every time her plane left the ground, I loved seeing the confidence it gave her.

"Mandy was captain of the debate team. Thanks to her strategy and poise, her team won a national competition on 'Elimination of Affirmative Action' and 'Should racially derogatory remarks be considered protected speech?' She was so persuasive.

"The day Mandy got into the Air Force Academy was the happiest day of my life. I was so proud of her. When I got home from work that day, she jumped into my arms like a little kid. Despite Susan's reservations, we were both thrilled by Mandy's excitement. We called Daniel at college and went out to dinner to celebrate.

"I don't remember exactly when the calls from the Academy started to change. Mandy's voice got a little flatter and she didn't quite sound her usual, confident, self. One Sunday morning we called and I could swear she had been crying, but she said she was fine. It was just a cold she said.

"There were a few times when the phone rang but no one was on the other end. Susan sensed something was wrong but I brushed it away." He was still angry with himself. He had been wrong and stupid.

"Then came the call from the school's Commandant. Mandy was in the hospital and it didn't look good. She had lost a lot of blood. I knew the commandant said something about what was wrong but it didn't register with me. We caught the next plane to Denver, because there wasn't a flight to Colorado Springs until the following day.

"It was so quiet in the car," his voice dropped. "As we drove down Interstate 25, it was already getting dark. The mountains looked like black cutouts against the dull winter sky. It felt fake you know? Like a kid's drawing or a stage set at a school play. The road was totally straight, which was probably good, since I was operating on autopilot anyway. About 40 minutes into the drive, it started to snow, slowly at first, and then picking up speed with the wind. The snow was driving straight into the windshield. I had never seen a storm like this. It was completely disorienting. By the time we hit the pass, we could only see a few feet ahead.

"I was anxious to reach the hospital." Joe remembered the shouting match in his head between the urge to go faster and his awareness that he had to drive slowly to get safely through the storm. His hands gripped the wheel as he stared into the oncoming snow, struggling to keep the car on the road. "We almost missed the turnoff to the hospital because Susan was reading the directions, but I was having trouble hearing her voice." He paused for a moment. Maria was transfixed, barely breathing herself.

"By the time we got to the hospital Mandy was barely conscious. Her face was so white that the circles under her eyes looked blue. When we called her name she opened her eyes a bit and smiled in recognition. Then her eyes darkened and she whispered that she was sorry. The heart monitor started buzzing loudly and the line went flat. People flew into the room and I was pushed back. I felt like I was frozen—I had no idea what to do or how long I stood there watching.

"All I know is that after all the commotion, the doctor turned to us and said how sorry he was. Susan started sobbing and still I couldn't move. It was as if I was watching a movie and there wasn't any sound. Or any air in the room. I stumbled out the door and sat in a chair in the waiting area. Someone brought me a glass of water. I realized Susan was sitting next to me crying. I wanted to hug her, to say something that would make her feel better, but my mind was blank and my body didn't obey my commands. I can't really blame her for feeling like I let her down, too." His voice cracked.

"There was a young woman in a cadet's uniform watching us from across the room. She caught my eye and walked over. She handed me a letter in a pale blue envelope, touched Susan's shoulder, and said something, but I was in a fog. We both stared at the envelope for a while and when we looked up we could see her retreating down the hall.

"The letter was from Mandy's roommate, Becky. She told us what had happened. In October, Mandy had been on guard duty late at night and an upperclassman assaulted her. Fortunately, two other plebes heard the commotion and helped her fight him off." Even now it made Joe furious that he hadn't been able to protect his little girl. "The older cadet threatened them that if they reported the incident, he would just say that Mandy had come on to him, and that the freshmen had started the fight and deserved to be expelled. The boys were willing to take the risk and stand by her but Mandy felt she could deal with the incident privately and put it behind her.

"She didn't say anything to anyone but Becky. She didn't tell us because she didn't want us to worry. She hadn't been on birth control and there wasn't any way to get a morning after pill, so Mandy prayed and hung around their room when she wasn't in class or on duty.

"When she realized she was pregnant, Mandy was beside herself. She had worked so hard to get there. She didn't want to be part of any scandal that might discredit the Air Force she loved or get the fellows who helped her in trouble. Mandy knew she'd be kicked out of the Academy for failing to report the incident, or for fraternization if she had the baby, even if she gave it up for adoption. She also didn't want to disappoint me." Joe was clearly in pain at the thought. "She was desperate to find someone who would do an abortion, which was illegal in Colorado since her life wasn't in danger. Becky's boyfriend knew someone who knew a girl who had had one so they got a number. To make sure that they weren't undercover agents, the woman made Mandy take a home pregnancy test while she watched, and sign a confession that would be destroyed after the procedure.

"The letter described the place but I couldn't read that part. The operation went badly so the woman dropped Mandy at the hospital before speeding off. Mandy made Becky promise that she would let her parents know what had happened.

"Susan blamed *me* for Mandy's death. For supporting the Republican Party even though I believed abortion should have remained legal, and the focus should be on educating young people with realistic information so they didn't get pregnant in the first place. For not using my clout as a GOP Pioneer to argue the point. For encouraging Mandy to go to the Academy and getting her sponsored. For my silence, when I should have written a letter or joined her at a Pro-Choice rally or talked to my influential friends. As soon as the funeral was over, Susan packed her bags and left." He sat slumped, not meeting Maria's eyes. "The last time I saw her, a few months ago, we still couldn't talk about it." It was awful to consider that Susan might have a valid point. He couldn't hide the connections from himself any more.

He forced himself to go on.

"At least there was some belated justice. We went to the Commandant. He was appalled. The two young men confirmed the story and it turned out there was security footage that corroborated them. The upper classman pled guilty to nine counts of violating military law including forcible rape, indecent assault, and conduct unbecoming an officer. He was court-martialed, given a dishonorable discharge, and sentenced to 16 years in a military prison. Unfortunately, my efforts to have him tried for manslaughter, failed since the prosecutors felt that the abortion that caused her death was Mandy's fault. At least the bastard is rotting in prison.

"The Commandant sent me a handwritten personal letter of condolence. He said that Amanda's death was a tragedy and a great loss to the Air Force. She would have made a superb officer. He told me he had a daughter of his own—and he could only wonder what she would do if she found herself in a comparable dilemma. I think he took a real risk in writing that letter, since Mandy's failure to report the incident and her subsequent illegal behavior placed her own character in question. But it was written by a father as well as an officer, proud of his service but deeply distressed at the dishonor done to both it and my daughter."

Maria listened in silence. When he came to the end of his narrative she didn't comment, she just leaned over and hugged him. He started crying. She held him. The fact that she wasn't judging him made him sob even harder. Miguel noticed and ran away from the other kids, his eyes wide with concern. "You OK, Joe?" He put his arms around Joe and Maria.

"It's fine, Miguel. Joe's telling me about a bad dream he had. Why don't you go back and play?" Maria smiled at the boy. Joe nodded. Miguel patted Joe on the knee. "Maria always makes me feel better when I have a bad dream." He ran off.

"Take a deep breath," Maria advised. "You'll be alright in time. It's amazing what people can survive." The effort of revealing something so personal exhausted him. He hadn't been that intimate with anyone in years. Fortunately, she didn't push the point or try to dig any deeper so he felt like he could resist the urge to walk away.

Things were looking up with the New Year. Joe and Maria had been able to save a little money and they were hoping to get a room somewhere, so Miguel would have an address and sufficient documentation to obtain a voucher to start school in the fall. He already knew how to read and do simple arithmetic, and was equally comfortable in Spanish or English.

Milton, Joe's supervisor, was asked to take care of the West Atherton home of one of the resident's families, the Slaters. They were spending January and February at their Aspen house skiing, and March to May at their Palm Beach house. Milton assumed responsibility for the maintenance of the 10,000 square foot main residence and grounds. The family left after a warm and festive farewell party for 100-year old grandma Slater, who wasn't entirely sure who everyone was, but nevertheless bestowed powdery kisses on anyone who came within reach. Milton invited Arthur and Joe (and their families) to stay in the guesthouse with him. Together, they could share the work, have a warm place to spend the rest of the winter, and earn a little extra money.

The group was thrilled with their good fortune. Each family took a bedroom/bathroom suite, and they shared a small common area and kitchenette. More simply decorated than the main house with its acres of marble, granite, faux painted walls, brocade oversized sofas, and massive four-poster beds, the guesthouse was light and sunny. Since all the furnishings and bed covers were white, they packed the bedding away in a closet and bought some sheets to place over the couch and chairs. The children were cautioned to play quietly and not call attention to their presence—it was better if the neighbors weren't aware they were there. During the day they kept the blinds drawn, and limited their use of the lights at night. Ironically, the lights in the main house were on a rotating schedule to make sure that it looked like the Slaters were home in order to ward off intruders.

Milton fired the lawn services company to reduce the risk of discovery. He had Joe and Arthur take over the tasks of mowing the lawn and tending to the gardens. Twice a week they took turns cleaning and dusting the main house. Both buildings were immaculate at all times, and with a washer/dryer available they reveled in the luxury of keeping themselves clean and tidy. Joe knew it helped his self-esteem to be able to look like his old self again, even if his wardrobe was limited and less expensive. Because they had a place to cook, they could eat better as well. He was happy to forgo the prepared food and frozen dinners that had been his mainstay after the divorce or the odds and ends since then.

It was difficult for him to analyze his relationship with Maria, since it didn't fit with any of his known or pre-conceived patterns. He felt entirely comfortable with her. He could tell her more than he had ever told anyone. They were affectionate without being sexual, which he found weird, but safer. It wasn't exactly romantic—she was too young and too vulnerable. He sensed that she was wounded at some core level, and that even while she approached him with love and an open heart, she guarded her innermost being from everyone except Miguel.

She didn't demand or expect anything from him, yet he was willing to share everything he had with her. She was his guide on some journey through completely unmarked territory. There were no guideposts or map and he didn't have a frame of reference for any part of his life right now. All he knew for certain was that his heart was full and calm.

He recalled a Bill Moyers series on Joseph Campbell that Susan had forced him to watch. At the time, he teased her that it was the kind of show the chardonnay and brie crowd liked. Campbell claimed that most people sought to "experience the rapture of being alive." Maria was the most alive person he knew and she had enabled him to share that experience of rapture.

At work, it pleased him to be of comfort to his charges. Several times he had sat with people as they died, holding their frail and spidery hands, so they would know they weren't alone at that final moment. He would listen to their labored breathing, willing them to a peaceful passing, and feel that final pulse as the life force passed from their bodies, the color and animation draining from their faces. It seemed to him that the body was just a shell that contained one's essence; for many of these people their conscious selves had departed long ago.

He, who had been so confident as to the rightness of the world, now questioned the morality of so many things he had taken for granted, such as the heroic care of older bodies just because it was medically possible. It seemed somehow perverted when you spent so much time with these carefully warehoused individuals and those dying slowly of terminal cancers. He preferred to imagine what they had been like in their prime.

As he and Arthur pruned the rose bushes at the Slaters' house, Arthur wondered aloud, "I'm not a communist or anything, but do you think it's reasonable that one couple with grown children should have two or three empty mansions, while so many sleep on the street? Were their lives so terrible when they paid a bigger share of taxes?"

Joe thought of the countless times he had sat with friends at the golf club or in their comfortable homes, bitterly complaining about the tax burdens they endured, and the obvious laziness of welfare cheats who would rather take government money than do an honest day's work.

"Everyone I knew before honestly believes that they are entitled to consume whatever they want as long as they can afford it. It doesn't matter if they have more money than they could possibly spend in two lifetimes. They deserve—as a God-given right—to accumulate as much as they can. If others don't fare as well, it's their own fault." His face burned with shame at the memories. "To imagine Miguel and Maria or Milton or Robert or the Sterns, or you, as somehow less deserving seems ridiculous to me now. In the abstract I could accept it. When put in terms of real people I know and love, it feels selfish and obscene. Like a sick joke."

"I never expected it could get this bad," Arthur concurred. "My younger brother became a plumber. I looked down on him because I was an engineering manager and had the professional life. I made fun of him for being in a union, and told him that organized labor had outlived its usefulness because they didn't change with the times. Then my situation changed with the times. I had to let go most of my experienced engineers and replace them with young H1-B visa holders because they were so much cheaper. The next year I was asked to train my successor, because they moved the entire department to Bangalore.

"Remember reading the management guru, Peter Drucker? We all bought into the idea that we were moving from a skill-based society and economy to a knowledge-based economy. The range and application of a skill, say like a tool and die-maker or a plumber, was limited, but knowledge workers could apply their knowledge to a wide range of tasks and jobs. So, look at us, my friend, with all our knowledge. The union may be gone, but now my brother, the plumber, is the one who can support his family while I'm emptying bedpans. I didn't dream my bosses would pay themselves so extravagantly and ship my job away to increase the company profits. And yet I know that I didn't speak up when it was happening to other people."

"Neither did I," admitted Joe. "In fact, I was responsible for eliminating jobs. I rarely weighed the human costs, only the financial and legal ones. At the time, I honestly believed I was doing the right thing, because I was saving jobs for others by keeping the company competitive. Do you think we only think it's wrong because it happened to us?"

Arthur considered the relative merits of the question. "Maybe it's the other way around. Maybe we needed to go through it so we could see why it's wrong."

★   ★   ★   ★   ★

He didn't share his revelations with Maria that night before he left for work. The ideas were too new, too unformed. He needed to process them a bit longer. Joe wanted to thank her for what she was giving him but he didn't quite know how to express himself. He didn't have a vocabulary sufficient to articulate what he was experiencing.

The next morning was payday. Milton counted out his money and offered to give him and Arthur a ride back to the Slaters in the gardening pickup. Joe was tempted but he wanted to stick around for a bit. Mrs. Elton, one of his favorites, had taken a turn for the worse and he wanted to hold her hand for a while. Her family wasn't expected until later in the day, and he didn't want her to be alone if she died before they got there. When her children and grandchildren arrived, he slipped out of her room.

Joe changed out of his scrubs and set out walking. It was a glorious day. He was rehearsing in his head what he wanted to say to Maria. She had changed his life in such amazing ways and he didn't know how to thank her enough. All those Sundays sitting in church seemed mechanical and stiff compared to how he saw God now. He thought back to Miranda's comments about the forces of the universe. They made sense to him now, too. Living a truly moral life is more dependent on how you live and treat others than where and whether you pray in a formal setting.

When he had had everything, he only saw life in terms of the patterns and images he'd been taught. He had been too afraid to look underneath the surface or challenge the rules. It was safer to go along, even when he didn't agree completely, and avoid arguing with people who wanted him to justify his stated opinions. It had taken the force of the universe to turn his life upside down, make him face his worst fears, and let him see that he could live through it. The world hadn't ended, even though it looked completely different.

When Joe arrived at the Slaters, he found his way to the guesthouse blocked. Milton was being stuffed into a police car with his wrists cuffed behind him. Neighbors had emerged from their gated estates and were milling around. Joe edged up to one man and asked what was happening.

"They found a bunch of squatters living in the guest house. Can you imagine? One of the other neighbors noticed some suspicious activity so she called it in. When the private police force contacted the Slaters to check, they said that only one person was authorized to be there. That's him, under arrest." The man was visibly outraged. "Bringing a bunch of poor trash to live here."

Joe tried to sound casual. "I just moved in down the street and hadn't noticed them. Were they really a problem? Where are they now?"

The man frowned. "You have to be careful these days, what with terrorists, thieves, and troublemakers everywhere. They took two women, another guy, and a couple of brats off earlier. I heard one of the cops say they were shipping them to a detention camp in Utah."

Joe's heart missed a few beats. This couldn't be. He tried to think about what to do. What if he said he was Milton's lawyer? They'd expect a card and a phone number even if they overlooked his casual attire. And even though he loved them more than any one else alive, he had no legal standing when it came to Miguel and Maria. As an attorney, he knew that under the Patriot V Act, the authorities didn't have to tell him anything anyway. He remembered when Justices Roberts, Thomas, Scalia, Alito, Yoo, Gonzales, and Starr had ruled it was constitutional for the president to suspend all civil liberties in time of war. Well, war had become perpetual.

He was devastated. He hadn't protected them any more than he'd been able to protect Amanda. He was completely impotent.

He was garbage. Joe turned and started walking away before the neighborhood busybodies realized they didn't know him either. Without paying attention to where he was going, his feet led him the couple of miles to the laundromat in Palo Alto. Miraculously, Robert—looking a little thinner and worse for wear—was exiting with a cart of clean laundry. Joe had never been so relieved to see anyone in his entire life.

Robert was frightened by the sobbing man lurching towards him and making incoherent remarks. When he finally recognized Joe, Robert's face softened. "Where have you been? I haven't seen you in months."

"I didn't know where you lived. I couldn't find you." Joe's relief turned to embarrassment as he realized he was blubbering like a baby. Robert gently took his arm and led him to a small house on Cornell Street. It was quiet inside and Joe posed the obvious question with his eyes. Robert nodded. "My wife died in December, not long after our Thanksgiving dinner. I'm sorry I didn't know how to get word to you. At least she's at peace now and not suffering any longer.

"The worst indignity was the investigation to make sure that I hadn't done anything to hasten her death, since she died at home. While we were waiting for the funeral director to pick up the body, the hospice workers and I were interrogated for a couple of hours by a panel of religious nut jobs. They wanted to make sure that we hadn't interfered with God's will and that she had been allowed to have the chance to accept Jesus Christ as her personal savior before she died. We're Jewish, for crissakes.

"Who the hell are these people? What makes them think they have the right to tell other people how to live and die? I try to tell myself they're well-intentioned but I don't think they have the slightest idea how incredibly offensive it is when they try to 'save the soul' of someone who holds different beliefs." Robert stopped himself. "I'm ranting again. I'm afraid I've become a bit of a bore. What's happened to you?"

Robert heated up a can of soup and sliced up some bread and cheese. As they ate, Joe told him about his winter's journey. Robert observed, " You sound like you've changed your perspective on life."

Joe nodded, "It's not like I suddenly think I'm this righteous person or that I was horrible before. I know I was a decent person. Yet I was so steadfast in my principles, I didn't allow room for any facts that didn't fit my preconceived notions. Maybe it was out of fear but I ascribed evil intentions to people who held another point of view. Now so much of everything I've always believed unequivocally has been turned upside down." Robert listened sympathetically.

"The worst part is that Maria and Miguel are gone. Not only can't I do anything about it, I didn't even get to say goodbye." Joe started breaking down again.

Robert gave him a glass of whiskey and made him a bed on the sofa. Joe slept for two days, getting up only to eat occasionally. He was afraid to go to work, worried that if the authorities had picked up Milton and Arthur, they might be looking for him too. Finally, Joe took a shower, shaved, and dressed in some clean clothes that Robert bought for him. As he scrambled some eggs, Robert said, "OK, let's talk about what you need to do next. What feels most unfinished in your life right now?"

"I have to try to find out what happened to Milton and Maria and the others. I know it's a long shot but I'd never forgive myself if I didn't make some attempt."

"OK, we'll try making some calls." Robert nodded, "Anything else?"

Joe thought about it a long while. "Daniel. I need to make peace with my son. I missed my chance to tell Maria what she meant to me. I didn't protect my daughter either. I didn't stand up for any of them when it counted. I need to ask him to forgive me. Of course, he may not want to talk to me. I'm sure he's heard from Susan by now about the way I left Aquamarine. She has every right to hate me. Hell, I hate me now.

"What kind of stupid system is this that just grabs people without due process? Where anyone can be accused of being a terrorist and all their possessions stolen by the government or their crumby lawyers? How did I not see this coming? Worse than that, I helped make it happen. Why was I such an idiot to care about my bank account more than my own principles?" Joe was stomping on the floor, filled with raw anger, frustration, and self-contempt.

Robert let him rage for a good 15 minutes and then pulled him back to center. "We will try to find Maria. Either Daniel will talk to you or he won't. You have options. You can try calling him, or you can just go see him. You can go alone or I can go with you. Whatever you need. Do you know his address and number?" Joe had to admit that he didn't even know for sure if Daniel was still in San Francisco.

Robert took charge and Joe surrendered to his help. First they tried tracking down Maria and Miguel. Robert, posing as an elderly uncle looking for his family, spoke with the private security service, the Atherton Police Department, and then the National Security Company that ran the Utah detention centers. As Joe had feared, they couldn't even get confirmation that the two were being held. To learn what had happened to Milton, Joe called a few attorney friends but none would return his calls. Apparently the word was out that Joe was practically radioactive—no one wanted to risk being associated with him.

They tried locating Ben Stern, sure that he would help, but the family had moved on without leaving a forwarding address. Joe prayed that good fortune had smiled on them and that the Sterns were back in more comfortable circumstances. It struck Joe how tenuous life had become for all these good people he knew. Ironically, Maria's life of dysfunction and strong character allowed her to treat the uncertainty with graceful acceptance, but those who had only known affluence were bewildered and unprepared, if not broken.

Daniel's old number was no longer in service, so they went to an Internet café and googled him. They found a current number and address in the city. Robert took him to buy some clothes and a decent coat at a second hand store. Joe got a haircut and then went to Robert's dentist. That was painful and depressing—a year and a half of neglect had taken its toll, but at least most of the damage wasn't obvious.

Robert had a former colleague who was going to San Francisco for a Sunday matinee concert not far from Daniel's place. He agreed to drop Joe off and, after the performance, if Joe was waiting outside, give him a ride back to Robert's. There were no excuses, no barriers; now everything was up to Joe.

★　　★　　★　　★　　★

Joe listened to the man's stories on the drive up, but his stomach was in knots. Joe tried to focus on his breathing, to simply be, and not spin disastrous scenarios in his head, but it was tough. When Joe rang the doorbell, he was sure he wasn't breathing at all. Daniel looked stunned to see him. Maybe it was a mistake to have surprised him. He was guarded when he saw Joe's knapsack but was taken aback when Joe blurted out, "I'm so sorry...for everything. I know I didn't understand what you've been saying to me all these years." Daniel's brow furrowed and Joe recognized the expression as an indicator that his son was working through a difficult problem.

"Guess we're skipping the small talk, eh? Mom said she saw you last summer. She thought you might have changed, but then you just took off. She and Stan are fine you know, in case you care." His tone was bitter. "The money didn't make up for you being a coward. Cash is not the answer for everything."

Daniel looked surprised when Joe said, "You're right. I deserve that and anything else you care to throw at me. For what it's worth, I'm not the same person I was then. I'd like to talk to you and hear your side of things, but if you don't want to, I understand. I'd like to stay with you for a few days, but I have a ride coming…" he looked at the wall clock, "in three hours if you want me to go.

"Where's your car?" Daniel inquired.

"I don't have one anymore." Joe replied simply. He decided not to go into the story of Simon. It would be too distracting. "I don't have a lot of the things I used to but I've been given a lot of other gifts I didn't have before." Daniel looked skeptical, but his face was softening. "We can talk for now, but let's not decide if you're going to stay here yet."

Joe looked at his son, seeing the little boy he had been, as well as the man he was now. "I'd like to hear how my actions or shortcomings feel from your perspective, if you're willing to tell me."

Daniel began, "I've talked to Uncle Edward about this a lot. He felt particularly betrayed because he had devoted so much of his life to getting the Republicans in power. I guess he was operating on the old model when they wanted government to stay out of your personal business.

"I don't think you really know what it's like to have so little voice in America when it comes to equality. My friends and I are mainstream members of society, paying our dues in all the typical ways, and frankly, probably to greater extents than most. Most of us don't keep shouting about our issues. We let majority rule. We live our lives at greater expense and peril than you all, since we cannot travel freely and safely to certain parts of our own country.

We have to go to unreasonable legal extents and assume heavy financial burdens to protect our families and our rights—and we often fail. Imagine how Edward's kids felt when they were taken away from the only parents they had ever known? Did you even try to help him stop it? As long as we're the good little fags down the street or look cute on TV shows, you let us play in your yard.

"I'm not sure the Democrats are always better, though at least they make the effort, and don't need to resort to such extremes to be satisfied. Republicans complain about the Democrats' type of intrusion; Democrats complain about Republicans' platforms of catering to the rich; you all go on defending all of your nits about money this and money that, policy here and policy there. These are so very trivial when compared to the simple right to be, to exist, to love who you want to love, to live in union with your spouse, to raise your children with the pride and safety and value of family, like everyone else. What's wrong with that?"

Joe started to protest, "You know I don't have a problem with you or Ed being gay. It never affected how I felt about either of you. You're just as much of an American as anyone else."

"Then you sold out your own principles," countered Daniel. "We will all be Americans when we all have equal rights and equal protections under the law. It's all well and good to imagine the Constitution is a gender, race, and religion-neutral document, but when it was written African-Americans were slaves and counted as 3/5 of a person, women couldn't vote or own property, and all homosexuals had to live life as a lie. Unfortunately, it's not a level playing field. We will all be Americans when we have the same rights you do; when our children can hear from their society that their families are valid; when you admit to your prejudices and move beyond them. Sure, some people are too touchy, but reducing every legitimate concern to a 'PC' joke doesn't help the situation. Just because you haven't personally experienced racism or sexual prejudice, doesn't mean it doesn't exist, or that you are 'victim' if you acknowledge it.

"As a lawyer, father, and brother, how could you have supported people committed to a constitutional amendment outlawing gay marriage? Our existence is no threat to marriage. Our unions are no threat to marriage. It's bullshit. We are not destroying the fabric of Atherton, San Mateo County, California, the Deep South, or the USA. Divorce, porn, Monday Night Football, reality shows that make a silly contest of picking a mate, 'news' that is nothing more than sensationalistic entertainment and titillation, and sheer indifference are threats to marriage. Why aren't you all pushing a platform that outlaws or discourages those? All your claims of values, democracy, and hope are empty, unjust, and unholy. Your claims of moral superiority are thin, since the morality of discrimination and torture is null. All other issues are inconsequential relative to basic human rights."

"I didn't know you felt this strongly or that I had let you down so much on a personal level," Joe admitted.

"That's because you never actually heard me. You'd act like you were listening, but I could see it wasn't really registering," Daniel said, venting years of pent up frustration. "Can't you see the pattern? Blacks are threats to whites. Aliens are threats to citizens. Free slaves were threats to the economy. Free trade is a threat to American jobs. Mixed blood is a threat to the ideal human. Women are a threat to men. Muslims and Jews are threats to Christians. Liberals are threats to Conservatives. Gays are threats to Hets. Most religions preach tolerance, yet far too many religious believers demonize those who do not practice as they do. Aren't the arguments all the same? All are based on hate, ignorance, fear and insecurity. Civil liberties and freedoms—and no, they are not the same—should *never* be a question of majority rule. Unfortunately, sometimes the majority chooses not to protect the minority. The benefits of democracy depend on how the right to vote is used."

Joe listened respectfully. It was obvious to both of them that Joe had not paid attention this way in the past, yet Daniel remained combative. "What happened to you that you're willing to listen now? Why should I believe you get any of this better than you did before?"

It was a fair question. Joe gave him a somewhat abbreviated version of the past year, with Daniel interrupting whenever Joe slipped into his old pattern of sounding like he was talking about someone else. There were a lot of interruptions. It was 6 PM before they looked at the clock again. "I guess you're staying the night," Daniel offered. "I have plans this evening but there's food in the fridge and some extra blankets. I need to think about this. I'll see you in the morning before I leave for work."

Joe nodded. He was disappointed, but supposed it wasn't reasonable to expect too much at once. Daniel had always been sensitive and, like Joe, needed time and space to make up his mind.

Alone now, Joe studied the apartment. What sort of man had his son become? It wasn't that tidy or well decorated—so much for that old canard. There were a lot of books—mostly non-fiction, heavily political. A range of authors. Daniel clearly wanted to know what every side was thinking. There were lots of photographs—quite a few of Susan, some with Daniel, Susan, and Stan, a couple with his brother Edward. There were a surprising number of candid shots that Edward had taken of Joe and Susan, with Mandy and Daniel as kids and teenagers. At least Daniel had some fond memories of his childhood.

There were also pictures of Daniel smiling and laughing with other young men. Joe realized with a wrench that he had missed so much of Daniel's life. Joe didn't know who Daniel's friends were or even what he did at his job. He wanted to find out.

★   ★   ★   ★   ★

When Joe woke around 10 AM the next morning, Daniel was already gone but he'd left a key and a note, "I'll be home for dinner around 6. I'll get food. – D"

Joe was quite pleased. This was a start. He decided to go out for a walk. Daniel's building was in a decent neighborhood, but as he walked towards Van Ness, the number of homeless people astounded him. Even his recent experiences hadn't prepared him for the intensity of the problem here in an urban setting.

He smiled and said hello as he passed, ashamed of all the times he had pretended street people didn't exist. He could see a lot more now: families in distress, those whose mental illness was obviously untreated, alcoholics, abandoned adolescents, and ordinary folks who looked simply bewildered at this turn of events. Most responded with a smile of their own, except for those who were too far-gone to notice him.

When he reached Civic Center Plaza, he saw there was a rally going on and he stopped to listen. Young people were reading poetry aloud. People of all ages, color, and manner of attire were carrying signs protesting the on-going War on Terrorism: How long can this go on? Peace is Patriotic. If You Love God, Don't Kill His Children. While the crowd was energized, it was definitely orderly as it circled the designated protest zone. Along the perimeter, a line of women passed and rang a bell for each of the 5,000 servicemen and women who had died since the last "Mission Accomplished" celebration for the Middle East campaigns. The ringing seemed endless.

Several hundred passersby and the usual FBI agents armed with video cameras were merely observing the crowd when all hell broke loose. National Guardsmen with dogs, shields, batons, and tear gas moved in. It was absurd. No one had been in any danger until now. Why was this protest considered so dangerous and subversive? Who wouldn't want both peace and an end to terrorism? He was carried along with the others struggling to stay on their feet. Some that weren't lucky were trampled or separated from their companions. People were screaming, reminding him of that day at Aquamarine, but on a much larger scale.

He intervened to help a mother who was being yanked away from her son. The boy was clearly terrified and was crying uncontrollably. Joe tried to break the guardsman's grip on the woman's arm but he was shoved aside and put in a line of people being processed for arrest. After an hour of waiting, Joe felt someone pull him out of the line. The guard handled him roughly and pushed him around the corner of a building. The panic rose in his throat. He was going to be killed. It was all over. He wished he had seen Daniel that morning to say goodbye. Slowly, the man lifted up the facemask on his riot gear. Joe couldn't believe it. The guard was Bruce McDermott. He had been one of the security guards in his building at the chocolate company years ago. He grinned at Joe, "I knew there had to be a mistake when I saw you. Walk down this alley and get out of here. I'll cover for you. Now go quickly." Joe thanked him and ran.

Shaking and disoriented, Joe tried to head back to Daniel's apartment but he couldn't find his way as he stumbled through the streets. As he stopped to catch his breath, a little girl in ragged clothes came up to beg. He reached into his pocket to hand her a few coins. Suddenly, a dozen other children materialized, crowding around him and all reaching out asking for money. To his own horror, he panicked and pushed them roughly aside. All he could think about was how to get away.

Looking up, he saw they had emerged from a vacant lot where a crowd of dispirited looking men and women sat huddled together. They were dirty and visibly malnourished and ill. Some were covered in sores as they coughed or lay about. The only shelters were cardboard boxes, and hardly anybody had blankets or tarps. It was like a scene from a horror movie or a third world slum, even filtered through the eyes of someone who'd been living on the streets. Such sights weren't supposed to exist in the United States of America. There wasn't even a natural disaster to blame.

His heart was pounding and it didn't slow until he found his way back to Daniel's apartment. He felt guilty about his own frightened reaction. Then he threw up. He hoped the woman had been reunited with her son and thought about Maria and Miguel in the detention camp and prayed that they all were safe. He didn't know what to think about the people in the lot.

When Daniel finally got home, Joe couldn't wait for him to put down the grocery bags as he told him about the protest, how he had avoided arrest, the begging children, and that scene in the vacant lot. Daniel didn't cut him any slack. He poked his father in the chest and said, "See, even now you look like one of the haves and it works to your advantage. Remember when we'd argue about what happens to the others who don't start from the same position of power?"

Joe nodded, so Daniel pressed his point. "What did you imagine was going to happen to all the people who were completely dependent on the government safety net that you and your friends cut? The ones who weren't creative, with lots of ambition and initiative—like your friend Maria? Who didn't have credit cards to overdraw, relatives to impose upon, or marketable skills like the Sterns? Remember the people left in New Orleans after Hurricane Katrina? Well, those people you saw today—and there are lots more like them around the city—are human beings stuck in that predicament. They don't get medical care, they don't get enough to eat, and they have no hope. There aren't enough private charities to take care of them. And to call this country 'a land of opportunity' is wishful thiking if you have the misfortune to be born into the wrong family."

"I figured they'd find a way," Joe protested. "That when they got desperate enough, they'd get off their butts and do something constructive." Then, hearing how his own words condemned him, he admitted, "I never expected…" his voice trailed off.

"Dad, look what's happened to you," Daniel said, not unkindly. "If you, with all your abilities, education, and work ethic could only get a job as an orderly, what prospects does some uneducated, unskilled slacker have? Let's agree to admit that some of these folks, OK maybe quite a few, are lazy and seriously flawed. Does letting them starve and die on the street of treatable diseases really benefit the rest of us? Even if you think selfishly, the public health issues of TB, measles, and whooping cough throughout the general population are reason enough to care."

"What can I say? I've been wrong about some things," admitted Joe. "At that march today, it was obvious. Our government is abusing power. I confess I didn't see it before because it wasn't happening to me, or people I knew. I'm ashamed to say that it wasn't until it affected my life that I could recognize the signs."

"Well, that's a first step, but the real question is what are you going to do about it?" challenged Daniel. "As you've said to me so many times 'complaining is just whining.' You have to take personal responsibility."

"I'm not sure what's in my power to do. Without money and status, I'm nothing."

"You'd be surprised," smiled Daniel, "maybe you're better connected than you think. Remember the Valerie Plame case and the CIA operatives who were purged from the agency for disagreeing with the Bush II administration in 2005? They're still around. I bet they could use someone with your personal assets."

"What personal assets? I've lost everything," Joe replied.

Daniel continued to grin, "Look in a mirror. You still look like the well-to-do white guy you always have been. When you open your mouth, you are educated and articulate. You know all the arguments and rhetoric that support those in power. It's only on the inside that you've chosen to change. No one would know the difference unless you chose to tell them."

"What would I have to do?" Joe asked suddenly concerned. "It's not anything illegal is it?"

"I'll make the introductions. You decide how you want to get involved."

★   ★   ★   ★   ★

On Saturday, Daniel borrowed a friend's car and they drove up to the cemetery in Mill Valley where Amanda was buried. Joe had wanted her final resting place to be a national cemetery befitting an Air Force cadet, but Susan put her foot down and insisted on Forever Fernwood, an ecology-friendly burial site. At the time Susan had been infuriated with him and wouldn't consider his wishes at all.

Daniel and Joe made somewhat awkward small talk on the drive up. As they walked through the wild meadow dotted with oak trees and flat markers of petrified wood, Joe saw two figures in the distance. Daniel said, "I hope you don't mind but I invited Mom and Stan to join us. I thought it would mean more if we could deal with this as a family."

Joe felt so nervous he was nauseous, but he was so relieved that Daniel hadn't rejected him that he chose not to react. He'd always hated surprises. Guess he had to get used to the unexpected even though it put him off balance. Susan was crying softly and Stan was comforting her. When he saw Joe and Daniel approach, Stan stepped back under the shade of a nearby tree so the younger man could hug his mother. Joe stood there awkwardly, and haltingly took a few steps closer.

"I'm so sorry for everything. For running away from Aquamarine. For not being there for you when Amanda died." Joe felt desolated and ashamed by the complete inadequacy of his words.

"She loved you so much," Susan said with a touch of accusation and envy in her voice. " She would have done anything you wanted. She was in all those stupid clubs to please you. She joined the debating society to please you. She went to the Air Force Academy to please you. She felt that if you were supporting the War then she should do her part. It didn't matter what I thought, or that none of her friends were going into the military. It didn't bother her that the reasons for these stupid senseless invasions and campaigns kept shifting. The worst part was I didn't fight you hard enough, because I wanted to please you too." She broke down sobbing.

"And now she's dead, not because of the ideals you believed in, but because of the restrictions and rules against things even you didn't think were right. She was trying to serve her country— and then some piece of shit destroyed her. If you hadn't supported those fanatics, she would have been able to get a morning after pill or a legal abortion."

"If she had only told us, we could have helped her. We could have arranged something," Joe said weakly. "I loved her too. I would have done anything to help her."

"But I think that's the point, Dad," Daniel interjected gently. "It wasn't realistic to think that the policies we didn't like wouldn't affect us, that we could pick and choose what was convenient at any given moment. Maybe you wouldn't have made a difference, but maybe if you hadn't been so willing to compromise for other reasons, Mandy might have felt like she had a choice."

Joe didn't know what to say. It was physically painful to conceive he could have contributed to his own daughter's death. It was so much easier to point to someone else, that he had to fight his natural impulse to shift the blame. He reached out to Susan and grasped her hand. "I know there isn't anything that I can say or do that can bring her back, but you're right. I should have spoken out when I had the chance to influence the outcome. I know I was afraid to call my own decisions into question. That seems ludicrous now."

Susan was looking directly into his face. He couldn't tell by her expression what she was thinking. "I did not fully appreciate," he said slowly "how much of yourself you compromised for me during our marriage. When I saw you in Aquamarine with Stan, you were so happy. Much happier than in the conventional life I wanted for us. You were kind to me, even though you had lots of reasons not to be. I didn't even have enough awareness to let you get angry at me and face up to what I had or hadn't done."

She hugged him gently. He could feel that even if she didn't want to be married to him that she still loved him and forgave him.

Joe released her and knelt down by Mandy's grave marker. He traced his fingers across the letters of her name over and over again. He forced himself to face the fact that she was never going to grow old and have the opportunity to do great things, or make mistakes, or follow the passions of her heart. His thoughts shifted to Maria. Mandy and Maria would have been around the same age yet their youthful experiences were so different. One had love and protection and every possible advantage a child deserved, while Maria had none of that. Yet they both became strong, confident young women, capable and courageous. For his part, he had failed to protect either of them. Maybe it wasn't too late to do something for Maria and Miguel and all the other young people he wouldn't ever meet. Maybe Daniel was right. He, unlike his daughter, did have a choice. He could face his own fears and take a risk to do something for someone else. He had God-given attributes and the good fortune to be born into a comfortable

American family. Life was not a level playing field and maybe he should use some of his gifts to benefit someone else.

He shook Stan's hand, hugged Susan again, and turned to Daniel, "I think it's time to meet those friends of yours."

★   ★   ★   ★   ★

Joe paced the living room of Daniel's apartment while they waited for the pick up. "Are you sure you can't come with me?" Joe asked.

Daniel shook his head. "They said it was better if I wasn't there for the first interview. You have to want to do this because you believe, not because you want to make something up to me."

"How do you know these people anyway?" Joe's voice was strained. "What makes you think we're not both being set up?" What if Daniel was being fooled? How could a kid know people who had been in the CIA? What if this was some kind of trap?

There was a soft knock on the door. Daniel opened it a few inches and spoke to the person on the other side, who handed him a paper bag. The door closed and they looked inside to see a dark wig, a gray sweatshirt, and a pair of dark sunglasses. When Joe put them on, he couldn't see a thing.

"OK, they want you to go downstairs in five minutes wearing the wig and sweatshirt. There will be a cab waiting for you. Get in, put on the glasses, and the driver will take you to the meeting place. Seems a little cloak and dagger, doesn't it?" Daniel laughed and then became serious again. "You have to be careful. But, don't worry. It will be alright."

Joe nodded. Daniel gave him a hug. "I'm proud of you, Dad," he said.

"But I haven't done anything yet," Joe protested.

"The fact that you're even willing to consider this means a lot to me. I've always believed you are fundamentally a good person, though I couldn't understand how you went along without questioning what seemed to me to be so obvious."

It was time. The cab, an armored SUV with dark tinted windows, was sitting at the curb. He stepped inside, put on the glasses, and the vehicle pulled out into traffic. The driver said, "Sit back and relax. We'll be there in about a half hour."

Ha, Joe thought. Like he'd be able to relax. The driver was making a lot of turns. Even if he knew San Francisco well, he wouldn't have been able to recall where they were going. What if they were going to ask him to commit treason or do something violent? He couldn't do that. He believed in the rule of law. He was not Joe Courage. What was he thinking when he agreed to meet these people?

When the car stopped, the door opened and four hands helped him out. He figured they were in a garage somewhere because he could see only dim light with his peripheral vision. They led him to an elevator. He could feel it move downward a few floors. He heard the doors slide open and he was brought into a room where his guides helped him sit down on a chair. It occurred to him that they were handling him politely even though he was feeling so nervous and threatened. His mouth was dry.

"You may take off the glasses now, Joe," a pleasant female voice commanded. He removed the glasses. He wondered if he could take off the wig too. He felt so silly. "Yes, the wig can go too if you like," the voice said with a tone of amusement. How did she know what he was thinking? He wasn't sure if he liked the idea of having his mind read, but he took the wig off anyway.

There were four people seated at a table in front of him. A fifth figure was sitting in a darkened corner in the back of the room. He couldn't make out the person's face, but he or she was dressed in running shoes and jeans. He couldn't even tell the sex of the person. A dark haired woman of about his age seemed to be the one who had addressed him. To her right there was an older woman, Joe estimated to be in her late 70's, and to her left were two solid-looking younger men, one black, and one white. All of them looked like perfectly ordinary Americans, no one you'd label as the radical fringe. Their expressions were polite and neutral; it was as if he were a candidate at a job interview. OK, maybe less judgmental than that. He didn't get the sense that anyone wanted to prove he couldn't do the job. Whatever it was.

He noticed that there was a small table to his right with a glass of water. As he looked at the water, the woman—who introduced herself as Helen—said, "Feel free to have some water. Would you like anything else?"

They started by asking Joe about his background, where he grew up, went to school, that sort of thing. They laughed at his anecdotes about his family, nodded sympathetically when he talked about his dog being hit by a car, and generally made him feel at ease. When they asked him about his entrée into political activities, they seemed genuinely curious. How had he decided to become a Republican?

"It wasn't really something I had to decide. My family and everyone I knew were Republicans. It was like being Christian—I never had to think about it or make a conscious decision. When I was growing up people around me didn't think much of Jimmy Carter, whereas Reagan, well Reagan was everything you could want a President to be. He was such a great guy. Everyone loved him. No one even suggested that maybe Carter was more representative of our values than Reagan."

Watching their faces, he suddenly had the sense that not everyone there might have loved President Reagan with the same enthusiasm, but for the moment, they didn't comment.

"Do you still see the Republican Party in such a benign light?" asked the African-American man.

"It's kind of a two part answer," Joe admitted. "I still believe in the core ideals of individual responsibility, limited government, free markets, and personal privacy, but I've seen that my Party isn't holding true to those. To hang on to power, those in charge cater to more extreme social positions and engage in repressive tactics. I'd like to believe that the majority of people would vote for us if we stuck with the basics." As soon as the words came out of his mouth, he wondered if they sounded naïve. And he was aware that, he had used the word "us." But what, exactly, did "us" include or mean to him now?

"I always told myself that my family and I wouldn't have to be affected by the more extreme fundamentalist beliefs, so it didn't matter if all those laws got passed. Even when my own daughter died as a result, I still wouldn't let myself see the contradictions."

"What about your son?" The question came from the back of the room. The man's voice was strangely familiar, but he couldn't place it.

"I don't think I had any idea until recently how much I hurt him. My brother too. He was a big shot with the Log Cabin Club, very connected, and he still lost his adopted children. He asked me to help him fight from within the Party leadership and I refused.

"It's embarrassing to say it, but until I lost everything, I was willing to keep reaping the benefits of policies that helped me, but made it harder for other people to survive, much less get ahead. Deep down, I knew we were taking economic advantage of middle and working class people by making everything sound so simplistic, but it was easier to just go along. Besides, everyone likes the world to seem simple, straightforward, and uncomplicated—it's less scary that way, isn't it?"

"Perhaps it is," said the older woman, Ruth. She reminded Joe of his grandmother when he was a little boy. "Why do you think so many Americans are willing to overlook the more repressive tactics?" she asked.

"It's obvious, isn't it? So they feel safer. If someone you trust is controlling everything, not only don't you have to worry, you don't have to take responsibility for what's happening. We've all been trained to trust our own authority figures. How can you let yourself believe that someone who you swear by would deliberately do something to hurt you?"

Oh my God, he was sounding simple minded. Did he actually believe that? He continued in a less certain tone. "When there are plenty of voices around telling you that they're right, why would you challenge them?" At least they weren't laughing at him. "You can always point to other countries that are worse." Nothing like being defensive eh?

Tom, the preppy guy who looked like he could be Joe's younger cousin, asked. "What's changed for you? Why would you be willing to challenge the status quo now?"

Joe considered the question. "A year ago, I might have been willing to take action in my own financial self-interest. I mean, how could the government steal my hard-earned money? Now there's something more important going on for me. I've met liberals and poor people who have turned out to not be misguided, lazy, selfish people. They aren't the ones who seem brainwashed to me now. I've seen other professionals like me who've lost everything, even though they did everything expected of them in the name of success. Paying a fair and proportionate assessment of taxes to get a shared safety net, basic services, and invest in future prosperity doesn't seem like such a bad tradeoff anymore. The market doesn't always produce the best results if it's the only driving force that matters."

"Why should we trust you?" asked the disembodied voice.

"I don't know. That's up to you. I can tell you that I still believe in personal responsibility. As a lawyer, I helped the rule of law subvert fairness. You know, bigots don't think they're bigots, and wealthy people who feel they never have enough money, don't feel like they're being greedy. They have good reasons to justify their actions. They surround themselves with other people who tell them that they are wonderful and fair-minded. They tell each other that every opinion is as good as every other opinion. And if some outsider suggests there might be some fundamental flaws in their arguments, they just call him a socialist and put him on the defensive.

Joe's voice started to shake as he thought of Amanda, Maria, and Miguel, "The bottom line is that I didn't protect people I love. I know I screwed up. I want to do something about it. My son, Daniel is willing to give me another chance to be in his life, even after letting him, his mother, and my brother down in a big way. I know I am a good person who loves his country, and if I can do anything to help put it back on track then I want to do that."

"Have you ever heard of Oskar Schindler?" Ruth asked.

"You mean the guy in that Spielberg movie who used his factory to save Jews from the Nazis during World War II? What about him?"

Ruth smiled slightly. "He was an ordinary man who defied the rule of law to do the right thing. He didn't shoot a gun or speak out in public, but rather used his position in society to act in a courageous way. It was the only time in his life he achieved greatness. Our resistance movement is taking a similar approach. We are asking regular people like yourself to take risks to stand up for the true values of our society." Ruth added, "I have to tell you that it may be dangerous even though we're committed to non-violent action."

"But I'm a suspected terrorist now, as stupid as that is. How can I help without causing even more problems? I could analyze legal briefs or something." Joe didn't feel very excited by the prospect.

"We had something different in mind." The man from the back of the room walked forward into the light, "We don't expect you to become 007 but we can make use of your natural skills and deeply held beliefs. We want you to be a Republican."

Joe's jaw dropped. It was his brother Edward.

★   ★   ★   ★   ★

Joe should have known it wasn't going to be that easy. Even though Daniel was ready to accept his conversion at face value, Edward was not. It was clear he still harbored bitterness towards Joe, not that Joe could blame him. Edward didn't stick around for the battery of tests they gave him—word associations, hooking him up to skin and eye sensors while they showed him short clips of current events, images of public figures, scenes of violent behavior. They told him they'd get in touch with him in a few days.

He put the wig and glasses back on. A different car dropped him off a few blocks from Daniel's apartment. He stuck the glasses in his pocket. His instructions were to go into the multiplex, watch an action flick, then go to the men's room and remove the wig and glasses and dispose of them in his used popcorn container.

As he left the theatre, he passed two policemen stationed outside. He couldn't help himself but he looked at them out of the corner of his eye and one of the men held his gaze. He hesitated a split second too long before he said hello. The cop's eyes narrowed, and deciding Joe looked suspicious, asked him to step over to the car and place his hands on the vehicle. When they patted him down they found the glasses and his ID card that still had his old address in Atherton.

The officer tried to look through the glasses. "What the hell are these? Steve, run this ID card will you? Stand here buddy and don't move."

Joe's mind went blank. Why hadn't he thrown the glasses out with the wig? How could he explain them? If he said they were from the eye doctor, they'd ask for the doctor's name. What if he said he used them to help him sleep? That was pretty lame. Why was he carrying them around?

The other policeman said, "Let's go down to the station. There are no outstanding arrest warrants on your ID record, but there is a pointer to the Homeland Security database. We'd like to ask you a few questions." He didn't exactly shove Joe into the back seat but he wasn't too gentle either.

This interview was decidedly less hospitable than the earlier one. A rep from Homeland Security met them at the police station on Vallejo Street. They sat in a small room. Joe wondered who was watching from behind the mirror.

"We see from your file that you've had some contact with Homeland Security before," the rep said. "It doesn't look like any action has been taken on your case other than asset audit and reclamation. It seems that your attorney, Jack Swenson, requested a postponement of your hearing until next year."

Joe thought his head was going to explode but managed to keep control of himself. That bastard was making sure he couldn't clear his name. If all charges were dropped, then Jack wouldn't have anything to hold over his head. What if he told this guy about the resistance movement? Would they give him back his money as a reward?

The police were asking about the glasses. Where had he gotten them? Why did he have glasses that blacked out all vision? What was he doing up in San Francisco?

His anger at Jack flared. Why wouldn't his brother forgive him after all he'd been through? Why should he put his life on the line when he'd lost everything? Fear and rage churned up inside him.

He stammered, "I...I...I'll tell you, if you ..."

Then he passed out.

★ ★ ★ ★ ★

Joe's head throbbed as he came to. His guilt over Mandy, his anguish about Miguel and Maria, and his anxiety for what would happen to Daniel if he talked washed over him. An officer pulled him off the floor back into the chair and shoved a plastic cup into his hand.

"Drink some water. Now what was it you were about to tell us?" When the cop leaned over, the man's nose was only inches from Joe's. He could smell the tuna sandwich the guy had for lunch.

He couldn't believe he was about to betray his brother, again. Some secret agent he was. He decided to do the honorable thing if it killed him. He owed it to all of them.

Inspiration dawned. "I'm sorry. I have severe migraines. I use the glasses so I can block out all the light if one hits me when I'm out in public."

The police decided to kick him loose. It didn't seem like he could do much damage.

Joe found himself amazed at the amount of preparation that was going into the operation. The plan was to fly him and several other recruits to a small airstrip near the resort where the Domestic Policy Council would be meeting. As was the practice at all Administration events, only carefully vetted Republicans were to be admitted. Registered Democrats, Greens, Independents, and Libertarians were completely shut out. The resistance volunteers had all been chosen for their general physical similarities to specific delegates who were coming from remote areas in Montana, Alaska, and North Dakota. The idea was to intercept delegates between the airport and the resort so doubles could be substituted. The agents would obtain information on the government's plans so it could be disseminated to the public through underground channels.

On board the four-seat Cessna, Joe studied the dossier of his double, Henry Walters. Same age, top school grad, also originally from a small town in Illinois. Joe could see the resemblance to his former self, especially in the expression around the mouth and the way the lips pressed together. He touched his face. It seemed like his expressions had changed a lot over the past two years. Would it feel odd to assume that much reserve again?

Sam, a fellow recruit, glanced at the photograph from the seat next to him. "What's yours look like?" He compared the photo with Joe's face. "Pretty close. Are you nervous?"

"I'm not sure if I'm more worried that they won't find Walters and I'll have to sit on the sidelines, or that they will and I'll have to go through with this. What if I can't pull it off? What if..."

Sam interrupted him. "Don't waste energy. If you get the chance, just keep thinking about that kid, Miguel, you told me about. Do it for him and all the other children who don't have enough to eat or parents to protect them. Take a look at my guy. I'd like to think I'm much better looking than he is." Sam grinned and Joe couldn't help but smile back.

"What made you decide to do this?" Joe asked.

Sam said, "It was my wife's idea originally. She's part of the group too. We don't have kids, but we do have a bunch of nieces and nephews. We had good jobs and could have looked the other way, but we decided to take the risk and become part of an active resistance movement. We love our country, and can't stand the idea of it becoming a place where anyone who disagrees with government policies is labeled a traitor. What happened to higher ideals like 'liberty and justice for ALL?' Just saying the words isn't enough if it isn't how we really operate the country.

"You can be sure the patriotic slogans will continue to be used even if they're used to convey the opposite meaning. Masters of the strategy, like pollster Frank Luntz, taught the Party a great lesson. Don't appeal to that which broadly or vaguely unifies, but that which specifically and bitterly divides. If you use the right words—'death tax' instead of 'estate tax'—and press the right buttons—such as 'right to life'—but neglect to ask what kind of life and for how long, then you can embark on a process of segmentation. Make people focus on divisive emotional issues and divert them from any larger sense of what creates protections for the larger society. Get enough people with different hot buttons on your side and you forge an electoral majority of 'us' against 'them'—an equation for continued domination. Think how many people respond to Ayn Rand's philosophy that 'the pursuit of man's own rational self-interest and of his own happiness is the highest moral purpose of his life.'"

Joe Winston could see how effectively the Party had appealed to his vanity and avarice, an appeal cloaked in the rhetoric of values and the supremacy of free markets. It justified his efficient concentration on making more and more money, allowing him to believe that what was good for him was inevitably good for the country. Since so many he knew had more, it was easy to think of himself as one of the regular folks. That perspective was less defensible now that he had met and lived with a few of the people who made up the other 98% of the country.

★ ★ ★ ★ ★

When they arrived, an intervention team was driving up with a guy in the back of a blue Suburban. It had been immobilized by use of a radio control device that had shut down the engine at a pre-selected spot, something that was child's play for the ousted CIA covert operations people who had joined the movement. One group was taking off the license plates and putting them on another SUV. They put the luggage and briefcase into the replacement car.

An intense young woman introduced herself as Jane and hustled Joe into the observation booth of an interrogation room with a one-way glass. As she turned up the sound, Joe could hear Walters yelling at the interrogators as they removed the blindfold and gag. "Who do you think you are? Do you know who I am? How dare you lazy scum think you can steal my car?"

Joe recognized the tone in the voice. It was just like he sounded when he had been inconvenienced. The guy stopped when one of the men in the room punched him in the jaw. A woman cut off a sizeable hunk of Walter's hair and walked out of the room.

"This is kidnapping, you know!" the man shouted. "You'll be lucky to get life in prison if they don't execute you. All of you."

"No sir, I don't think so," a burly man in a blue windbreaker told him. "We just gave you a ride when your car broke down. And I bet you will come away with only pleasant memories of our rescue." The smile he gave his "guest" was more intimidating than cheerful.

The former Hollywood hair stylists and make-up artists who were part of the team came into the observation room a few minutes later. "We're going to get started while you watch the interview so you can get on the road soon." They started to apply brown dye to Joe's hair and eyebrows. The make-up artists were debating over which green contact lenses to use. "Those are too bright. Try the other set."

Jane pressed the intercom button. "Please have Mr. Walters stand up and turn around. Take his shirt off." A short young Hispanic man went through his pockets and took out Walters' wallet, keys, and identification. Walters went apoplectic. The women conferred. "You're a little thinner than Walters so we're going to put some padding on you. Don't go swimming as part of your undercover operation, or pick up any political groupies," she teased Joe.

It took a shot of a newly improved variant of sodium pentathol before Walters relaxed his aggressive tone. The sight of the needle suddenly seemed to get through to the man that this wasn't a routine car-jacking. "Are you going to torture me?" Walters whimpered in genuine fear.

The questions mostly focused on whom Walters was expecting to meet at the conference, whom he knew, and what he had told people his role was going to be. Joe concentrated as hard as he could, jotting down extra notes in the electronic organizer he was to carry.

After the excess dye was washed out and his hair dried, they held up a mirror to Joe. The women wore very proud grins. It was spooky how much he looked like Walters. He stopped himself from smiling and put on that prim expression.

They had him undress to apply the padding and slipped him into a set of Walter's clothes. He got his last minute instructions from the interrogators, and walked out as Sam was entering the other observation room. "They got *my* ugly bastard. I'll see you at the Lodge."

As Joe drove the remaining 45 minutes to the resort, following the calm voice of the car's GPS system, he reviewed the facts about Walters. Fortunately, all those years of living in his head made it pretty easy to go back there. He could see the difference was how much sensory input was coming in. He hadn't realized how much he had missed before, even though he always considered himself quite observant.

When the valet took his car, Joe had to stop himself from thanking him. He strode in without waiting for the bellman to bring in the bags. He handed Walter's credit card to the clerk at the front desk. He'd been practicing the signature since they'd found a match, so it was good enough for an untrained eye.

"Here's your electronic room and billing key. If you go over to the registration table on the mezzanine, they'll give you your materials and gift bag." Joe went up the escalator, glancing around for people he recognized. He had been told to try to avoid close contact with anyone who knew him well, but to test the effectiveness of his impersonation with someone who knew Walters, and another who had met Joe briefly in the past. If the disguise didn't work, he was to come up with an excuse of being ill and abort the mission immediately.

A plump, middle-aged woman gave him the electronic tablet and a large leather satchel that contained gifts from the companies underwriting the Policy Conference. A Hermes cashmere sweater, a pair of Oakley sun glasses, and an assortment of fine cotton shirts in Walter's size, were among the items visible on the top. As Joe turned he saw a party organizer from Memphis, Karl Jones. Joe had met him at several fundraisers and at the 2009 inauguration but didn't know him well. Joe walked over, looked purposely at the nametag, and introduced himself, extending his hand, "Hi Karl, I'm Henry Walters. Do you know where the dinner is being held this evening?"

Jones smiled graciously and pointed to the ballroom on the other side of the atrium. They chatted for a few minutes and it was clear Jones didn't recognize him. OK, one down.

As Joe approached the elevators to go to his room, he felt a hand on his shoulder. He tried not to stiffen. "Henry," the other man exclaimed. Joe glanced at the nametag as he turned around. Evan O'Brien. Joe remembered that as a name Walters had mentioned earlier. He smiled and shook O'Brien's hand. "Hello Evan. I was just going up to my room, will you be grabbing some drinks before dinner?" O'Brien nodded in the affirmative and said, "You look like you've been working out, lost a few pounds, eh?" Joe forced himself to leer, "I've been playing tennis a lot this spring—new female tennis pro. I'll see you later."

Joe managed to avoid running into O'Brien in the bar and at dinner. The food was awesome looking, but he was so nervous he couldn't taste the food— a shame since it had been ages since he'd had veal chops smothered in fresh porcini mushrooms. Fortunately, he'd found a table with folks who didn't know either him or Walters, so he could relax a little. Exchanges he had heard a million times before now sounded strange. He felt so hypocritical when the words came out of his own mouth, and found himself irritated when someone else said something mean spirited. It seemed as if these people had never met someone gay, or a poor person, or a liberal, except as a character in a bad TV movie. Of course, now that the liberal Hollywood elite had been blacklisted, most movies were either heavy handed and violent, or sanctimonious and boring. Hmm...was he climbing onto his own soapbox?

After dinner, as Joe returned to his room, he saw a man inviting the maid doing turndown service into his room for a nightcap. The fellow had obviously had a few already, and was very insistent even as the young woman was making her best effort to politely evade his grasp. Joe knew he wasn't supposed to get involved but he couldn't stand by and do nothing. He loosened his tie and opened his top button and staggered down the hallway. He stumbled into the fellow, breaking his grasp, knocking over the woman. "I'm so sorry. It was a grrreat party," he slurred as he helped the woman to her feet. For a moment, their eyes connected and he glanced down the hallway. As he stood up, he faced the man and apologized profusely, giving the maid a chance to scurry to the stairwell. The man looked annoyed but didn't bother to follow the woman. He muttered something about "lesbian dyke" and shut the door to his room.

Joe was sweating when he arrived back at his own room. He thought about calling Sam to get some reassurance, but assumed the phone system was monitored. He showered, hoping it would clear his head, but he slept fitfully and had to take another shower in the morning. Henry had a great electric shaver so at least he didn't have to worry about cutting himself. The cologne wasn't to his taste, but it seemed like a small sacrifice to make. Anyone who smelled like this on purpose must want people to know that he was completely indifferent to sensitive types with allergies. He made himself a mental note to thank the thoughtful person who had substituted a brand new toothbrush. He laughed as he realized how central personal hygiene became, when you didn't have ready access to such basics.

Joe debated whether to wear the luxury items in the gift bag— it had been a long time since he'd worn Sea Island Cotton Shirts—but he decided the resemblance would be enhanced with Walters' own personal uniform. The suitcase was packed with five identical sets of navy polo shirts and khaki trousers. Didn't this guy have any imagination?

Joe went down for breakfast and Evan O'Brien invited him to sit at his table. Joe was getting nervous as O'Brien started asking about Walters' family when Sam, now with a sandy moustache and glasses, slipped into the chair next to him. "Henry, how are you? It's been way too long." Sam, wearing the nametag of Albert Johnson, introduced himself to O'Brien and the others at the table. Joe dug into the bacon and egg breakfast. Maybe keeping his mouth filled with food wasn't the most ingenious way to avoid talking to O'Brien, but it seemed to do the trick.

Joe had been told to go to the session on Voter Management Techniques. He took a spot near the loudspeakers so he could get a good recording. The PowerPoint slides were already in the electronic tablet. The first 10 minutes were fairly predictable, self-congratulatory, comments by the moderator, before the panel started getting interesting.

The first speaker talked about the specific plans for field operations, which had been refined since the 2004 and 2008 elections: misleading flyers that gave people the incorrect address for their polling place, too few voting machines in minority neighborhoods so people had to wait on long lines for many hours, poll watchers eager to challenge the registration of minorities and young women who looked like they could be intimidated. These tactics had to be carefully adapted at the local level to reflect the subtleties of the community.

The second speaker elaborated on successful efforts at the state level to block paper ballots and optical scanners in favor of touch screen machines. A combination of media handling, favorable bid processes conducted by partisan state elections officers, and subsidies of Party-controlled equipment manufacturers, meant the optimum equipment was in use nationwide. He closed his presentation with a description of the untimely accidents that had befallen some activists who had brought legal challenges, and advocates of Open Source software that would be open to review by any and all U.S. citizens. The audience clearly found these anecdotes humorous, so Joe chuckled along uneasily.

In the past, the implications and inconsistencies would not have even registered in his brain, now they were terrifying.

The final panelist took the national perspective and covered the status of the Electoral College. Population had been declining steadily in the heartland. When leading statisticians had proven that the votes of Californians, New Yorkers, and other populous states counted less than the rural Plains states, there had been a grassroots attempt to eliminate the Electoral College and revisit the wisdom of the Senate allocation of representation. The Congressional majority leaders had squelched substantive debate. The Supreme Court firmly squashed any legal appeals to challenge the formula claiming clear intent by the Founding Fathers in the Constitution.

In his summary, the moderator recapped the main themes of the speakers, adding that the greatest threat to continued stability was public financing of campaigns. Without the overwhelming financial advantages enjoyed by the Party, and the spin control that shaped popular opinion, disruptive special interest groups might mislead the public.

Later that evening, before the entertainment started, Joe met Sam and the others at the pre-arranged location in the laundry room. The operation had been successful in placing five doubles. Each was to transmit their day's information, notes from informal and overheard conversations, and all the presentation slides via a computer that had been hidden in a linen basket used by housekeeping. As Joe was putting the computer back under a pile of towels, the door opened and they all froze.

In walked the maid he had rescued the night before, laughing with several other women and security guards still behind her in the hallway. When she saw Joe, she stopped short, turned, and casually suggested the group go out to the patio instead.

The men debated whether they should continue but Joe felt fairly sure that this woman wouldn't tell anyone what she had seen. He had to convince the others, who like him, weren't exactly CIA regulars. They were average guys who had come to see that the administration's vision wasn't all it had been cracked up to be. He had never been a hero or served in the military. The most dangerous thing he had ever done, was tell a bunch of Susan's feminist girlfriends that men were naturally better at math and logic.

They split up and went back upstairs. Joe really needed a scotch after the close call. A table of true believers drinking ginger ale glared at him disapprovingly but Joe didn't care. He glanced at another table and saw Kipp Sanders from his old church holding forth in a loud voice. Kipp had been an asshole before, and it was clear nothing had changed in the last two years. Joe attempted to slip past unnoticed when Evan O'Brien stepped in front of him. "Hey, Henry, we haven't had a chance to talk."

The sound made Sanders look up. His eyes narrowed as he looked at Joe. "You look familiar. You remind me of someone from my church in Los Altos. I heard he left town after getting mixed up with a terrorist group."

O'Brien laughed. "You must be mistaken, this is Henry Walters from Billings. I've known him for years. Henry, I can't believe you would have a secret life in California."

Joe fought to control his panic. His mind raced to find something to say. Should he say he had a cousin? What if they checked the national identity database? Should he say anything? He and Sanders had had a lot of arguments; the man might remember his voice. He shrugged, and trying to imitate Henry's sneering tone to the interrogators said, "They say everyone has a double. Maybe our ancestors came over on the Mayflower together. Who do you think you are? No one's ever dared to suggest that I look like some towel head terrorist." He stomped off, not daring to look around.

He went into a stall in the men's room barely breathing. Think. Think. Could he get his keys for the SUV from the parking valet and simply leave? The resort was in the middle of nowhere. There wasn't any public transportation. It was too far to walk to the next town. Why had he left Walters' personal communicator upstairs? Then again who was he going to call anyway? He was afraid to find Sam, not wanting to blow his cover too. He couldn't endanger the operation. They were getting useful material that could potentially have a real impact. But, what were the chances that Sanders would just let it go?

As Joe walked nonchalantly from the men's room, he saw Sanders talking to the security guards. As a way to involve and reward the gun crowd, this venue boasted its own 'well regulated militia.' He forced himself to walk slowly and to breathe. In that moment, Joe made a decision. If they thought he was working alone, perhaps the others could either keep going or at least get away. This effort was bigger than he was and more important than any one individual. He hoped Edward would forgive him, and pictured Daniel meeting Maria and Miguel as he ran for the front door. As he intended, he never made it outside.

Epilogue

As knowledge of the government's true plans leaked out, spread by word-of-mouth, blogs, podcasts, email, and through underground channels, millions of American citizens wondered whether they were being too passive. People whose lives had unraveled questioned whether things would get better after all. Those hanging on by the slimmest of threads realized the tenuousness of their positions might require action before it was too late. Many who still had jobs and savings who were hoping the pendulum would swing back, asked themselves if they weren't morally obligated to give it a little push. Individuals who had been making their own private contributions, within the constraints of their lives and jobs, began to hope that a sea change could be possible. Those who had resisted directly and indirectly were encouraged to take greater risks. The leaders of various movements, from greens to gay activists, libertarians to militant atheists, evangelical environmentalists to anti-war protesters re-evaluated whether their differences with the silenced Democratic Party and each other mattered more than their common goal of reclaiming a decent, fair, and free civil society. People started asking more questions, which in turn pushed what was left of the independent media to ask still more questions, and resist simplistic and obfuscating rhetoric.

Even those who benefited the most, but who had never bought into the whole picture, started to crack open their minds to the possibility that maybe it would be in their interests to have a strong opposition in order to hold the most powerful corporate and political forces in check. A few considered they might have to give voice to their own misgivings even if it meant letting go of some of their advantages. They realized that choosing to continue to ignore the implications of what was being done in the name of "security" or "morality" or the status quo, might threaten their very souls. Others preferred to focus on the negative market implications of the questionable union of religious fundamentalism and crony capitalism.

Word of the resistance and its heroes even made its way to the detention centers in Utah. As Daniel had promised Joe, he used Uncle Edward's underground network, not to mention his own considerable force of will, to locate Maria and Miguel. Daniel was able to gain access by posing as a subsistence farming specialist who could help inmates grow their own food in marginal climates, thereby saving the government additional costs for their incarceration. The protective security measures of facilities used for non-violent offenders and their dependents were oriented toward keeping people in, not out, so Daniel and his associates drove their white panel truck containing literature and tools in through the front gate. As his colleagues toured the grim fields, Daniel was able to slip inside the wooden barracks for women and young children. He found Maria sitting quietly, smoothing Miguel's hair. He approached her but before he could identify himself, she smiled. "I know who you are. You look just like your father."

Wordlessly, he sat on the bunk beside her and handed her an envelope. She opened it and took out a letter. After reading it, she put it aside and turned to Daniel. "I know your father may have disappointed you, but he did the most difficult thing that any human being can do. He admitted and learned from his mistakes, faced his worst fears, and then genuinely found his soul."

Daniel nodded. "I know. I'm incredibly proud of him. None of this would be happening if it weren't for him…and for you. You helped him see what was most important in the world."

"He taught me, and Miguel. Not just about books or how to speak more clearly either. He helped me understand what people in power care about and what frightens them deep down. Now, I have to build on his lessons." She stood up and took a deep breath.

Daniel followed Maria to the common room where she sat at a long table and addressed a group of men, women and children. While she was not the eldest or most distinguished-looking, she possessed an air of quiet authority. Everyone was listening to her intently.

"As we've all been hearing, a window has opened and we have to take advantage of it. Our government claims to cherish the rule of law, yet most of us were brought here without due process. Our leaders say they value the sanctity of life, yet all of us have lost loved ones prematurely to hunger, illness, disaster, and war. Those in power preach personal responsibility yet they raise their children to be dependent on the sweat and ingenuity of others. They send our children abroad to their deaths, in the name of the democratic rights and freedoms they deny to us at home.

"We need to acknowledge that all of us have both good and dark sides. Each of us is as capable of greed and ill will as we are of generosity, love, and an open heart. Whether we trust in God, the universe, or in our own consciences, each individual must deliberately choose to act with compassion, honesty, and kindness every day. All religions advocate ethical behavior, unconditional love, and tolerance, yet some of us misuse our beliefs to inflict pain on one another. Our country has been a beacon of light to the world but we've also committed genocide, engaged in slavery, and unleashed nuclear devastation. Loyalty is not the blind belief in an illusion of perfection. True loyalty and patriotism is seeing the good with the flaws and transforming that understanding into a sincere desire to evolve and improve.

"The rest of the world has good reason not to trust us—we are not the America we are capable of being. We have to recognize our shortcomings and move beyond them. If people get the government they deserve, then we need to take responsibility for allowing our government to say one thing and do another. And if we want a different kind of society, then all of us have to do something about it—even if the very idea terrifies us. If we operate from a place of uncertainty and fear, then we'll continue to slide into the darkness."

She paused, her gaze resting on Daniel. "A dear friend of mine helped me understand some very important life lessons. If you have all the money in the world but you don't have people you love in your life, you are poor. If you have all the education and advantages in the world, and yet choose to disregard the suffering of others around you, then you are willfully ignorant. On the other hand, if you transform loss or pain into something positive to give to others, you feel incredible joy. We have to translate our fear and complacency into courage to act, each and every day. The ideal of liberty and justice *for all* is just a fantasy if we wait for someone else to hand it to us. God will bless America, but we have to do our part too."

A man asked, "Yes, but what can we do about it? Especially now that we're here."

Maria answered, "Start with the smallest gestures. Treat each other with kindness. Show the guards that we are people like them, who love our children and want them to have shelter, enough to eat, and a chance to learn. Ask the guards about themselves. Chances are, they share some values with you, whether it's caring about the environment, believing in personal responsibility, or allowing spiritual freedom. Maybe they lost a loved one in one of our many wars. Make a connection so they can see your humanity and more importantly, so that you can feel theirs. Encourage them to ask why someone so like themselves is locked up here."

After her talk, they walked back to the barracks and sat down. Daniel broke the silence, "I think more people should hear what you have to say."

"Why would they listen to me? I'm such an unimportant person."

Daniel smiled and shrugged. "I have a feeling that the time is right for a message like yours. How do you and Miguel feel about tight spaces? Do you think he could stay quiet for a couple of hours?"

"If a runaway slave could do it, so can we," she said pulling out the book that Joe had given her for Christmas. "It has always been my inspiration that basic human decency and courage can overcome the worst situations. I've been reading this story to Miguel his whole life. I know he'll do it for Joe."

"You do know that even if we manage to get you out of here, the most difficult part is just beginning," Daniel warned.

She nodded and went to find Miguel.

As the guards searched the truck on the way out, they didn't notice the 18-inch difference between the dusty floorboards and the undercarriage. The white van drove off into the desert.

★　　★　　★　　★　　★

Quietly, slowly, a general strike was organized for Friday, July 3, 2015. The theme was Total Peace. People were encouraged to simply stay home, just for one day, to reflect on what it means to be an American and what is truly great about our country. Enough people called in sick to impact even the comforts of the Divinely Entitled. Millions of lattes went un-steamed. The lack of hospitality workers, wait staff, and dish washers resulted in closed restaurants and resorts. Airplanes didn't fly. Gas stations were unmanned. Multiplexes, theatres, concert halls, and museums were dark. Construction halted. The offices of military recruiters were empty. Elective surgical procedures and general visits to doctors' offices were postponed. Caddies, greens keepers, and golf pros were unavailable. Parents took care of their own children and elderly relatives, scrubbed their own toilets, and prepared meals out of the contents of their cupboards and freezers. No pizza was delivered. The economic impact was noticeable and the political overtones glaring, even to those who tried to pretend it wasn't happening and folks were merely leaving early for the holiday weekend.

Wealthy people who were sympathetic to the concerns of the less entitled donated to a fund to provide income to those who couldn't afford to lose the day's pay. Special soup kitchens and picnics were set up for the hungry, manned by those courageous enough to take the risk of being videotaped by Homeland Security. Prayer services and candle light vigils at churches, synagogues, temples, and mosques drew more than the usual parishioners. Downloads of the songs of Pete Seeger and Woodie Guthrie were so numerous, traffic on the Internet slowed. Impromptu concerts were held as people, leaning out their apartment windows joined in singing "This land is your land, this land is my land…." American flags flew alongside rainbow flags on millions of flagpoles. No small gesture of hope and patriotism was too corny. People actually *listened* to friends, spouses, and relatives who didn't see the world the same way. Millions of soldiers, police, and security personnel followed their consciences and there were few scuffles or incidents.

The unusually quiet streets called attention to false promises and unmet expectations. The strike was only a small step that changed nothing immediately or dramatically, but it put the leaders of the country on notice that it was not acceptable to starve the populace to feed the voracious appetites of a few, nor to trample the spiritual diversity of a nation to conform to a single belief system.

Acknowledgements

I would like to thank the many friends, acquaintances and complete strangers who shared their stories and strongly held beliefs with me as I was writing this book. I tried very hard to accurately reflect the goals and good intentions of the Republican Party as well as the inner conflicts many of its members are facing. Reverend Matt Broadbent, Brian O'Leary, James Shaw, Nicci Kobritz, Anna Kiachian, David E. Gold, Richard and Alyce Johnson, the women of Hope House, Maria from the Tampa airport waiting room, the conservatives on Paul Blumenstein's email list, and the veterans and dedicated staff of the VA Hospital in Tampa gave me invaluable insights into other worlds and perspectives.

I owe a tremendous debt to the people of HD1 in Denver whom I met during the 2004 presidential election and who reinforced my desire to fight for our democracy. I would also like to thank Jeanine Valadez and Reynette Au, who when they wrote their impassioned email to a large group arguing about the 2004 election results, never imagined it would form the basis for Daniel's rant to his father. The Parent Partners who worked for the Wraparound program in Contra Costa County gave me a chance to "see God" in the faces of people who give to others out of their own pain. I am continually inspired by the writings of Paul Krugman, Bob Herbert, Hendrik Hertzberg among many others who are speaking truth to power. A more extensive list may be found on www.raisethebar.com/doublethink/references.html

Historian, scholar, and swimmer Edith Gelles was particularly influential in encouraging me to attempt (and complete) this project along with Aggie Potter, Suki Parker, and Haley Vertelney who heard about every plot twist in real time (either at the pool or on horseback). Other reviewers who were generous with their candor were Allison Amick, Wanda Cavanaugh, Joanne Sperans,

Andy Stern, Betty and Frank Stern, Charlotte Gilbert-Biro, Barbara Bowen, Russ LaBarre, Diana Neiman, Alice Lankester, Susan and Phil Yost, Donna Dubinsky, Kris Onken, Dorothy and Bill Conlon, Lorraine MacDonald, Kathi Wilson, Roy and Kathy Bukstein, Maryann Rodgers, Janet Schwartz O'Leary, Lauren Cetlin, Reverend Helen Cummings, Giovanna Cerutti, Tony Glaves, Harry and Laurie Vertelney, John Fiddes, Joanna Hoffman, Judith Coley, Lee Pantuso, Tikki Dare, Cathy Boe, Linda Geiger, Katherine Boshkoff, Marianne O'Connor, Katie Povejsilk and John Marshall Collins.

Kevin Arnold and Barbara Callison opened my eyes to the intricacies of the book business for debut authors, and novelist Dorothy Bryant pointed me to great resources. Literary Agent Kirsten Manges was incredibly helpful answering my questions so I could bring the book to life in time to meet the 2006 election cycle, including introducing me to my editor, James O'Shea Wade of the Independent Editors Group. Jim is tough, funny, and always willing to graciously argue a point. He saw immediately what I was trying to accomplish and shares my enthusiasm for the best possible America.

My talented friends and colleagues helped me with their creative skills: Peter Fox, Ark Stein, Dan Griffin, Ann Benett, Barbara Resch, Wanda Cavanaugh, Rick Smith, Marshall Cetlin, Jenna Kang, Deanna Orr, and Charlotte Falla.

This book is dedicated to the memory of my parents, Anne and Michael Schwartz who always taught me to stand up for what I think is right; and most of all to my life and business partner, Bill Conlon. He has been unflinching in his honesty, unconditional in his love, and has supported me in this journey every single step of the way. This book would not have seen the light of day without his hard work, attention to detail, and encouragement.

J.E. Schwartz
Palo Alto, California, March 2006

ABOUT THE AUTHOR

J.E. Schwartz lives in Silicon Valley and provides marketing and systems consulting to corporations, non-profit groups, and government agencies. This is the author's first novel.

Quick Order Form

Postal orders: Raise the Bar Press
                    345 California Avenue, Suite 2
                    Palo Alto, CA 94306 USA

Please send _____ copies of Doublethink by J.E. Schwartz at $14.95 each plus $3.00 shipping and handling to:

Name: _____

Address: _____

City: _____ State: _____ Zip: _____

Daytime telephone: _____

Email address: _____

Sales tax: Please add 8.25%sales tax on books shipped to California addresses

Enclosed please find:

_____ Books at $17.95 each   _____

       CA Sales tax (8.25%)   _____
       ($1.48 per book)
       Total: _____

Credit card and international order:, order online at
http://www.raisethebar.com

Telephone orders for 10 or more copies only: 650-327-2902
Retail orders of 10 books or more receive a 10% discount
Shipping and handling charge based on size of order.